BLOODLETTING   &

Vincent Lam

MIRACULOUS

CURES

{ *stories* }

DOUBLEDAY CANADA

COPYRIGHT © 2006 VINCENT LAM

LIBRARY AND ARCHIVES CANADA CATALOGUING IN PUBLICATION

Lam, Vincent
Bloodletting and miraculous cures / Vincent Lam.

ISBN 0-385-66143-6

I. Title.
PS8623.A467B5 2006   C813'.6   C2005-904928-6

JACKET IMAGE: © BETTMANN/CORBIS
JACKET DESIGN: CS RICHARDSON
PRINTED AND BOUND IN THE USA

Published in Canada by Doubleday Canada,
a division of Random House of Canada Limited

Visit Random House of Canada Limited's website: www.randomhouse.ca

BVG   10   9   8   7   6   5   4   3   2   1

TO MY PARENTS, ANDREW AND ROSALIE,
AND MY WIFE, MARGARITA,
WHO MAKE EVERYTHING POSSIBLE.

*"Medicine is a science of uncertainty
and an art of probability."*

SIR WILLIAM OSLER, 1849–1919,
renowned Canadian physician and educator

HOW TO GET INTO MEDICAL SCHOOL, PART I

—
—
—

DESPERATE STRAGGLERS ARRIVED LATE FOR THE molecular biology final examination, their feet wet from tramping through snowbanks and their faces damp from running. Some still wore coats, and rummaged in the pockets for pens. Entering the exam hall, a borrowed gymnasium, from the whipping chaos of the snowstorm was to be faced with a void. Eyeglasses fogged, xenon lamps burned their blue-tinged light, and the air was calm with its perpetual fragrance of old paint. The lamps buzzed, and their constant static was like a sheet pulled out from under the snowstorm, though low enough that the noise vanished quickly. Invigilators led latecomers to vacant seats among the hundreds of desks, each evenly spaced at the University of Ottawa's minimum requisite distance.

The invigilators allowed them to sit the exam but, toward the end of the allotted period, ignored their pleas for extra time on account of the storm. Ming, who had finished early, centred her closed exam booklet in front of her. Fitzgerald was still hunched over his paper. She didn't want to wait outside for him, preferring it to be very coincidental that she would leave the room at the same time he did. Hopefully he would suggest they go for lunch together. If he did not ask, she would be forced to, perhaps using a little joke. Ming tended to stumble over humour. She could ask what he planned to do this afternoon—was that the kind of thing people said? On scrap paper, she wrote several possible ways to phrase the question, and in doing so almost failed to notice when Fitzgerald stood up, handed in his exam, and left the room. She expected to rush after him, but he stood outside the exam hall.

"Are you waiting for someone?" she asked.

Shortly after they arrived at the Thai-Laotian café half a block from campus, Ming said deliberately, "Fitz, I simply wanted to wish you the best in your future endeavours. You are obviously intelligent, and I'm sure you will be a great success."

The restaurant was overly warm, and Fitz struggled out of his coat, wrestled his sweater over his head, leaving his hair in a wild, electrified state. He ran his hands over his head, and instead of smoothing his hair this resulted in random clumps jutting straight up.

"Same to you," he said, smiling at her almost excitedly.

She watched him scan the bar menu. When she asked for water, he followed suit. She liked that.

She said, "Also, thank you for explaining the Krebs cycle to me."

"Any time," said Fitz.

"I feel guilty that I haven't been completely open," said Ming. She considered her prepared phrases and selected one, saying, "It didn't seem like the right time in the middle of exams."

"Nothing in real life makes sense during exams," said Fitzgerald. He tilted in the chair but kept a straight back. Ming reassured herself that he had also been anticipating "a talk," and so—she concluded with an administrative type of resolution—it was appropriate that she had raised the topic of "them."

She leaned forward and almost whispered, "This is awkward, but I have strong emotional suspicions. Such suspicions are not quite the same as emotions. I'm sure you can understand that distinction. I have this inkling that you have an *interest* in me." She didn't blurt it out, instead forced herself to pace these phrases. "The thing of it is that I can't have a romantic relationship with you. Not that I want to." Now she was off the path of her rehearsed lines. "Not that I wouldn't want to, because there's no specific reason that I wouldn't, but I— Well, what I'm trying to say is that even though I don't especially want to, if I did, then I couldn't." The waiter brought shrimp chips and peanut sauce. "So that's that."

"All right," said Fitzgerald.

"I should have told you earlier, when I first got that feeling."

"You've given the issue some thought."

"Not much. I just wanted to clarify."

Fitz picked up a shrimp chip by its edge, dipped it in the peanut sauce with red pepper flakes, and crunched. His face became sweaty and bloomed red as he chewed, then coughed. He grasped the water glass and took a quick gulp.

Ming said, "Are you upset?"

He coughed to his right side, and had difficulty stopping. He reminded himself to sit up straight while coughing, realized that he wasn't covering his mouth, covered his mouth, was embarrassed that his fair skin burned hot and red, wondered in a panicky blur if this redness would be seen to portray most keenly his injured emotional state, his physical vulnerability in choking, his Anglocentric intolerance to chili, his embarrassment at not initially covering his mouth, his obvious infatuation with Ming, or—worst of all—could be interpreted as a feeble attempt to mask or distract from his discomfort at her pre-emptive romantic rejection.

Ming was grateful for this interlude, for she had now entirely forgotten her rehearsed stock of diplomatically distant but consoling though slightly superior phrases.

"Hot sauce. I'm fine," he gasped, coughing.

There was a long restaurant pause, in which Ming was aware of the other diners talking, although she could not perceive what their conversations were about.

She said, "I've embarrassed us both."

"I'm glad you mentioned it."

"So you *are* interested," she said. "Or you *were* interested until a moment ago. Is that why you're glad that I mentioned it?"

"It doesn't matter, does it? What you've just said has made it irrelevant. Or, it would be irrelevant if it were previously relevant, but I'm glad you brought up your feelings," said Fitzgerald. He picked up the menu.

"Don't feel obliged to tell me whether I needed to say what I just said."

"It was great to study together. You've got a great handle on . . . on mitochondria."

The waiter came. Ming felt unable to read the menu, and pointed at a lunch item in the middle of the page. She got up to use the bathroom, and wondered in the mirror why she had not worn lipstick—not taken a minute this morning to look good. Then, she reminded herself that she should have actually taken measures to appear unattractive. Nonetheless, Ming examined her purse for lipstick, finding only extra pens and a crumpled exam schedule. When she returned, they smiled politely at each other for a little while. They ate, and the noodles fell persistently from Fitzgerald's chopsticks onto the plate, resisting consumption. Ming asked if he wanted a fork, and he refused. After a while, as Fitzgerald's pad thai continued to slither from his grasp, Ming caught the waiter's eye, who noticed Fitzgerald's barely eaten plate and brought a fork without Ming having to ask.

Fitzgerald ate with the fork, and craved a beer.

"We're great study partners," said Ming, still holding her chopsticks. "I want to clarify that it's not because of you." She *had* to get into medical school this year, and therefore couldn't allow distraction. Her family, she said, was modern in what they wanted for her education, and old-fashioned in what they imagined for her husband. They would disapprove of Fitzgerald, a non-Chinese. They would be upset with Ming, and she couldn't take these risks while she prepared to apply for medical school. The delicate nature of this goal, upon which one must be crucially focused, superseded everything else, Ming reminded Fitzgerald. He stopped eating while she talked. She looked down, stabbed her chopsticks into the noodles, and twisted them around.

He asked, "What about you?"

"What do you mean, me?" she said.

"Telling me this. Did you feel . . . interested?"

"I thought *you* might be."

"You might say that I've noticed you, but I accept the situation. Priorities." The imperative of medical school applications carried the unassailable weight of a religious edict.

"Very well," she said, as if they had clarified a business arrangement.

The bill came. Fitzgerald tried to pay and Ming protested. He said that she could get the bill next time and she insisted that they should share.

She said, "See you in January," and left. He had not even put his coat on, and afterwards she felt badly, decided she should have been calm and walked out into the street with him. Not just *should have*. She wanted to have done that, to have at least allowed herself to pretend, for the length of a city block, that there was something between them. Except that her cousins and family's friends were numerous on campus, and might notice her and Fitzgerald walking together without any academic justification for each other's company. Not that those of her own age would disapprove, and not that they would do anything less themselves. They would be enthusiastic about such gossip, and it was the talk that could be dangerous.

Fitz struggled into his sweater, took it off again, sat for a little while, and then ordered a pint. There came the relief and ease of the first drink. With this sense of mild well-being, and having abstained completely over the exam weeks, and with no more tests to write and Ming having fled, why not have another? So another beer, and with it the open hurt of feeling sorry for himself. This was the part he liked least, when he wanted to cling to something. This feeling was a lingering shadow of what he had felt when his mother went away, and reminded Fitz of how his father had become cold except when morose in drink. This was the worst part of it, both familiar and unhappy. What was new to Fitz was that he felt a pain at not having Ming. The pain of rejection was a significant shade different from the longing of desire, he noted, although drawn from the same palette. This sombre phase could generally be gotten through with a few more, and therefore justified the third drink. A washroom break. With the third pint came the brink between anger and the careless release that could sometimes be achieved and was the goal of the drinking. Fitz tried to will himself into this easy release, to tip over the meniscus of anger that grew like water perched higher than the rim of a glass, but it didn't work today. It didn't spill over so that he could relax, and instead he grew angry at his mother for crashing her car, at the doctors for not saving her, at his father for being his father, at himself for drinking, at Ming for being scared. After a fourth pint, the waiter brought him the bill and Fitz paid it with no tip, angry at the waiter for presuming that it was time for the bill. He told himself not to think about Ming because the anger didn't help him deal with the hurt of rejection. He let himself out into the street where it was still snowing, that drifting quiet veil that sometimes persists after a storm.

—

During the previous month, Ming and Fitzgerald had studied at the same table in the library. For self-identified "med school keeners" (the label was inherently self-designated even for those who publicly denied it), study tables were the monks' cells of exam time. Adherents arrived early in the morning and sat silently except for whispered exchanges. There was a desperate devotion to the impending sacrament and judgment of the exam. The faithful departed late at night, and returned upon the library's opening. At first Ming and Fitzgerald sat at the same table coincidentally, but gradually the third table from the corner window became their table. One day they courteously acknowledged that they were studying for the same examinations, and then later that day murmured about phosphorylation reactions.

Sometimes, Fitzgerald closed his eyes and mouthed words while he memorized. Ming pretended to look out the window, allowed herself to briefly watch the half-image of his reflection speaking silently. She could see that he was immersed in the material, that he was trying to get inside it. She admired this, and longed for Fitzgerald because of it. Ming had decided to be occupied primarily with the facts in her textbooks, and less with comprehension. Ionic channels were not a wonderful riddle to her, as she knew they were to Fitzgerald. They were simply a means to an end, that end being a perfect set of grades and a medical school admission letter. Hers was the more common attitude in the life sciences faculty, and so Ming regarded Fitzgerald as being pure and noble, if strategically unwise.

Midway through the exams, they grew into a twice daily session of going through questions. Fitzgerald proposed that they use these question sessions as breaks, and so they visited the library cafeteria twice a day. Ming considered going to the cafeteria to be an indulgent use of time, but she decided that it was acceptable as long as they discussed only academics, and as long as she didn't spend too much time actually enjoying Fitzgerald's company.

They ate, clarified the puzzles of cell membrane physiology, and talked about their need to become physicians. Others were not genuine, they agreed, and transparently wanted to become doctors for money and prestige. Ming and Fitzgerald wanted medicine for the right reasons, they told each other: service, humanity, giving. Because their motivations were clean, they were certain they deserved it more than those among them. They did not ask why they wanted to serve, be humane, or to give. These simply felt like the right motivations, and being correctly motivated should improve their chances of success. This was enough, and these sentiments felt easy and immune from questioning. If forced to reflect, both Ming and Fitzgerald would have had to admit that these convictions were, at their core, somewhat improvised. They did not challenge each other, but instead reinforced each other's sense of moral correctness as a virtuous conspiracy of two.

Their consuming ambition was the same as those of their classmates, but they agreed that most of the people around them were fake. Ming did allow that, although she did not want to pursue medicine for the money, earning a good living was important to her.

"I like being obsessed by things," said Fitzgerald one day. "It suits me." He did not tell Ming that he supposed that if his attentions had happened to fall upon something other than medicine, he would have been equally engrossed with it.

Ming paced exams like a marathon. In a three-hour examination, she finished her initial draft within a strictly self-enforced two hours. For twenty minutes, she returned to uncomfortable questions she had indicated with a lightly pencilled star. After reworking her response she erased the star because she didn't believe in changing an answer more than once. For another twenty minutes, she focused on the crucial phrasing of the questions, ensuring that her answers corresponded. They altered questions subtly from the previous years' versions in an attempt to throw off those who studied from the prohibited, but widely available, pool of old exams. Ming was vigilant that a four-point question receive no more than four indisputably correct facts in the answer; it was possible to lose marks by including incorrect extra information. She sat straight, with her ankles crossed under her seat.

In her assigned seat behind Fitzgerald, Ming sometimes glanced up at him, saw him curled over his
papers. In some sessions he wrote furiously until the
invigilator came to take the paper from him. At other
times, he finished writing within an hour and then fid-
geted while everyone else worked. Fitzgerald constantly slipped his shoes on and off, and once
accidentally kicked his right shoe two rows across. The
invigilator retrieved it, and pulled out the insole to
check for any hidden papers before returning it to
Fitzgerald with a recommendation that his shoes stay
on his feet.

Ming called Fitzgerald late that night, hours after she
had rushed away from her half-eaten pad thai. He
woke to the phone ringing, his head pounding with an
early evening hangover.

She said, "You've been honest, so I should be. I am
attracted to you, and now that we both understand
this problem, we shouldn't study together or even see
each other."

"Does that make it more clear?"

"It's only that the whole thing will go wrong."

Fitzgerald pointed out the competitively lonely
nature of their faculty, spoke in a seemingly spontaneous and heartfelt way about the improbability and
importance of human connection, and said, "Why don't
we be friends, of an academic nature." It was at this
moment, as he said this in a comforting manner, that

Ming became certain that she was in love with him. They concluded that since they were adults with common priorities, and agreed that a relationship was inadvisable, there was no reason why they couldn't help each other study. After hanging up, Ming felt pleased in a longing, distanced way. She could be in love with Fitz in this protection of an agreement, with an understanding between them that there would be no romance, and so, she decided, she would not be hurt.

The graded biochemistry finals were the last set to be distributed in the second week of January. Fitzgerald flipped through his paper, adding up the numbers. Ming opened her locker and thrust her own exam into the bottom of her knapsack. She was unsure whether to ask Fitzgerald the sensitive question, the private issue. Some people made a show of displaying their victories, or their self-flagellation at a disappointment. Ming felt that grades were fundamentally secret successes and defeats. On the other hand, Fitzgerald lingered near her. No, she wouldn't ask. She was not afraid of him doing better than her. It was just that he might feel that she was being nosy in the publicly competitive way that she hated, or would think that she cared, which should be avoided.

"I won't make the cut-off," said Fitzgerald. He looked up.

In the way that a mother asks a child to show her a boo-boo she said, "Show me."

"I needed to ace this," he said, handing her the paper.

Ming was embarrassed by his grade, by his lower lip drawn tight, and by her own result.

"The cut-off changes every year," she said. It was believed that a magic grade point average was required in order to get an interview. Ming searched for an error in the addition of marks, hoping to find that ten points had simply not been added. She could give this to Fitzgerald like a gift, although this happening would be like finding a hundred-dollar bill lying in the street. Among the medical school applicants there were theories about MCAT scores, varying schools of thought about curricula vitae, and tales circulated about what so and so's brother and such and such's sister were asked in their interviews. Small groups of people who sat shoulder to shoulder in every lecture shared underground treasuries of old exams, but denied their existence to anyone outside their number. It would have been commonly agreed that Fitzgerald's grade of seventy-eight was a liability.

"How did you do?" asked Fitzgerald.

"Okay."

"Most people wouldn't be so modest."

"I lost two marks, but made them up with the bonus," she said. She had to tell him. There was an accepted notion of *I'll show you mine if you show me yours*, and she felt good telling him. Whenever Ming got her marks, the numbers first gave her a sense of relief, and only once this moment passed did she allow herself to feel some pleasure. Then came the fear that if she became pleased and complacent, she might fail in the future. She reminded herself of the ease with which perfection could be lost, and was wary of being satisfied with her grades. Now, it felt good to tell Fitzgerald that she had received a perfect score. Still looking at his exam, she said, "Get this regraded."

"Found something?"

"I can't find marks, but you *understand* this stuff. You're losing marks on detail. The Krebs cycle—you know it better than I do. The problem is the way you study and write." She said this not only to be kind, but because she found his answers elegant and insightful. Ming's own responses were always factually complete in point form, convenient to check off for a perfect score. Fitzgerald seemed to disregard the assigned value of questions, and in some three-inch spaces he cramped his writing into tiny letters in order to include the essay-length breadth he felt was appropriate. In another section where a page was allotted, he wrote four lines and drew a diagram that, to him, encapsulated the entire issue.

It was Ming's cousin Karl who had taught her the rules of academic success: be meticulous about details because it's easier to lose two marks than to earn eight, understand what will be asked and prepare to deliver it, expect that the next test will be harder and that this is your reward for success. When Karl was eighteen and Ming was twelve, it was as a big favour to her father that her uncle had agreed to allow Karl to use some of his valuable time to tutor the B student, Ming. Karl was the shining boy who filled her uncle's mantelpiece with academic trophies. He was on scholarship in his first year of university biology while Ming blundered through junior high.

Ming's father impressed upon her the importance of learning from her cousin, of not bringing shame to her parents. She admired Karl's easy confidence and the way he grasped everything he wanted—each award, each prize. He taught her a system—a way of breaking knowledge into manageable packages that might be related but didn't have to be, that didn't even have to matter, but the facts of which must be internalized, mastered, and displayed without so much as a momentary lack of confidence. To lose sight of any of these lists, subjects, or compartments would be to fail, and if you failed any part—whatever else had been learned would not matter when the time came to see if you would be allowed to write the next, tougher test.

"Well, congratulations, Doctor Ming," said Fitzgerald, his grin too wide. She knew he genuinely intended it, but that it was hard to smile through his frustration.

"That's a bit premature," she said. She rolled his biochemistry final into a tube in her hand and said, "How was your Plato?" This was his humanities elective, and she did not take the same course so there could be no comparison.

"Top of the class," he said.

"Wonderful."

"In the philosophy department, that's a seventy-one."

"You need to strategize your electives," she said. Hers was introductory psychology, a course that fulfilled its reputation of providing an easy A+.

"Next year," he said. Each year, a few were admitted to medicine. Some rejected applicants decided that they had other things to do with their lives, and the remaining aspirants continued to fill out application packages and resubmit them. "I'll be more strategic next year."

"If you don't get in, no one deserves to get in. This grade point business is a stupid, arbitrary system," she said, profoundly believing this as someone who had completely mastered it.

"I'll be happy when you get in," he said. "Really, truly. Lots of people say that, but I really will be pleased for you."

"Thank you," she said. Ming believed that he *would* be happy for her, though many would say so and it would be fake. She wanted to tell him about how she tried to save seats for him in the lectures without wanting him to see that she was doing so, about how she liked seeing him ride his bicycle around campus in the snow—pants tucked into his socks—and about how certain things scared her just enough that she couldn't indulge her present impulse to lean toward him.

Instead, she said, "I'll jinx myself, talking as if I'll get in. Don't say 'Doctor Ming' or it'll end up being a joke." She looked at her feet and said, as Karl had once told her, "We have to dissect your study techniques."

The following day, Ming went through Fitzgerald's December finals and pointed out that he had mostly lost marks through a flagrant disregard for testable trivia. She introduced him to her scheduling system, in which each week was divided into a chart with half-hour time slots.

Monday
7:00: Wake up, wash.
7:30: Breakfast and pre-read a lecture chapter.
8:00: Bus to school.
8:30: Lecture.
9:30: Pre-read next lecture.
10:00: Second lecture.
11:00: Review morning lecture tapes while eating lunch.
12:30: Relax.
13:00: Third lecture.

Ming crossed out each time slot as it was completed.

Fitzgerald's note taking had previously been limited to what he felt was conceptually relevant, summarized by diagrams. Often, details were not included in the diagrams because they did not seem important to him. A tape recorder and a yellow highlighter were the core of Ming's system. After each lecture, she listened to her tape of it and ensured that every testable fact mentioned in the lecture was included in her notes. While studying, she highlighted notes as she committed them to memory, until her entire notebook was a glaring neon yellow.

"It's not that concepts are unimportant," Ming reassured Fitzgerald, "it's simply that they're not essential to scoring top marks." She had mentioned that her cousin Karl was a surgical resident in Toronto, but did not explain that this was Karl's study system. Why should she tell Fitzgerald, an "academic friend," everything?

Each night they spoke on the telephone—always at the end of the evening so that there was no disruption of the sacred studies, nor a time limit. Conversations began with questions about the day's lectures, but veered off more and more often so that they had to remind each other of their primary obligation to help the other study. They talked about what they would do, see, and allow themselves once they had fulfilled their delayed gratification of becoming doctors. Ming thought of the two of them doing these things together, far away from her family, yet she was careful not to refer to "we" while discussing these fantasies. Although everything was fragile and crucial right now, it would all be perfect once they achieved the state of being medical students. It floated before them like a transcendental and elusive plane of existence. They allowed that it would be a challenging profession, but it felt obvious that once admitted, the difficult thing would be done.

Occasionally, they ate lunch in restaurants that did not have many windows. Ming was careful to place textbooks on the table, so that each other's presence could be easily explained if she was seen by any of her cousins or family's friends, who seemed to be everywhere on campus. Dinner or a movie were out of the question. Between classes, they studied in vacant classrooms. Once, while looking for an empty classroom, they both reached for an elevator button at the same time, and after their arms brushed, warm, went silently into the room, sat down, opened their books, and didn't speak for an hour.

At night, the phone sometimes clicked softly, and then the sound became hollow with a shadow of breathing. When this occurred, Ming stopped talking and waited for the phone to click off. Fitzgerald learned to do the same. If the other line did not click off after several moments, Ming and her father would converse briefly in Cantonese, and then she would say to Fitzgerald in a voice that was halfway between meek library mouse and breathless seducer, "Thank you for helping me with my study problems," and all three parties would hang up.

Ming was offered four medical school interviews, and Fitzgerald none. She felt that this placed a protective expiry date on their relationship, and wondered whether they might hold hands sometimes—couldn't this be entirely platonic and also somewhat comforting? More and more, she wanted to grasp his palms, his fingers. She thought of him while studying, which scared her. Fitzgerald posed unusual questions to professors during lectures, which frequently provoked tangential answers. Ming found herself rewinding her tapes to listen to him ask these questions, and it bothered her that she wanted to hear his voice.

Because of the way in which her interviews were scheduled toward the end of March, Ming convinced her parents that the obvious thing was for her to travel to Toronto on Friday for her Saturday morning interview, then spend the weekend there and go to Hamilton for her Monday morning interview before returning to Ottawa. She insisted that she needed to travel without them in order to concentrate. Ming hadn't asked Fitzgerald, nor had he made the suggestion, but between them they had decided that he would come to Toronto with her.

"You can help me prep for my interview. Afterwards, we'll have dinner together," said Ming. It was her reward to herself, she decided, this extravagant pleasure which was only possible in a city where she was a stranger.

"You get to choose the restaurant."

"We might as well stay in the same hotel room."

"Because of the cost."

"I specified two twin beds."

"Needless to say," he added quickly.

After a pause she said, "Not to imply that you would imagine differently."

He was her best friend and study partner, she reasoned, and therefore it was normal that she would want his company. Besides, it was her parents' own fault that they would not understand this, therefore she would not tell them.

"Next question," said Ming. It was one o'clock. That morning, they would travel to Toronto. They lay in their respective beds, in their separate homes, talking on the telephone. Ming was curled on her side in the dark. Her muscles ached as if they had been stretched beyond a natural length and then allowed to recoil into tightly wound balls. She imagined Fitzgerald lying on his back, the sheet of paper on his knees, the light from the reading lamp yellow on the page. She knew the paper he held, because she had given him this list of interview questions from previous applicants' Toronto interviews. It had the pebbly look of a photocopy of a copy of a copy. He read questions, which she answered like lines in a play. Ming foresaw the aloneness of saying goodnight, and wished that she could hold him.

Even so, she felt panic as if being attacked when, at that moment, he said, "Do you think that if things were different, we could be lying together right now?"

"Fitzgerald, this is the worst possible time for you to say that."

"Sorry."

"The hotel has two beds, and the only reason I agreed to you coming is because we're unemotional friends, and you're supposed to help me with my interview. Not get me all screwed up." She spoke as if the idea of Fitzgerald coming to Toronto was entirely his doing.

"But don't you wish we weren't afraid of each other?"

"We need to go through all the questions once more."

"It's better if you answer them spontaneously."

"For you, that's the way. For me, I need to be prepared," she said.

"It's more honest if you just go for it."

"You think they want honesty?"

"They'll throw you questions that aren't on this sheet."

"Fine, Mr. Interviewer. Make up something, then."

Laughing, Fitzgerald said, "Miss Ming, do you really, truly, deeply care about humanity as you claim in your essay?"

"Doesn't everyone who sits in this stupid chair?"

"Tell me, Miss Ming, what's the most terrible thing you have done in your life?"

She had been thinking of this, of wanting to tell him about that which answered this question. It would be a trial run of telling it to a man she was in love with, as it would seem somehow necessary to tell such a theoretical man. This would be ideal, she had already reasoned, because Fitzgerald resembled a person that she might fall in love with. In this instance, however, their pre-set constraints meant that nothing would be lost by discussing this thing that she carried like a full bowl of water on her head—so careful to not spill it and yet every moment wanting to smash it into the ground.

Ming said, "Do you really want to know?"

"I must know, Miss Ming. We only admit the purest of character."

"Forget the interview shtick. I want to tell you something."

He said, "You want to confess that you fantasize about me." They had both come to accept an ongoing flirtation of feigned seriousness. It allowed them to vocalize their desires in a way that—by being absolutely straightforward—they could treat as a joke.

She pulled her legs up to her chest. "I want to tell you something true and awful, which I really hate. Will we go on being friends?"

He said, "We'll be the same people."

"Except that there's a part of me that you don't see yet—that's very dark—and you might think I'm a bad person."

"You mean the fact that you're withholding the truth—that you're deeply and soulfully in love with me, as I am with you," said Fitzgerald. Again, this reality was spoken directly to discount itself. This time, she felt, it sounded slightly too honest to function as the usual throwaway, and given what she was about to tell him, she felt angry at Fitzgerald for saying these words which mocked them both. Now scared, she said, "It's awful, that our friendship has become important. I wanted to keep everything sterile. I wanted to go to medical school and start fresh."

He retreated, saying, "It's best that there's . . . nothing between us, then."

Briefly, she thought of making something up, of confessing to something silly. But Fitzgerald had a good instinct for knowing what wasn't true, of hearing what didn't fit. Besides, maybe she would tell him and he would hate her. It would be tidy and finished. She said, "I had this, you know, this relationship."

"Sure," said Fitzgerald.

"Maybe for you it's no big deal," she said. Then, "I'm being touchy."

Ming's chest pounded, and her breath felt as if it was coming through a small straw. She was afraid that her next word would crack, and was angry at herself for being close to crying, for not letting the silly fake-interview question slide away. She had come to assume Fitzgerald's kindness, but now felt trapped in actually needing to trust it. She said, "It was from when I was twelve until not very long ago. With Karl, who taught me to study."

A short silence, which seemed to stretch. A click, then the hollow tone.

The other line had been picked up. She could not see—little points of light swirled in front of her. The click had occurred only after she had finished speaking, hadn't it? Or had it just clicked off? Had the other line been open all this time, and had it just clicked off? Ming's stomach was tight. Was her father listening now, or had he listened? Wait . . . the telephone silence had that hollow sound right now. Was she fooling herself—what was a sound with no one speaking? Then, as she tried to discern the nature of the silence, as she wished that she could reach across the quiet to take Fitzgerald's hand, Ming's father said in Cantonese, "Little daughter, you have an important trip tomorrow. Sleep, please."

"Goodnight then, Fitzgerald," she said in a buoyant public voice. "He was pretending to interview me, Dad. Thanks again, Fitz, take good notes for me."

At two o'clock Ming called back. "So?" she asked.

"We were friends before, and now it's the same," said Fitz.

"And?"

"And you are very honest. I shouldn't come to Toronto, though."

"That's fine," she said, "I don't know why you wanted to follow me around."

"You need to focus on your interview. I don't want to distract you."

"I'm curious as to why you think that if you had come, which I agree that you should *not*, you would have been distracting. We have an agreement. Nothing romantic, and so I'm confused that you would think that *I* might be liable to be distracted by *you*."

"Then we agree," he said.

———

At three-fifteen, Ming called Fitzgerald again, tried to keep her voice clear. She needed to tell it, the way a scab must, at times, be picked off the body and made to bleed before the finger is satisfied.

"At first it was Karl's hand on my knee as he explained the periodic table. I didn't think much of it, although it felt strange—he's my cousin, after all."

When she wrote her first perfect exam paper and showed it to Karl before showing her father, he pecked his lips on hers. It was brief initially, but the congratulatory kisses became longer and slower. In the wetness of lips, Ming could see Karl's weakness in his desire, and began to enjoy this power at the same time that she began to enjoy the kisses. Physical pleasure did not do away with her habit of rinsing and spitting ten times (she counted) immediately after Karl's departure, or the "letters to self" detailing why she was a filthy slut. She discarded these in the garbage at the bus stop on her way to school. One afternoon before she wrote her entrance exams for Dunning Hall Girls' Academy, Karl told Ming that he was busy, and might not be able to tutor anymore. Terrified of losing her new academic success, Ming pleaded with him to make time for her, and he agreed to come over that afternoon. She had begun to pretend while they were kissing that they weren't really cousins, that she was adopted, or he was. That day, she didn't stop his hand when it slid up her leg, underwear tight at the waist with his strong hand pulling on it. Although this was frightening, she was more scared of losing him, and she liked it that he fumbled, that he wasn't sure where to go. Later, when he slid the condom off, it looked exactly like a snake shedding its skin. Only then did it occur to her that he had been prepared, that he had brought a rubber. Ming told her parents that she wanted to become a doctor, which was also Karl's ambition. Pleased, they doubled their severity in urging her to study.

Karl was accepted into medicine in his third year of biology. To celebrate, there was a twelve-course family banquet, the pan-fried lobsters sizzling and turning on the Lazy Susan. Ming's uncle proclaimed a generation of success, with Ming as the next doctor. She learned of Karl's failed second-year application from his sister, who whispered of this shame to her. Karl was a whirlpool of family approval whom Ming increasingly feared and hoped to imitate. He dated, and she was jealous. He told her that what they had between them was a special thing, and she tried to believe this.

In Ming's last year of high school, Karl went away for a month of rural training, and Ming felt cleaner and lighter. She aced chemistry without his help. When he returned, Ming told him that she didn't need his tutoring anymore. Karl threatened that he could influence her medical school application. He said it with such bravado that she recognized that this was not the first of his lies. The study sessions ended.

Now, Karl was doing his surgical residency in Toronto,

and they avoided each other at family gatherings. He had put his hand on her breast once this year, in an upstairs hallway during a birthday party, and she had threatened to scream.

It was four-fifteen in the morning.

She said, "You thought I was so perfect."

"You seem to have everything under such control."

"I cultivate that notion. I used to stand in front of the mirror and call myself *slut, bitch.* Not out loud—I was afraid someone would hear, so I mouthed the words. I felt like I deserved to be called names. Then Karl told me how good I was when we did what he liked, and when I brought home my grades my parents were happy and proud."

"You were a kid. How could you know what to do?"

"That idea should absolve me, except it also takes something away. I looked forward to seeing him, although he was my nightmare. I got stuck. If I don't recognize that I enjoyed certain things, even the sex, then I was a stupid lump. No. I was there and made decisions, but was I coerced? Of course. I got things, but only some of them were what I asked for. These thoughts go round and round. You know how I distract myself? I study. Every last little detail, and it fills my head. Karl taught me how to study for marks—how to write all these stupid tests—and now I forget myself by stuffing my head full."

There was quiet, and then after a little while

Fitzgerald said, "You know I love you." Again silence, and then, "I might as well say it."

"It may be the same for me, but I'm afraid of it."

At seven in the morning, when she woke up, Ming realized that she had not asked Fitzgerald whether he was coming to Toronto. Ming's father delivered her to the train station, the long line of travellers snaking under the black maze of girders. She saw Fitzgerald buying a ticket at the booth. Her father, for whom Fitzgerald was an invisible telephone threat, was oblivious as Fitz walked past them toward the end of the line. At the platform, Ming's father squeezed her and told her how much honour she would bring to the family if she succeeded. Ming boarded, and sat alone until she had waved her father goodbye. Only then did she find Fitzgerald. At nine-thirty, the soft clanking rhythm of the iron wheels on the joints of the track came quicker and closer as the train escaped Ottawa's southern suburbs. Exhausted from the sleepless night, Ming grasped Fitzgerald's hand, and rested her head in the cleft between his shoulder and chest, amazed at the way the sides of their bodies fit together. It was a physical relief for them to touch. He kissed the top of her head and, as she fell asleep, Ming breathed in deeply this sweetly unfamiliar warmth.

TAKE ALL OF MURPHY

—
—
—

THE THREE STUDENTS STOOD BESIDE THE WRAPPED body lying on the metal table. They all wore clean, new laboratory coats that still had creases down the arms and over the breast pockets from being folded and stacked in a box. These white coats were the same size, even though the wearers were of varying build. All three medical students were size medium, but differently framed. Ming had her cuffs rolled up twice.

They had come in from the hot early afternoon of an autumn day, a remnant of summer. They had entered the basement by an unmarked inner staircase, and then approached the lab through a plain, combination-locked door. There were fourteen dissection rooms, eight tables per room, three students assigned per table, checking the tags to find their cadaver, whispering and shuffling like white-coated ghosts in the basement anatomy lab. No windows. Instead, a dry fluorescent light flattened every surface.

"You want to go first?" asked Ming.

"I don't mind," said Sri.

"Me neither," said Chen, holding the blade hesitantly between his thumb and second and third fingers.

"Well, to me, it doesn't matter," said Ming. "What about you?" she asked, turning to Sri. When he paused, she said, "If it's a problem for you I'll start the cutting."

To Sri, Ming seemed both overly eager and fearful regarding the task, and Sri did not want their dissection to begin with this mix of emotions. Sri felt only fear, which he believed was a better way to begin this undertaking, and so he said, "I'll start." He gripped the blade handle firmly.

"Not if you don't want to," said Chen, seeing Sri's discomfort. "I can."

"I'll start." Sri shifted closer.

That morning, they had been briefed in the lecture theatre by Dean Cortina: "A few of you might be upset initially. You may temporarily excuse yourselves if necessary. In any case, I would rather you be a bit emotional than, shall

*we say, overly cavalier. Keep in mind that distasteful inci-
dents regarding cadavers have, in the past, resulted in
expulsion."*

*She reminded them that there was to be no eating or
drinking in the dissection rooms, although snacks could
be consumed in the anatomy museum as long as it was
kept tidy.*

"I think it's easier if you hold it like a pen," said Ming.
When Sri said nothing, she added, "All I'm saying is
that if you hold it like a. . . . Well, never mind, suit
yourself of course, it's only that—"

"Just let me do it," said Sri. "Let me stand there."
He moved to stand where Ming was, without waiting
for her to make way. She shifted, avoiding collision.
Ming and Chen were quiet.

Sri began to cut the cotton wrap, a stringy damp net,
discoloured yellow in its folds. It smelled tough. First
he cut downward like when you lean with the first finger on a boned meat. This dented it, but the fabric was
swelling inwards instead of giving. He turned the
scalpel upward, and lifted the edge of the fabric to slip
the blade beneath it. He sawed back and forth, and the
threads twisted when severed.

"What about scissors?" whispered Chen.

Dr. Harrison, their anatomy demonstrator, appeared
at their table, congratulated them upon entering the
study of medicine, and said, "This fine cadaver is your
first patient. Dignity and decorum are crucial. You

must be mindful of this gift you are given, and treat your patient nobly." He paused. "Nobility. You may give him . . . or her?" Harrison checked the tag. "Ah, him, a name if you like. Or not. That's up to you. No frivolous names. Questions? No? Very well. Continue, then." All of this he managed to say with his hands crossed neatly in front of himself, and then he was at the next table, nodding seriously.

The fabric now open, Ming took scissors and cut it wider in a quick, impatient motion, spreading the fabric up to the neck and then down to the navel. The damp skin of the cadaver's chest was a shocking beige within the yellowed fabric.

"There," said Ming.

"Are you going to do it?" said Sri, not offering the scalpel. He hadn't moved, and she had leaned across him to open the swath of cloth.

"I was just trying to help, you know, get things going."

"I already said I'll do it."

"As you prefer."

Sri now held the scalpel like a pen. He looked at the manual. The manual was very particular, and Sri wanted to follow it with clarity. The incision should begin at the top of the sternum, extend downward to the xiphoid. *A central incision,* it read. Ming opened the fabric, pulled it to either side, the nipples purple on the rubber-cold skin. Still not moving, Sri stared at the manual's exact instructions. There was a dotted line drawn from the top of the sternum in the illustration, an arrow pointing toward the navel but stopping short of it. Sri straightened the veil, covered the nipples. He gripped the scalpel hard, like a dull pencil.

"Right down the middle," said Ming. "Like a zipper. But if you're going to take forever—"

Sri grabbed the scalpel handle like a stick and buried the short, triangular blade in the midline of the chest. Flesh gripped the blade, and through the handle Sri felt its texture—thick and chalky. Steel scraping on sternum. Sri thought of a beach—of writing with a stick in hard sand thrown halfway up from the tide, with the water not far away. Through his knuckles, Sri felt fibres tearing. The cadaver's flesh pulled hard at him now. Halfway there. It ripped at Sri, to cut this skin. He tore it, forced his way through. He pulled open the cotton shroud. This old, wrung-out chest with small lopsided man-breasts. Above the left nipple were four tattooed hearts in purple, the shape of the designs twisted by the skin's movement through its years. A clean, jagged tear through the centre—the sternum white beneath. Sri was amazed by the pale ivory of this man's bone.

The three of them stood erect at the shining cold table. The man now lay slightly unwrapped. The cloths wound around themselves up and over his neck, then tenderly wrapped the face. They had been told the heads would all be shaved. The table was indented, and the indentation traced down to a hole between the feet.

The hole opened into a spout over a bucket so fluids could escape as they ran down the table. On the steel was the man-form in soaked cloth. His chest was gashed now. The chest was not shaved but thick with cold hair. Hair parted now by one crooked stabbing cut that peeled open the front.

"Good job, Sri," said Chen.

"Feels funny."

"I guess it's my turn."

There were eight dissection tables in the room. Whispers shuddered up from the floor as the familiar touch of skin became distorted. One hushed voice: *Haven't we all seen bodies before?* At another table, one student held the cloth up while the other two cut at it. All of the students wore new lab coats, which they had been told they would need to discard once the dissection was done.

One day when Chen was in Dean Cortina's office to discuss student loans, she said to him, "I remember my dissection group. Oh, what year, I don't want to tell you. I remember some comments that were made . . . regarding dissection material. You see, in my time it was all people from the jails or found dead in fights or ditches. No identification and so forth. What you would call bad people. Yours are different, all volunteers. Elderly, upstanding citizens mostly. Ours were young people with fast lifestyles. Virile, some might say. Although I guess it's really no different once they're cadavers.

"Anyhow. I remember some guy saying, 'Wow look at this one, what a broad.' I didn't like that, you know, I didn't think it was right. On the other hand, I remember we dissected a big man. Muscular, built, and someone called him an ox . . . as if to say what a powerful man, a big strong man. So they called him an ox. Vernacular to be sure, but it was out of respect and to say he must have been impressive. I thought that was all right. I didn't like someone saying 'what a broad,' though. What was he looking at? That sort of sexual appeal was not the right way to think. I spoke up, oh certainly I did, I said to this guy who was laughing, 'You wouldn't like a man calling your sister a broad.' He was angry. He was pissed off and he said, 'My sister is alive so shut up.'"

Dean Cortina laughed. "So I said, 'It's not cool to call your sister a broad because she's alive?' Boy, he was upset."

Chen didn't know quite how to respond, so he agreed in a polite and very general way, and left without resolving the issue of his student loan.

On the day the ribs were cut to get at the organs, the room shrieked with hand-held rotary saws. Bone dust—it was in your hair, on your lips afterwards.

"Smells like barbecue," shouted Ming.

Sri leaned off the saw, held it, still buzzing, in front of him, and regarded Ming is if amazed at her. As if about to speak. Instead, he diverted his eyes from her and said, "Where's the manual?"

Chen walked out quickly, his hand over his mouth, almost running. When he came back he was red and wet in the face, his hair pushed back and damp. "I'm fine. Are you finished cutting?"

The chest opened to show the heart's chambers, where the great vessels now lay at rest. These sinuous vessels coursed to the lungs, and splayed into the organs and limbs. The lungs were fringed with the gritty black of tobacco.

"Aren't there people who fill their dead with stones," murmured Chen, "and sink them to the bottom of the sea?"

"You're thinking of concrete boots. Gangsters did that." Ming didn't look up as she peeled away a strip of fat.

"No, after they die naturally. As a burial ceremony. They take out the heart and lungs and fill this," he patted the inside wall of the chest, "with stones so the body sinks."

"What do they do with the organs?" asked Ming.

"I can't remember that part. Who are they?" He turned to Sri.

Ming also turned to Sri, "Do your people do that?"

"We burn them."

"Must smell," said Ming.

"What do you think?"

"I guess it smells. Like cutting bone. Like—" she laughed, "forget it."

Sri said little for the rest of the lab time, and his quietness spilled uncomfortably over the other two, so

that all three worked in a thick silence for the rest of
the day. Cutting through layers, spreading tissue, saying only what was necessary.

Sri changed all of his clothing at the lab. Many people kept a shirt or coveralls in their lockers for dissection, but Sri changed everything—his underwear, his
socks—in the men's room. Always in a stall, preferably
with no one else in the washroom. That day, he heard
footsteps come into the bathroom a moment after he
had taken off his shirt. He kept still, a reflex. The footsteps were not followed by running water, or the hissing of urine on porcelain. He waited.

"Uh—Sri? Is that you, Sri?" It was Chen.

A pause. "Yeah."

"You're cool, right?"

"Yeah."

"Great. I'm glad. Ming's got a tough exterior. Right?
All bluff, you can see that."

"I said I'm cool."

"I'll see you, then."

No footsteps.

Sri crossed his arms, his naked chest prickling in the
concrete block basement. "It's fine, Chen. Thanks for
asking."

"Right. See you."

Footsteps, the squeaky door.

When they started the dissections, there were bright
mornings to come in from, and warm afternoons to go

out to after the day's work. As the weeks passed, they entered the basement on cooler mornings with a hesitant light, and departed into a fading golden afternoon. The leaves swelled with colour until they became too heavy with the intensity of reds and oranges and fell to the ground. Each day, more human anatomy was exposed, more of the organs lifted from their shy hiding places into their first glimpse of light. It was as if the actual daytime no longer existed. Night was just ending as the students arrived in the morning, just beginning as they left. The daytime of sun had been replaced by the fluorescent-bathed, whitewashed-concrete daylight of the basement, as the inverted parts of bodies were given belated and temporary glimpses of light.

Sri proposed that they name their cadaver Murphy. A dignified but comfortable name, he argued. Ming refused to use any name. Chen took neither side, suggested that each do as they please. Sri referred to "Murphy's aorta, Murphy's kidneys." Ming made a point of saying "the cadaver's aorta, the cadaver's kidneys."

Beneath the shield of diaphragm, the liver and spleen were wet and heavy. There was a stickiness to the smell where the formalin had seeped into hepatocytes and gelled the lobes of the liver into a single pungent mass.

One day the bowel tore. A line of shit squirted onto Ming's coat. It smelled like formalin, an acidic sweetness, and another smell. She wiped it off, leaving a mark, finished tracing the mesenteric circulation, and laughed when she threw the coat into the garbage. "I wanted a new coat anyhow," she said. The cuffs of her fresh coat were again too long, and soaked up fluids until she rolled them back. It became easier to dissect, as over the days the cadaver became more fragmented and the pieces more separated from one another. There was less to pry apart—it was more detail work now.

They unwrapped one arm from the wrist upward. The hand was wrapped separately. Ming held up the arm, holding the hand as if in a victory grasp. Along the flat back of the forearm was a lightning bolt tattoo—once straight lines, now soft arcs. Each branch of the lightning bolt underlined a word: one *Golden*, the other *Flash*. Chen rolled back the moist, yellow gauze. Above the elbow was a ring of small figures: crosses? No, airplanes. In addition to the thumbprint-sized fuselage and wings were the remnants of little propellers, now faded into age spots and the creases of oldness. Above the airplanes in official type was tattooed *RCAF—17th Squadron*. Above this was a Spitfire with an open shark's jaw. The tail of the Spitfire was ajar due to a thick scar across the fuselage that had been sewn shut dirty, long ago. The ring of airplanes stood wing to wing on the front of the arm above the elbow, and then there was a gap on the inside of the arm.

"Go, killer," said Ming triumphantly. Then, when they looked at her, "All those planes. He must have shot them down. You'll have to call him Lieutenant Murphy."

"A pilot?" said Chen.

"There's some planes missing," said Ming. "He didn't get enough to go all the way around."

Sri touched the tattooed arm. "I guess the war ended."

"It's good they started the tattoos from the outside," said Ming.

Chen bunched up the gauze and snipped it. He continued to unroll, revealing a rich and delicate crucifix within a heart, large over the hump of shoulder. In gothic letters under the crucifix: *The Lord Keeps Me— Mark 16.* The gauze was off the arm. Ming opened the manual.

"Okay, so down here, and then across." She pointed with the blunt edge of the blade.

"Mark. From the Bible, right?" said Sri.

"It's one of the four books in the second half," said Chen.

"What is that part?"

"Um . . . I don't know. The overview is simple: Jesus died on the cross to save us, rose from the dead after three days. As for Mark 16 . . ."

"It must mean something," said Sri.

"I'll look it up for you," said Chen.

"Why don't we cut around it?" Sri's small finger traced one arm of the cross. The cross expanded to curve across each side of the arm with its faded blue wrought ironwork.

"The manual shows," Ming said, "to cut here."

"It is a shame," said Chen, "to cut this apart." The manual's illustration advised an incision directly over the tattooed arm.

"We can easily cut around." Sri spun his scalpel in the fingers of one hand, which he often did until someone reminded him, or he remembered, that it was not a pen.

"What are you going to do," said Ming, "save this?"

"It's bad luck," said Sri. "Cut around here." He traced the ornate heart with the handle of his scalpel.

"It's a nice cross," agreed Chen.

"You guys." Ming didn't look up. She traced the incision lines on the arm. "It's not going to work. Don't you want to see the bicipital groove?"

"You should respect a man's symbols," said Sri. "My mother told me that. Look at his arm. These are his symbols."

"Don't your people burn the corpses anyhow?" said Ming, grabbing the tattooed arm.

"He's not my people."

"Let's get on with it."

"But that's not the point," said Sri.

"So what's the point? You afraid of lightning bolts?"

"I'm not afraid of you." He twirled the scalpel nervously, met Ming's stare.

"Why don't you cut around," said Chen, breaking their locked eyes. "Then dissect the subcutaneous layer? It'll be the same."

Dr. Harrison was an origami man. In his room of eight tables, they first learned how to make paper boats.

"Let me show you how to tuck in the corners so that it'll be tight and waterproof," he said. Each day in the lab, after dissection, came the origami.

"All right, my friends, I hope you've learned well and are ready to set your knowledge free." Each day, every student had to select a page from the lab manual, cut it out carefully at the spiral binding, and fold it into that day's paper figure. After the boats came paper frogs. Then the paper balls you needed to blow into. They were advised to choose a clean page. They learned that it was easy to make swans after knowing how to make a boat, if you had the trick.

"If you want to take more than one page out of your manual, you may do so," Dr. Harrison said. "Of course, I may test you on that page. Only anatomy manual origami is allowed." It was understood that you should make notes before removing a page. You had to take out at least one page.

The swans were hung over the cadavers with twine, and if you forgot something you could look up and see whether it was printed on the wing of a twirling swan.

Halfway through the semester, the days were ending earlier. The sky turned blood to black in the late afternoon. Sri and Chen came in from a dinner break—veggie dogs. Ming didn't take breaks, instead munched granola bars in the museum section of the basement.

They had to stay late because it was the evening before the anatomy midterm. Most of the class was still in the basement, and Sri and Chen found Ming rummaging through the bags of body parts, searching. She explained the situation to them, frustrated but not apologetic.

"What do you mean you lost the right side of the head?" Chen asked quietly.

"No, I didn't exactly lose it. It's simply not where I left it," said Ming.

"You put it in the head bag?" asked Sri.

"Anyway, we've got the left side. We can look at someone else's right."

"The exam's tomorrow," said Chen. The right and left halves of the head had been dissected differently, and the parts needed from the right had been removed from the left.

"Just think for a second. Are you sure you left it here?" asked Sri, fingering the bag that contained the left half of the head.

"I'm sure. I covered it. I sprayed it. It was right here."

"You're always in such a rush," said Sri. "Maybe if you slowed down. . . . You know how long I spent dissecting those cranial nerves?"

"I bet someone took it," said Ming.

Sri replied, "Right. Make up a story. You were looking at it, so it was your responsibility to put it back. With the rest of Murphy."

"Who made you boss? And he's not a Murphy," said Ming. "Probably someone borrowed it—it'll turn up."

"You lost the head," Sri whispered, leaning forward and looking at Ming, "and I named him Murphy."

"It's only half. And I did not lose it. I left it right here. It's not where I left it. That's not 'losing' it."

"Obviously you don't care," said Sri.

"Just study it from the manual."

"I made the cranial nerve page into a swan," said Chen. He rested his latex-gloved hands on the table.

Ming said, "Should have chosen a different page."

At two in the morning, only Sri and Chen were in the lab, sitting over the borrowed right half of a head. All the other tables were covered in sheets, and sprayed with the fresh pungency of formalin.

"You know she won't apologize, but you probably should," said Chen.

"Why?"

"Because we've still got the pelvis and legs to do. It'll be better if you make peace."

"This is very bad."

"Sure, you guys are upset, so just smooth it out."

"It's not just her. Losing half his head is bad. And why did she insist we cut through Murphy's cross and heart?"

"She follows the book, Sri. She reads it, she does it."

"My mother told me you should respect a man's symbols. We should have cut around the cross. Did you look up that Mark thing?"

"Sorry, I forgot. What was it again?"

"Mark 16."

"I'll check it for you. Did your mother say anything about losing half a head?"

"Never came up."

They looked down at the open half-head they had only been able to study after midnight when another group had finished with it. Ming had decided to study from the anatomy atlas. "Ready for tomorrow?"

"Ready as ever, I guess," said Sri.

"I guess we're done here. Hungry?"

"Kind of. I need something filling to help me sleep."

"Let's go."

In the night, walking under blowing elms, they smelled themselves more clearly, their skin sticky in the armpits and elbows. In the creases of their hands. In the washroom of Nona's, while the round lady heated their calzones, Chen washed his face with his hands, and the more he washed the more that odour seeped from between his fingers and under his nails. Under the low-wattage light, he used the tepid water and hard soap to wash his hands raw.

After the midterm, Sri went to Dean Cortina and asked to switch to a different group. He said, "One of my partners is great but I have a communication problem with my other colleague."

"The course is almost over, and we can't change the groups. I'm glad you said colleague *because that means you think like a professional. Take this as your first*

professional challenge," said Dean Cortina. "I remember my anatomy group, and I don't want to tell you how many years ago." She sat back in her big chair. "We had a communication problem. Men are odd about penises. They don't want to talk about them but they secretly believe them to be very important, perhaps sacred. So we got to the penis on our cadaver, and the men wanted to skip it. 'We'll look at the book,' they said. 'No way,' I said, 'we need to see the inside of the penis.' Corpus spongiosum, all that jazz. Besides, the poor guy's body was lying there. A big man, powerful, and it would have been a shame just to let it go to waste. What did we do? We talked. We talked like professionals, and I saw that it was this one guy's turn to dissect, and there was no way that this man was going to cut up a penis. So I said, 'What if I do it?' and I did it, and I think we all understood the issue better. Does that help?"

Sri couldn't think of anything to say. He thanked Dean Cortina and left her office.

When they got to the penis, there was no problem or hesitation. It was Ming's turn to cut, and she went right through it with one long arc of the scalpel, so that was all there was to it. She said, "You guys okay?"

"Sure," said Chen.

"Someone want the testicles?"

Both Chen and Sri declined politely, and so Ming did the rest of that day's dissection—producing a fine display of the epididymis and the spermatic ducts.

—

Late after the final exam, some of the class was still at the upstairs patio bar of The Paradise. Many of Dr. Harrison's group were there, setting liquor-doused paper napkin swans alight in blue bursts. It was their private party, and they were trying to stay warm beneath the stars, helped by flame-ringed overhead heaters that smelled like burp. Someone had vomited on the toilet seat in the men's room and then simply closed the stall door, so now there were lineups for both washrooms. Others sat in booths, and in a far corner Sri had just bought Ming a vodka tonic. He was feeling good about himself for having bought the drink, and she was feeling big for accepting it.

She said, "Guess what, I found the right side of the head. It was in the bag with the omentum." Ming couldn't remember exactly how it got there, but of course no one had looked at the omentum before the midterm and so she recently had found it while studying for the final, looking for a kidney. Then she remembered she must have put it there. A moment of inattention, she explained.

"Where is it now?" asked Sri.

"Still there."

"With the omentum?" The omentum attached all the intestines into a fan-shaped sheet. "Why didn't you put it with the head?"

"I don't know. The bag wasn't handy, I guess."

"You guess. So you just left it with all the guts and everything," said Sri. "I'll have to go get it."

"What?"

"I'm gonna go get it," he shouted. No one turned to look, in the way that drunk people do not notice each other as being out of the ordinary.

"You're all screwed up," said Ming quietly. "Do you dream about your Murphy?"

"Me? You should have nightmares, the way you treat him."

"Hello? Dead? Remember? I don't have dreams, because I don't have hang-ups about the stupid corpse."

"You—"

"You what?" said Ming. "You don't like that? Corpse? Piece of Murphy meat?"

"You're just such a—"

"Just say it. What am I? You want to say it. Call me a name, go ahead and relieve your repressed little self. Say it."

"No. Let's just stop. No."

"Go for it, pick a name. Bitch? Witch? Name your name."

"I didn't say anything, you're picking the words now."

"You're such a wimp, I have to call myself names just to clarify what you think of me," said Ming.

Chen was pushing sideways through the falling dancers. He arrived in time to hear Ming say to Sri, "Just fuck off. See, I can say what I think." She stalked off, weaving across the floor.

"You guys," said Chen to both of them but now just to Sri.

"It was better for a minute. Believe it or not. I bought her a drink. Then she told me she found the head. Okay, but she didn't put it back! I can't believe she just misplaced it like that, like it doesn't matter, and then she didn't even put it with the other half? It's with the omentum."

"How many have you had?"

"My mother told me that alcohol can build and then burn bridges between people."

"Your mother."

"Well, it's done now. I'm gonna go get the head."

"Aw . . . Sri."

"I gotta get it, put it back on."

"Whaddya mean, come on, wait——"

Already walking away, Sri said, "I gotta go——"

"Hey, wait." Chen, still holding a beer, went down the stairs after his friend.

In the anatomy lab, Chen summarized the story: "Yeah, I looked it up for you. Mark 16. So after Jesus is crucified the women go to wash and prepare Jesus' body with spices. On the road they realize they won't be able to move this huge stone door in front of the tomb. But when they get there, surprise! The door is open and there's no body. *Don't be scared,* says the shining angel who's there. *Jesus has risen, so tell the disciples that he will comfort and lead them.* The women are scared. Jesus appears to Mary. She tells people about seeing him, but they think she's crazy, so he has to keep on showing himself to people until they're convinced. Anyhow, Jesus says that things are really going well, and all his people will do incredible, wonderful things, and be protected even from drinking poison. He says that his followers will be healers by putting their hands on people. Then he goes to heaven to sit with God." Chen put his beer down next to Murphy.

"Is that really what it says?" asked Sri.

"Roughly. I looked it up, but I am paraphrasing."

"It's good stuff."

"You still want to put the head back on," said Chen.

"Yeah."

They unwrapped the stump neck and took the left side of the head from inside the chest where they had left it to keep it moist. They found the right side in the omentum bag, and the right and left sides didn't match up exactly anymore because of the dissection. They put the two pieces on top, and Chen could see that Sri wasn't happy, so he wrapped some gauze around the neck to hold things in place.

"He's a bit dry."

"Needs a drink. Bless you, Murphy." Instead of taking the formalin spray bottle, Sri took the rest of Chen's beer and poured it gently and slowly from the lips to the open belly.

"You don't drink, do you?" said Chen.

"Not usually."

"You have a knack for it."

"Why do you think Murphy chose Mark 16?" Sri closed his eyes. "It's a weird passage. Is that the end of the Jesus story?"

"I guess a pilot would have figured there wouldn't be a body left for anyone. Nothing left for his girlfriend, or mother. Maybe Mark 16 made him feel better about that."

"He was wrong," said Sri, bowing his head, his arms stretched to the usually shining table now dull with the running of liquid. Beer dripped into the bucket between Murphy's feet. "He's here for us."

Sri wound a strip of yellowed fabric up the neck, pulled it tight over the chin so it wouldn't bunch, then softly over the eyes, and the coldness of the eyelids vanished under the cloth. Murphy's hair had continued to grow for a little while after being shaved, and Chen held up the stubbled head so Sri could work. Sri wound the fabric around the top of the skull, and tied it onto itself snugly with a slipless knot under the angle of the jaw. Sri stood back and noticed that the tip of the right ear protruded. He tugged gently at a fold of cotton and settled it around the ear, where it would stay.

HOW TO GET INTO MEDICAL SCHOOL, PART II

—
—
—

MING'S PARENTS THOUGHT THAT SHE VOLUNTEERED at the Ottawa Children's Hospital on Mondays, Tuesdays, and Wednesdays. Both she and Fitzgerald were there on Mondays and Tuesdays, but on Wednesdays neither of them went to the hospital. Instead, they went to the ski hill that was abandoned for the summer, where they would not encounter their classmates or Ming's cousins, and spread a blanket in the tall grass whose blades glinted in the flat light. The sun pulled sweat out of them, and there was a humid adhesion of skin on skin. When it became too hot, they put on their clothes and walked in the shade of the woods. A ski chalet had burned to the ground during the winter, and when they walked past it Fitzgerald kicked at the charred pieces of wood.

Ming received an acceptance letter from Toronto's Faculty of Medicine in July, and her parents put a down payment on a small condominium north of Bloor Street that backed onto a treed ravine. Her family held a banquet and called her *doctor*, but Fitzgerald did not attend. In Ming's home, he had been a faceless voice on the telephone and now was even less present. During summer holidays there was no studying, and therefore no excuse for him to call. Wednesday was their day. The Wednesday after the banquet, as they walked to find a picnic spot, Ming told Fitz that she hadn't enjoyed it without him.

He said, "Why do you sound so happy, then?"

"Don't you want me to be? My family is happy for me."

"You've achieved what they wanted. Another family success."

A deer crossed the ski run, nervous in the open, sniffing up and down the hill. They stopped walking, and the deer crossed their path and then folded into the woods. Ming said, "We were having a perfectly nice day until now."

"I'm sorry," said Fitzgerald. "You deserved a party. You did it." He reminded himself to be only happy for her, but felt that his exclusion from the celebration entitled him to possessiveness.

"Getting an acceptance seemed like such a big deal. Now I'm mostly just tired and relieved."

One hot, grasshopper-buzzing day at the beginning of August, Ming and Fitzgerald sat at the top of a steep ski slope, swinging in a green metal lift chair. They had once decided to have no romance, and they now referred to that as the "strange phase" of their relationship. A few months later, when they travelled to Toronto for Ming's medical school interview, they had decided that it was dishonest to deny that they were in love. On that trip, they held each other but slept in separate hotel beds, and agreed that there should be no sex. For Ming, this would be too close to her anger at Karl. Three weeks later, after this prohibition had been put aside upon Ming's initiative, they conceded that since they had become lovers there was no point in discontinuing a natural enjoyment between two people in love. Now, they sat facing down the hill, without the retaining bar of the ski lift chair. They ate cheese sandwiches and drank iced tea. Ming told Fitzgerald that she could not imagine loving anyone else, now that she had found someone to be honest with.

He said, "That's why people get married."

"You think so?" she said, drinking from the silver flask. "Aren't there lots of reasons, both good and bad?"

"Why don't we get married?"

"The circumstances are not ideal," she said.

"But are they ever, for anyone?" said Fitzgerald. Ming was moving to a different city in three weeks, and they had come together in halting lunges, preceded by a mutual denial of their deepening attraction. Instead of discouraging Fitzgerald, these events made it seem even more important to make and extract a commitment. "You just said you couldn't imagine loving anyone else. Let's hold on to that. We'll get married." He took her hand.

"Fitz, it's something for later."

"Then later. Put it this way: could you think of marrying anyone else?"

"Right now, no, I can't," she said, putting her other hand over his.

"These connections happen only once. We can't throw it away because of the problems around us. Later is fine, but let's commit to our feelings now."

"You'll be a good husband," she said. Ming took his arm, sat closer, and looked across the landscape of hills cut in a strange way into ski slopes. She had not yet told her parents about him, and said that she needed to wait until she had moved away from home. "It's stupid, but I wish you were Chinese. They'll threaten to disown me. That happened to my sister."

"But that would just be a pressure tactic, to make you choose between me and them."

"They won't, ultimately. In the end, they can't lose me. I don't think so, anyhow."

"What happened with your sister?"

"She broke up with her boyfriend."

"Oh."

"But that was different. I only met him once. It wasn't serious, I'm guessing."

The five-hour drive from Ottawa would give her the distance she needed in order to tell her parents, said Ming. She spoke with the assumption that Fitzgerald would be admitted to medicine in the following year. This was easier for her to say, and he said "if" while she said "when." He did speak as if he would move into her condominium. Ming suggested that he might have to live on his own for a little while.

She said, "My parents did buy it and everything."

"You could move out. We could get an apartment, so it would be our own place."

"Or something."

At the end of August, Ming's parents moved her to Toronto. They filled her freezer with white plastic containers of ginger beef, sesame chicken, and other favourites of Ming's. Fitzgerald took the train to Toronto on the same day that Ming's parents drove back to Ottawa. The night before Ming's first day of medical school, he said, "Now you'll tell them?"

"I'm tired," she said. "Right now, I need to be on my own, plant my feet."

"It should be easier, now that you're far away."

"You don't get it, do you? That it won't ever be easy." She turned away in bed.

"I just said easier."

—

In September, Fitzgerald returned to Ottawa. At first, he and Ming were both anxious to speak every evening. They fantasized about travelling, about being together, about when Fitzgerald would visit. During the school day, they anticipated these fantasies—which became satisfying in themselves. By October, Ming's class was dissecting the abdomen, and she suggested that they speak every second night.

"The volume of information is overwhelming," she said.

"But I'll miss you."

"Do you realize I've been cutting apart human bodies for the last month?" said Ming. The first rite of medical school was the anatomy lab, the opening of skin into the organs.

"You mentioned that," he said.

She described the dissections on a daily basis. She complained that one of her dissection partners, Sri, was a sentimental wreck who couldn't even cut open an arm, who did nothing but slow her down. Chen, her other partner, was tolerable. Every minute was important, she said, and she had realized that she was spending too much time on the telephone. "I didn't learn the thorax well enough, because you need me too much. How much do we have to talk? Human anatomy is important—it's for real now." Whenever Fitzgerald mentioned her classmates she corrected him, because they were "colleagues."

"Right." Fitzgerald wondered whether his biology and biochemistry lectures were no longer real—perhaps they were only the means to an end. He had previously enjoyed the ideas and concepts but now, even as he became more obsessive about the details and patterns of facts, he hated knowing that his marks were soaring as a result of Karl's study methods. He tape-recorded lectures, applied a meditative attention to details and trivial facts. His weekly time sheet was crammed with reading, eating, listening to tapes, memorizing, and working on medical school application packages. He worked with a desperate and fastidious zeal, imagining that each A+ brought him a step closer to Ming. One night, Fitzgerald told her that he wished they could stop studying, and instead could lie in the grass at the ski hill. Ming reminded him that achieving the last twenty marks required twice as much effort as getting the first eighty.

Fitzgerald said, "Another saying from Karl." Ming's cousin Karl's systematically mind-numbing method of achieving near-perfect scores was Ming's lesson for Fitzgerald.

Ming was silent.

It was the first time Fitzgerald had mentioned Karl. Until now, only Ming had ever brought Karl into their conversations. Fitzgerald had often thought of Karl while being coached in study techniques by Ming, and he knew that Ming had to push Karl out of her mind when they were in bed. He did the same, but had not told Ming of this. He said, "Sorry, that just came out. I've been studying too much."

"I'm showing you how to get into medical school. Isn't that enough? Is it my fault that Karl taught me how to do it?"

Fitzgerald felt his heart beating. He said, "It's as if his shadow is on me when I'm studying."

"Well, you've never met him so you can dismiss your excess of imagination. I've got his shadow on me, and one of us is enough."

"I guess learning is learning. Sorry."

After his midterms in October, Fitzgerald asked Ming when he should visit.

She said, "There's no good time. Only less bad times."

"When will you tell your parents?"

"Now that I miss them, it's hard to hurt them."

"Then you're glad to be away from me."

"No. But it is a relief to be further from our secret."

"And easier to study your anatomy and your dissection than to face our relationship, our problem."

"You have this amazing belief that things have something to do with you," she said. "Don't you see? I have to be as committed to renal anatomy as I am to us."

In the first week of November, Ming told Fitzgerald that she and Chen had gone out for dinner in October. He lived in the same building. Occasionally, she said, they grabbed a quick bite after class.

"We're nothing more than colleagues, but I wanted to mention it. I wasn't going to tell you, because it's nothing. Chen and I hung out once, maybe twice. Then I thought to tell you, because otherwise if you found out you might misunderstand and think that it was something."

"He's Chinese?" said Fitzgerald.

"Who cares," she said.

"You kissed him."

"Don't be ridiculous," she said. "This is why I wasn't going to mention it."

A week later, Ming said that perhaps she and Fitzgerald should "slow down." Also, there was something that she regretted, she said. A tiny misunderstanding, which she and Chen had already clarified. Chen hadn't exactly known about her commitment to Fitzgerald, and so there had been a kiss, although entirely one-sided, and she had stopped him as soon as it started, so it wasn't really that she had kissed him at all.

Fitzgerald called three times a night. He called at random times and asked Ming where she had been when she hadn't picked up the phone. He fell behind in listening to lecture tapes, until she reminded him that he had to study if he wanted to get into medical school and come to Toronto. We should cool down, she said, see what happens in the next year.

"Slow down, cool down, it's all you say now."

"I'm going to answer the phone once every two days. I got call display."

A week later, Ming said that Chen had tried to kiss her again, and she hadn't stopped him. Did Fitzgerald want to break up because of her lack of faithfulness, she asked. She would understand. She explained all of this in one very long expectant breath, with no pause. Fitzgerald said that he wanted to come see her.

"Our first plan was the right one, to just be study friends. I wish we hadn't got so off track," said Ming.

"I need to see you. You owe it to me." He felt an urgent need to bed her harshly and memorably if it should be the last time.

"If you're going to be angry, it's better for us to make a break."

Fitzgerald said that he needed her to get through everything—the exams, the interviews. Ming warned him not to twist things into being her responsibility.

"Don't make me into your mother," said Ming. A long, mutual silence. Then, "Sorry, I shouldn't have said that, I'm not sure why I said that."

"Is that what you think this is about?" asked Fitzgerald. He had once told Ming that the loneliness he felt after his mother died was like living in a house frame that would never be clad with walls or a roof.

"Look, that was wrong of me. Pretend I never said it."

"That hurts, you know? And then it hurts more that you want to pretend you never said it."

"You're not going to lay a guilt trip on me," said Ming, suddenly hard again. "I don't do guilt."

"No, you don't, do you?"

"Let's stop."

"We're not done talking," said Fitzgerald.

"We *are* done. What else do you have to say?"

"Lots."

"Do you have anything good, anything positive to say, or are we just going to hate each other more? I'm sorry I mentioned your mother, which was wrong. I'm sorry I'm sorry I'm sorry. That's all I can say on that subject."

"Well, you meant more, but now you won't own up to it."

"Let's stop, let's not hate each other."

"Hate? I thought we loved each other. I don't know why you're bringing hate into it. As for my mother—"

"Good night."

"No, don't you, Ming—"

"Good night, Fitzgerald."

When he called back, the phone rang until it went to her answering machine. Five minutes later, he dialed and the phone rang until her machine picked up. An hour later, her machine answered still.

Ming answered his calls every second night. She told Fitzgerald that she still thought he was a beautiful person, as if this was a dreary but proven scientific principle and therefore she could not deny it despite its uncomfortable implications. She maintained that he was the only person she could trust telling "everything" to, which meant the intimate aspects of her tutoring by Karl. Fitzgerald wanted to ask whether he, too, would become an uncomfortable secret, but feared that the asking would make it come true. At the end of each call one of them would be crying, and the other angry. In December, Ming said that although it was a "fact" that she loved Fitzgerald "as a person," they should no longer speak.

"You need me more than I can deal with, and more than you can handle, frankly."

"But if you weren't trying to run away, I wouldn't need you so bad."

"It's not my fault. I won't allow that."

"What about next year, when I come to Toronto?"

"If you come to Toronto, next year is next year. I suppose anything is possible."

In the following weeks, Fitzgerald left monologues on Ming's answering machine, emotional diatribes examining their relationship's dynamics. He left messages saying he wanted to discuss medical school application issues with her, and when she didn't call back he left further messages in which he discussed his thoughts about her possible responses to his issues. Sometimes he described his day's study progress, subject by subject. Fitzgerald pleaded with Ming to call him. He addressed the reasons he imagined she might have for not calling him, and promised that if she called, he would be calm and neither of them would cry. He would be silent for a few days, and then call to leave a message saying that he was finally getting beyond their relationship, that it was wonderful that things had cooled down a bit to give them both space, so it would be great if she would call and they could talk like good old friends. Like colleagues, he said.

Fitzgerald began calling to hear her voice on the machine. In the middle of the day, when he felt lonely, he would call just to hear the recording.

Hi. You've reached Ming, but I'm not here. Leave a message.

One day, at two in the afternoon, she picked up the phone.

"Hello?" she said.

"Hi."

Her voice was sticky. "I was napping. I just grabbed the phone. Why are you calling in the afternoon?"

"I'm addicted to the idea of you."

"Oh, I didn't check my call display," she said with a mix of annoyance and apology, as if to explain why they were actually talking.

"We're meant for each other. We decided."

She said nothing, and then came the dial tone.

The next day, Ming's number was out of service. The new one was unlisted.

It was an early March day in Ottawa. Fitzgerald rode his bicycle under a noon sun that chewed gleaming wet facets into snowbank peaks as streaks of black sediment crumbled toward the curb. Fitzgerald had just checked the midterm exam results, and was near the top of each of his classes. Tomorrow he would go to Toronto for his interview. The invitation had come from the Faculty of Medicine in a stunningly ordinary white envelope.

Fitzgerald pedalled away from campus along the canal, through lakes of slush toward the red light at the intersection of Sussex and Rideau. He chewed upon the imperative of acceptance into medical school, and scripted the shining, clear conversation with Ming that would set aside all the misunderstandings that had separated them. For months now, Fitzgerald's mind had alternated between studying and allowing his speculations to spin like wheels stuck in a rutted path of Ming and medicine, digging the tracks deeper and deeper. Everything would fall into place once he was accepted to the University of Toronto. That was it, the end point after which career, perfect words, heroic acts, and true love would come naturally as a matter of course.

She might call tonight to arrange to see him in Toronto tomorrow. He prepared himself for the things she might say, thought about what response would show tenderness, strength, and more maturity than when they last spoke five months ago. Fitzgerald pedalled slowly, timing the lights. Spinning his legs backwards, he judged the crosswalk with its orange hand flashing, then the traffic signal that turned yellow as he came closer, then red. Now his light was green, and he stood up out of the saddle in order to sprint through the intersection. As his rear wheel gripped the asphalt and he surged forward toward the green light, Fitzgerald saw the bus running the red, and now he was in the intersection with the bus, gigantic and fast, rushing at him. He grabbed the brakes with a spasm of his hands, and the bus swerved, its rear wheels locking, sliding sideways and throwing a fan of slush. He flew over the handlebars of the bike into the air with a sense of vast calm—an empty mind in the sudden knowledge that he was very near his death.

The humming noise of the bus whirring away.

Round red lights receding.

The heat of blood on his face, and the cold ground that had ripped through his pants to open his knees raw.

Cars honked. *Move on.*

The bike was unrideable. The wheels had pancaked into the frame when it was run over by the bus. Fitzgerald was alive through the luck of being thrown far enough forward. He chained the bike to a street sign, called the transit commission from a pay phone, told them what had happened, and they gave him a file number. He called the police, and they gave him a file number. He asked what he should do, and the constable asked if he was injured. Cuts and bruises, he said. Keep the file number, she said, and hung up. He took a bus home, glaring at the driver. After picking the gravel out of his face and knees with a shaving brush, Fitzgerald lay down.

The house was quiet. He thought vaguely of his father, who had said he was going to Luxembourg this week on business, or Lausanne? Some European place that began with L. He didn't pay attention anymore, and so the two of them were quiet bachelors living in the same house. Fitzgerald remembered his mother, and his tears stung in the scrapes from the bicycle crash.

Only then, lying on his own bed with his face oozing, did he think of Ming. In a distant way, it occurred to him to call her, to tell her about the moment when he was airborne in the intersection of Sussex and Rideau and believed that he would die. He didn't have her telephone number. A letter. He would send a letter, and she would feel sorry, would wish that she had been there to comfort him, and would feel guilty at her neglect. But why send a letter when he was going to Toronto tomorrow? Then he realized that he had felt cleaner and lighter in the four hours since the accident, that he hadn't thought about Ming or about medical school (was it really the first four hours in months?).

He fell asleep.

Fitzgerald slept until the next morning, and barely woke in time to catch the train, still tired. Lake Ontario's surface was a rippled grey as the train hummed toward Union Station, and Fitzgerald felt a blank surprise that the world continued—that the bus had rushed away into a winter afternoon, that today he would still have to explain himself at his interview. If the bus had found its mark, he decided, the world would have been much unchanged. Someone else would have become a doctor, perhaps a better one than himself. Fitzgerald reminded himself that he only had an interview, not an admission, and so he still might not become a doctor. Today, this did not seem to be as disastrous a possibility as he had previously believed. He tried to summon his conviction that all of this was crucial, but felt only vaguely amazed at having spent so many hours listening to static-hiss recordings of lectures, straining to write minute facts in his cramped notes.

Dr. McCarthy was the dermatologist who, in her private office on Edward Street, welcomed Fitzgerald on behalf of the University of Toronto's Faculty of Medicine. There was also a young Asian man in black jeans and a green scrub top who wore a crisp white lab coat and whose stethoscope was slightly askew on his neck. An impressively battered aluminum clipboard was propped between his hand and hip.

Dr. McCarthy said, "We always involve a trainee in these little sessions. This is Karl."

"I'm a surgical resident," said Karl, as if it should be evident that this exercise was entirely too banal for his important schedule.

"What did you do to your face?" asked McCarthy. "Karl, take a look."

Karl grasped the edge of the bandage and said, "The best way is fast—to rip it right off." He yanked the plaster, and with a pain more vivid than the original injury, Fitzgerald felt the fragile scab rip cleanly away with the bandage.

"Hmm," said McCarthy. She frowned slightly at Karl.

—

Fitzgerald explained about the bicycle and the bus, telling the story as if his only concern at the time of the accident had been his medical school application.

Dabbing at Fitzgerald's raw chin with a plastic-bristled surgical scrub brush, McCarthy said, "Although I'm a dermatologist, you didn't have to rip off half your face to come see me. We had already invited you for the interview." She seemed very pleased with this remark. The scrubbing burned, and Fitzgerald winced at the pain. She made him take off his pants so they could examine his knees. She had Karl scrub the knees, and he was rough—perhaps because he had expected to interview a candidate rather than change dressings.

"What did you like about Ottawa U?" asked McCarthy.

"I had a chance to develop my study techniques."

"And what did you learn about studying?"

"That knowledge acquisition is all about discipline," said Fitzgerald. He said to Karl, "You're from Ottawa?"

"So it seems," said Karl.

Fitzgerald said, "I'm a friend of Ming's."

"Oh, what a small world," said McCarthy. "You have mutual friends. But you have not met, correct? We can't have the interview be biased, of course."

Both Karl and Fitzgerald smiled blandly at McCarthy, which she took as confirmation that they were strangers.

As Karl hunched over, scrubbing hard at Fitzgerald's knees, hurting him, Fitzgerald imagined jerking his knee up into Karl's jaw, Karl's head snapping back. Could he make it look like an accident, like a sudden reflex of pain? It would be for Ming, he told himself. But they would know. They were doctors, therefore all-seeing, and they would recognize whether a knee-jerk was reflex or assault. And why should he do this for Ming, when this impulsive act might keep him from success, and she had drifted so far from him that she had changed her phone number? His knees had gone from scabbed and scruffy to raw and oozing with bloody fringes.

Karl said, "One thing you learn in medicine is that wounds heal. Almost all bleeding stops with pressure." He scrubbed hard, and Fitzgerald tensed his thigh. "Also, there's some pain."

He should drive his leg upward. It was Karl's fault that Ming had learned to exclude, to be hard. Of course, it was Karl's study system that had brought Ming to medical school and himself to this interview. But the method was irrelevant. To study was to work. To work was to make it one's own. As he neared the decision to do it—to knee Karl in the jaw—Karl finished wrapping his knees in gauze with a rough flourish. Karl stood and the opportunity for violence was gone. Fitzgerald looked at Karl and said, "Ming taught me that the first eighty marks are easy to get, but you lose it on the last twenty, so you live your life for the last twenty. Bleeding must be the same. The few cases that don't stop are the tough part, right?"

McCarthy said, "Before we discuss the management of hemorrhage, tell me about 'knowledge acquisition.' Is that what they call academics now? Like buying a house, or a hostile corporate takeover. How is it, Fitzgerald, that you 'acquire' knowledge?"

Fitzgerald told himself to turn away, to look away from Karl's gaze. "Maybe 'acquisition' is not right, since that implies taking it away from someone else. I guess when you know something well enough that you can use it from the gut, and it affects the way you think, then it's an idea that you own. 'Ownership' might be a better way to think of it."

"Owning ideas is all about discipline?" asked Karl.

"Why don't you get dressed," said McCarthy. Fitzgerald was standing in his boxer shorts and dress shirt, his face and knees freshly wrapped in gauze. After Fitzgerald had dressed, McCarthy asked him what quality he felt was most important in a physician. Trust is most crucial, said Fitzgerald.

"In that case, what should I ask you in this interview, if I wanted to know whether I could trust you?" said McCarthy with a tight grin.

"Ask me anything, and I could make up something that would sound good," said Fitzgerald. The interview continued for another half-hour. McCarthy bantered and Karl read questions from his sheet, sullen and cautious. At the end of the session McCarthy gave Fitzgerald sample tubes of cream for his abrasions and said, "I still don't know if we can trust you."

"The only way to find out is to let me in and see what happens." He said it plainly, somewhat tired.

After the interview, Fitzgerald went to the bathroom, splashed water on his face, ran his fingers through his hair. He got in the elevator and Karl caught the closing door, stepped in with him.

"We haven't met," said Karl. "I'm sure of it, so don't tell me we have."

"But I know you. Ming and I are close friends."

"You want to know how you scored today, close friend?"

"No," said Fitzgerald.

"I wouldn't count on Toronto." Karl stood directly in front of Fitzgerald, and behind him the elevator buttons flickered in sequence as they descended to the ground floor. "See, all it takes is one bad score—an exam, an essay, an interview—and you're out. Bye-bye. McCarthy liked you, but I think you've got the wrong attitude. Besides, whatever you think you know about me, you don't."

The floor numbers progressed downward.

"Feeling pretty guilty, huh?"

"I don't know what you're talking about, but don't count on Toronto." Karl turned away from Fitzgerald and gazed at the elevator door, leaning back on the railing.

Fitzgerald stepped in front of Karl, faced him. "Does the surgery program director know about your teaching experience, about how you got your start in tutoring?" They were at the fourth, then the third floor. "Imagine the embarrassment if there was some reason you couldn't be left alone with kids, perhaps needed special supervision during your pediatric surgery rotation. It's terrible how people talk."

Second floor, then ground level. The door rumbled open slowly, an old elevator.

"How'd I do?" said Fitzgerald, putting his arm across the elevator door. "That interview score. How'd I perform?"

Karl raised the aluminum clipboard as if about to hit Fitzgerald with it, but instead pointed its corner between Fitzgerald's eyes and said, "If you end up in Toronto, just remember that someone will see your mistakes."

Fitzgerald moved his arm, allowed Karl to pass, and watched him disappear around the corner.

An hour later, standing on the Dundas subway platform, Fitzgerald removed his tie. His sports jacket was constrictive and lumpy under his winter coat. He rolled the tie carefully and pushed it into an outside pocket of his coat. He rode the subway to Summerhill station, stepped off the train, and stood on the platform as people walked past him. He sat on a plastic bench that looked like a square mushroom, pushed his hands deep into his coat pockets, and watched two more trains arrive and depart. The three tones of the bell sang out before the doors whooshed shut and the second train hurtled away with a rising clatter.

Fitzgerald climbed the tiled stairs to the exit and clanked through the turnstile. Outside, the cold air felt like morning water. He was afraid. His breath steamed around him as he walked.

First, he buzzed.

He tried Ming's apartment twice.

The screen said *No Answer*. It was four-thirty-five in the afternoon. He rang again, punched the numbers on the keypad with a determination he hoped would make her appear. The transmitted electronic bleeping continued until the screen flashed *No Answer* again.

From his inner jacket pocket, Fitzgerald removed the keys. He opened the front door, went up the elevator, and his feet were light and fast as he walked down the hallway to Ming's door.

He knocked using his fingers, making a short little rhythm.

Silence.

He knocked again, rapped with his knuckles.

Still quiet.

The tip of the key trembled as he tried to bring it to the lock, and then with two hands he steadied and pushed the toothed key into its slot. It went in easily, without jamming or catching. He turned it. It turned smoothly, a soft click. She had not changed the lock.

He opened the door and called out, "Hello?"

No one.

Again, "Ming? It's me."

Quiet.

When he had last seen the apartment, it had been almost bare—furnished by her parents with one station-wagon load of prefabricated Swedish furniture and three brush-painted scrolls. Now, Ming had settled in. There were sandals and a single black pump in the hallway. In the kitchen, oven mitts that were supposed to look like slices of watermelon hung from a drawer knob. Medical pathology books and dissection notes covered the surface of the coffee table. Fitzgerald removed his shoes and winter coat, put them in the closet, and sat in the armchair that faced the couch.

On top of the study notes was a half-finished cup of tea, its inner surface ringed with brown circles. The apartment smelled of ginger and garlic. A large print of Van Gogh's *Starlight over the Rhone* hung above the couch, and Fitzgerald stared at it for a long time. He examined the rippled lines of the light reflected in the water, and the hunched stance of the man and woman. Why were they looking at the artist, and not at the deep cobalt water shot through with the light of reflected stars? They faced away from the riverbank, away from the dark liquid at the heart of the scene. They stared out at the viewer, who could be none other than an eye looking down from the black night.

She shouldn't be surprised, he thought.

He had written, he told himself, sitting there in his socks.

For weeks, he had sent letters reminding her of his interview date, asking if they could meet. She didn't write back. He wrote notes in which he addressed possible objections she might have to seeing him. *Was she afraid of hurting him?* If so, he wanted nothing more than to see her. *Perhaps she felt that because their relationship was over, they shouldn't see each other?* If this was her concern, he wrote, she should feel completely comfortable because he had accepted that the relationship was done, that their romance was finished, but it hurt him to not be able to see his closest friend. *Maybe she was too busy?* They would meet quickly, eat a meal like old friends—didn't she have to eat? *Did she feel that everything between them was in the past?* He wrote that although the past was gone, he didn't discount the future. Since he would be in Toronto for his interview and neither of them was deliberately travelling to see the other, this would be a perfectly neutral meeting—not evoking the past but also not requiring a future. *Did she hope they would simply forget each other?* Impossible.

He had written these things to her, but no reply had come. She should not be surprised to see him. He had tried to express the important but casual and enjoyable nature of a meeting. He didn't write that he would simply come to her apartment, enter, remove his shoes, and wait. Why not? Perhaps he didn't really think he would do it. The idea had run in his mind like a movie: she would be surprised at first, but then seeing him in her home would allow all of the old feelings to come back to her. She would hold him, she would thank him for seeking her out, she would swear to never turn away from him again.

Maybe he didn't think any of this could be real. It was unreasonable to break into her apartment, and so perhaps he never really thought he would be sitting here like this, flipping through her pathology notes, smelling her kitchen, patting the bandages on his face to see whether they had soaked through. That's what it was, he reminded himself, breaking and entering. Was that why he had not written about this possibility? Perhaps he had suspected that she had forgotten about his set of keys. Perhaps he had thought that had he mentioned anything about coming over on his own, she would change the locks. He hadn't written that he would be sitting here on her couch, that he would pick up her half-finished tea, go to the microwave, heat it up, sip it—that he would wish to feel like a soothed child because she had also sipped from this cup but would find that it was just stale, microwaved jasmine tea gone bitter with the leaves steeped too long in cold water.

Five-ten.

He wondered about the one black pump on the floor. Where was its partner? He looked for it in the hallway closet, pushed through her sheaf of clothing, smelled the jackets, the sweaters—her smell had changed. Less pungent, maybe from less home cooking? Or did he remember it differently? Had she been in such a rush to get the shoe off? He looked into the bedroom briefly, the sight of the bed painful, but thankfully there was no trail of footwear leading to the mattress. He closed the bedroom door, heart pounding, still holding the tea. In September, after her parents had left, they had a perfect week, a week of playing house. It was before her classes started, and they made love on their first night in the apartment, having assembled only the bed—the rest of the furniture still in its unopened flat-packed boxes. They filled her kitchen from the stalls in Kensington Market, and went to Centre Island twice to watch children playing. Ming had been the one who would point to kids, especially mixed-race children, and say that their kids might turn out like that.

Five-twenty.

He finished the tea anyhow, hopeful. It had a quality like warm, wet dishwater.

Five-twenty-five.

Fitzgerald gathered up some of the heart dissection notes from the coffee table. They were very instructional, like diagrams that show how to assemble model airplanes, except in reverse. They indicated where to cut, where to separate the muscle, how to open the heart in order to best observe its valves. He saw that Ming had added to the notes, that she had coloured each of the coronary vessels with a different marker. She had written words next to an asterisk. This was to remind herself to look something up.

* *Mitral Regurgitation.*
* *Collateral Circulation.*

Then, he noticed a smiley face in the bottom right corner of a diagram of the Purkinje system. A smiley face? Ming did not draw smiley faces. She was serious, focused. Who had done this? Fitzgerald flipped the pages. On another sheet, an unfamiliar hand had written *Dinner at Italia—six-thirty?* There was a little bulbous-drawn heart. Was this the individual known as Chen—Chen the kisser, Chen the interloper? Fitzgerald felt betrayed that Ming had never mentioned little cartoon smiley faces and hearts. This was wrong, that he would have been replaced by someone who doodled on anatomy notes. He continued to leaf through the papers.

Five-forty-five.

Fitzgerald replayed the movie in his mind, what he had imagined might happen. It was scripted as such:

Jilted but faithful lover, FITZGERALD, *sits waiting in apartment. His true love,* MING, *enters, removes her coat, and then sees* FITZGERALD *sitting in her living room.*

MING: You scared me. How did you get in?

FITZGERALD: That doesn't matter, but it's crucial that we see each other. What were you afraid of?

MING: Of myself, of you, of . . . the future.

FITZGERALD: Fear is natural.

MING: I'm glad you came, though. It's been so long. You look older. And wiser. I've seen you . . . looking this way in my dreams.

FITZGERALD: I've been thinking about the time we had, and about the time we might still have. We have to move forward, either together or apart.

MING: I've missed you. *(Tears begin to appear.)* I've distracted myself with other things . . . even other men . . . I'm so sorry. But I've always missed you. Late at night when I couldn't sleep, I knew you were there.

FITZGERALD: All is forgiven, my love. We're together again.

Lovers embrace. Lips slowly meet. Camera fades to black.

Six-oh-five.

The couple in *Starlight over the Rhone* stared at Fitzgerald from above the couch. Their facial features were indistinct, the direction of their gaze unclear. He had assumed that they were a couple, a man and woman bound together in life. But he now wondered that this might not be true. They could be brother and sister, or a man with his mother, or old acquaintances walking together along the river after having encountered each other by chance.

Fitzgerald went to Ming's desk, sat in her chair. A jumbled layer of notes and books stretched from the coffee table across the couch, onto the surface of the desk. A small pile of letters was half-hidden by an open anatomy textbook. He flipped through the telephone bills, the bank statements, and found one of his own letters. The bills and statements were opened, but his letter was not. At the bottom of this little stack were six of his letters, envelopes intact. He pulled open the drawers, rifled through the highlighters until he found a clump of his correspondence gathered with an elastic band, everything since the phone had been disconnected. None had been read since January.

Six-ten.

The phone rang, and a man's voice said into the machine, "Ming? It's me, Chen. Pick up the phone if you're there. What kind of salad dressing do you want? Guess you're not there. Well, I'm coming down to start dinner."

A new film scene shot itself in Fitzgerald's mind.

Interloper, CHEN, *enters room where faithful but jilted lover,* FITZGERALD, *sits reading mail at the desk of lost woman,* MING.

CHEN: Excuse me, who are you?
FITZGERALD: I should ask the same.
CHEN: I'm calling the police.
FITZGERALD: You don't know what you're doing.

CHEN *lunges for telephone in kitchen.* FITZGERALD *rushes to stop him. They struggle.*

FITZGERALD *(while grabbing* CHEN *in a headlock):* Ming promised to marry me.

CHEN: So you're the loser who keeps hounding her. Get a life!

CHEN, *who is secretly a kung fu master as well as a brilliant medical student, suddenly breaks the headlock, flips* FITZGERALD *on his back, and pins him to the ground with his legs while he calls the police using a tiny and very fashionable cellphone. With a quick flip of his knee,* CHEN *knocks* FITZGERALD *unconscious.* FITZGERALD *wakes up in prison, in a cell with three smiling, burly men.*

She had said that Chen lived in the same building. How long would it take him? Not long. Fitzgerald stuffed his feet into his shoes without tying the laces, grabbed his coat, and slammed shut the apartment door just as he heard the elevator ding down the hallway. He bolted in the other direction, then saw that this was a dead end with only two other apartment doors. The staircase was beyond the elevators. He turned and walked slowly, seriously, along the hallway. He held the bandages on his face and did not look at the man who passed him carrying a head of lettuce, a tomato, and two bottles of salad dressing. The man said something to him, something pleasant that strangers passing in narrow hallways say to each other, but Fitzgerald couldn't tell what it was.

One afternoon in September, Fitzgerald and Ming met accidentally on the lawn of King's College Circle in front of the Faculty of Medicine. They had been walking toward each other, and had noticed one another only once it was too late to discreetly change direction. The grass was singed brown in half-circles at the edges of the lawn where the sprinklers had not reached, and there was no shade of trees where they stood squinting at each other.

"Congratulations," she said.

"On what?"

"Getting into medical school."

"Sure," he said. It didn't seem very important, now that it was done and he was one of hundreds in his class who had accomplished the same thing. The congratulations felt like nothing more than a common courtesy. He said, "How are you doing?" Ming's hair was pulled back in a hasty ponytail that clung to her sweaty neck. Her stance was broad. Seeing her suddenly here, small-framed, her arms crossed, her right hand tapping her left elbow, made him feel as if he had dreamed their whole relationship.

"Better, now," she said.

"How's second year?"

"Tough. Lots of work."

Young men wearing T-shirts translucent with sweat ran at each other on the field, kicking at a soccer ball and panting.

"I wrote to you, for a while," he said. He stood, sweating, squinting against the sun. Ming's shoulders slouched more than Fitzgerald remembered. He was surprised that this was the person to whom he had told himself he was irrevocably attached, that conviction amplified by his resentment and anger at her absence. What surprised him was that he would have expected to feel more emotional, to experience some mix of elation and anguish at seeing his beloved. Instead, it felt as if he were meeting a celebrity at a grocery store. To see Ming now was to discover that the enticing onscreen femme fatale had a very ordinary and chaotic selection of groceries, chapped lips, and slightly dirty fingernails.

"I decided to not read your letters," she said. She regarded him with a hard clamp of her jaw. "I guess you know that."

The length of her silence, without her leaving or walking away, made Fitzgerald think that she was expecting something of him. Even though her hard presence now made his memories seem like a mirage, Fitzgerald knew the set of her mouth well enough to know that she was waiting for something from him. There was something she wanted him to say.

Fitzgerald thought of the long winter when he had wanted to see her, the months during which he had imagined the way their words would again link and hold them. After his interview, that had faded. His acceptance into medical school had been a vaguely important event. Once it was done, he couldn't quite articulate how he had gotten to that point. He stopped writing to Ming, and the desperate winter was now embarrassing to think of.

She said, "You didn't lock the door. Things were moved around. It was obvious."

"Right," he said. All of that now seemed incredible; that he had propelled himself to her apartment, broken in, sat there anticipating nothing that he could even clearly remember as being real. Now he was amazed that he had never considered the obvious—that she would know he had been in her apartment. He said, "I'm sorry."

"You should be." She continued to look at him. "Anyhow." Her mouth relaxed.

So that's all she wanted. An apology for breaking into her apartment. A very reasonable expectation, he thought. He said, "I'm sure you have things to do."

"Yes, actually."

"I won't keep you," he said.

"Same." She raised her hand, and waved slightly. "Bye." She walked past him.

Suddenly, he felt the tightness of wanting to love Ming, and that roaring feeling of wanting revenge for her abandonment. All of this filled his centre in the instant that he could no longer see her. Should he turn to look at her? Would the reality of her shrinking figure dispel these emotions, or would turning around to watch her depart make him want to run after her, to chase his screen idol? Perhaps it was best simply to stand here in the sun for a while, to sweat in the heat, heart pounding. Droplets of sweat traced his torso like fingers. For an instant, he imagined that Ming had not walked away at all, that she was standing right behind him, watching him. His back cold with sweat. No, no, that was not her. She would be halfway across the field by now.

Fitzgerald dared not turn.

He closed his eyes, and the sun was still bright through his eyelids. He heard the stutter of the sprinklers coming on one after the other on the field, the shouts of soccer players running through them. Slowly, he sat down on the grass. He was feeling almost normal again. He felt a lingering temptation to turn around and gaze at Ming, close or distant, just to prove that he could do it and it would be okay, but he decided not to.

His eyes were still closed and Fitzgerald could hear the sprinklers come to life closer and closer to him. He lay on his back and waited for them to swing around and spatter him with cool water.

CODE CLOCK

—

—

—

"WALK BRISKLY. DON'T RUN. I NEVER RUN," NIGEL says.

They are in the hallway already, having abandoned the patients and consults in the emergency department.

The overhead voice repeats, "Code blue, 4A West, room 467."

Past the fracture room, through the back door in radiology, they turn the corner to the elevators.

The *up* button.

Where is the elevator? Fitz thinks but does not say. He

looks toward the stairs, then at the doors that should be sliding open. *It would have been faster if we'd walked, but now that we've stood here for maybe fifteen seconds, even twenty? Now it's probably faster to take the elevator. But it's still not here.*

"Code blue, 4A West, room 467."

The elevator is coming. Stay cool, stay calm, and get into a good headspace.

Ding!

Stepping in.

Whoossh.

Stepping out.

"Code blue, 4A West, room 467."

Both Nigel and Fitz consciously hold in their steps to keep from breaking into a jog. Their feet tick-tock in the empty nighttime ward hallways.

"You want to run the code?" says Nigel.

"Sure."

"You ever run one?"

"I've been at lots."

"You sure?"

"I'll do it," says Fitz. "Left. West wing."

"Huh. You run the next one."

"Whatever."

Fitz walks faster.

"Walk briskly, don't rush," says Nigel. "My rule is when you come into a code, your heart can't be faster than the clock."

———

In the room, it's the second bed.

They see the stillness in him.

"Okay, what's happening? Who called it?" says Nigel.

"It's Mr. Dizon," starts the nurse in blue. Fitz at the bed already, his hand in the groin feeling for a pulse and his stethoscope on the quiet chest. "I was here for Mr. Singh's meds, and he said Mr. Dizon seemed quiet."

Fitz feels a stillness beyond the lack of motion.

"VSA," says Fitz, "I'm going to start bagging. Who's going to compress?"

"How long has it been?" asks Nigel. "And where's the crash cart?"

"Can you compress?" shouts Fitz at the nurse in blue.

The blue nurse says, "The cart is coming. I called you two minutes ago." She folds her hands together over the quiet chest and begins to pump it down, down, down.

Fitz has the mask on Mr. Dizon, and his fingers draw tight to pull the jaw into the plastic cushion on the Laerdal bag.

"But how long has it been?" says Fitz.

"Well, I was on break, and then I finished and actually I was going around to see Mr. Singh, and Mr. Dizon isn't even my—"

"How long?" says Nigel.

"Well, I was here just a minute before, but then Mr. Singh didn't mention anything, so—"

"I'm not saying anything's wrong," says Nigel. "I just need to know how long. Where's the crash cart?

Does anyone know how long since Mr. Dizon has been seen with vital signs?"

A nurse in green appears, pushing the crash cart ahead of her. The green nurse is out of breath, and she flutters through the pages of the chart to make an entry.

Nigel grabs the paddles from the cart, scrunches the man's gown up around his neck, and slaps the paddles onto the chest where black stitches stencil a vertical scar.

"Ten minutes," says the green nurse, speaking into the chart. "Mr. Dizon is mine, and I saw him ten minutes before Maria called the code. Here, do you want the chart?" She writes the time, ten minutes ago, into her notes. She shows the chart to Nigel. "I'm Sharon, this is Maria, and you are?"

"PEA in two leads," says Fitz, his gaze on the monitor, addressing everyone and no one.

"I'm Dr. Nigel, and this is Fitzgerald, my medical student. Why is this guy here?"

Sharon notes the names on the chart.

"Post-bypass. Came to the floor this morning."

"Sharon. You got the clock? Twelve minutes." There is a flashing red timer on the cart, which Sharon sets at twelve. Fitz is at the head of the bed. His left hand squeezes the mask onto the face. His fingers achingly pull the jaw up, so that the mouth is tight into the plastic of the mask. His right hand pumps the bag. His thumb can feel the lung's resistance succumb to his hand's blowing motion. The little yellow valve flips open as he squeezes, and falls shut when he allows the bag to refill. Maria is over the chest, her left fist in her right palm, pushing, pushing, pushing motion into the stillness.

"One of epi," says Nigel, "two bicarb."

Sharon draws epi from an ampoule, injects it into the IV port in the bend of the arm. Now looking for the bicarb.

Fitz feels his hand cramp. He stretches his fingers between bagging. "You want me to tube him?"

"Sure," says Nigel. "You comfortable?" meaning, *do you know what you're doing?*

Fitz says, "Can I get some help? Move that chair, we have to push the bed forward. Sorry, what's your name? Come on, come on, everyone, let's make some room."

"I'm Sharon."

"Sharon, get me a Mac-3, check the light, 8-0 tube with a stylet."

Soon, Maria feels herself falling onto the body instead of pushing into it. She is tiring. She can see the monitor and can see the compressions showing on the screen, but no other rhythm. Fitz asks her to stop compressions while he gazes at the tracing. Maria climbs onto the bed, kneels. Fitz says to resume compressions, and she does so on her knees. The compressions shake the whole bed, and Mr. Dizon shakes with it. He is limp, though stiffening against those around him.

—

"Time? Where are we?" asks Nigel.

"Fifteen minutes," says Sharon. She fits a rigid stylet into an 8–o endotracheal tube.

Fitz takes the tube and bends the end like a hockey stick. How is it that this tube finds its way beyond the teeth, into the back of the throat, and then through the trachea? Fitz can't quite resolve it in his mind, the anatomy, when he thinks of it. He says, "Have we got suction?" He thinks, *I'm comfortable. I am.*

"Another epi," says Nigel.

Fitz unlocks the bed's wheels and pushes it out from the wall. Maria crouches on it, elbows locked, pushing into the stiff chest.

"Hold compression. I'm going to tube him," says Fitz.

The motion stops. Maria slides off the bed, flexes and stretches her arms.

Fitz tilts the head back, thrusts the chin up into the air, draws Mr. Dizon's face into a pose of prayer. Fitz crouches behind the top of the bed, his right hand cups the head and his left hand grips the angular, L-shaped laryngoscope. The blade of the laryngoscope slides in easily, and with it Fitz pushes aside the tongue and slips it deep, into the small fold where the blade tip rests. Now he's at the entrance to the trachea. *Where are the vocal cords? The cords are the door to enter.* Fitz pushes the blade up. Straight forward and up, toward the ceiling. The tongue is pushed up to the left. *I always forget how heavy a head is,* he thinks, *until I'm trying to straighten an airway.*

"You want some pressure?" asks Sharon.

"I'm okay." Fitz can see the arytenoids.

Fitz tilts the forehead back further, extends the neck, lifts up. The pillowcase slackens as the head floats upward.

"Let me look," says Nigel, and nudges him.

"I'm okay."

"Jeez, just let me look."

"I can see the false cords. Give me some cricoid pressure."

Nigel presses his right thumb and forefinger on the thyroid cartilage of the neck. It looks as if he is about to strangle the man. "Fine. You position me, I'll hold it." Nigel steadies the head with his left hand and pushes on the neck with his right.

"I'm almost there." Fitz has his right hand on Nigel's, pushing and angling, flexing slightly and trying to line up the cords with the teeth and throat.

Nigel says, "Let me do it."

"Hold on." Seconds pass, a thin sweat running to Fitz's cheek. "One sec." Fitz hears Sharon's pen scratching on the chart. "I've got it. Tube." He can see the white, almost ribbon-like vocal cords. When they take the tube out afterwards, people often have a hoarse voice, these little ribbons traumatized. *If* they take the tube out.

Sharon holds out the tube to him, and he glances up briefly to take it.

"Damn." As he looked up his position had changed slightly. He repositions, his forearm tight and trembling with the laryngoscope. Fitz tells himself, *I am absolutely comfortable.*

"Have you got it?" says Nigel.

"Yeah, I've got it." He slips the tube down the back of the mouth and thinks he sees the tip at the door of the vocal cords.

"Are you sure?" says Nigel.

"Absolutely," says Fitz.

He isn't sure. *Relax.* He breathes. *Doesn't matter, probably.* Fitz looks steadily down the blade of the scope, the fibre optic light bright now on the cords. The tube passes through. *In.* As it goes in, the deflated cuff pushes gently past the cords; he can feel that slight hesitance upon penetration, and then in. The feel of it, once in, reassures him. *Trachea, not esophagus.*

"I'm in. Cuff up."

Sharon plunges the syringe to inflate the cuff.

"You got a good look? Saw the cords?" says Nigel.

Fitz switches the bag from the mask to the mouth of the endotracheal tube, and listens to the chest with his stethoscope as he pumps the bag.

"It's in," says Fitz.

"Okay. Time?" asks Nigel.

Sharon says, "Eighteen minutes since we called you."

Nigel says, "Pick it up next time, Fitz."

"He's a big guy," says Fitz.

"Tape it in," says Nigel.

"'Course," says Fitz, having forgotten the tape until reminded. Then to Sharon, "Another epi."

"Then flush the line," says Nigel to Sharon.

Fitz's gloves stick to the tape as he fastens the tube, now slippery with the throat's froth.

More CPR, more drugs, and it's still PEA.

"Should I tap him?" says Fitz.

"Fine," says Nigel.

"Hold CPR," says Fitz. He takes the big syringe, the long needle, and slips it under the rib cage, aiming for the heart. He pulls back on the plunger until he hits blood. Nigel thinks, *This never works.* Fitz sucks the purple fluid into the syringe, pulls out fifty mils, just in case this frees a heart trapped by a pocket of bleeding.

The man is still in PEA.

But if you don't do it, you don't know that it wouldn't have worked—because maybe this time it could have worked, thinks Nigel.

"Continue CPR," says Fitz, holding the warm, purple-filled syringe.

It is quieter.

The three of them watch Maria.

"Time," says Nigel.

Maria's compressions are becoming slower, more hesitant.

"Twenty-one," says Maria, breathing hard into her movements.

Fitz turns to Sharon, "Bolus a litre."

"Make it half. Bolus five hundred, please," says Nigel. "Hold CPR."

Without the compressions, they interpret the monitor. It has lost its faint electrical impulse, has become a straight line—asystole.

"We could pace him," says Fitz.

"What for?" asks Nigel.

"To try."

Nigel shrugs. Then he says, "This isn't practice, Fitz."

Mr. Dizon's arms are rigid, and jerk at the compressions, becoming resistant to them. All of this is a rhythmic clanking, the castors of the bed shake, shake, as Maria perspires, pushes into his chest again and again. Now a muffled cracking noise, the ribs snap, always sooner or later they break. Maria stops, slips off the bed, looks around.

"Continue compressions," says Fitz.

"I'm too tired," says Maria.

Fitz and Nigel look at each other. Fitz looks at Maria who stands sideways, tired.

"You bag," says Nigel to Maria, taking the Laerdal bag from Fitz and tilting his head toward the chest. Fitz switches with Maria, who has a streak of sweat down her back under her long hair. Fitz pumps, rocks his whole upper body into the chest. Maria squeezes the bag every few seconds. The clock flashes red. Fitz pounds his first compressions, causing more dull, wet cracking, and now the compressions become easier with the whole chest soft.

"Give him one of epi," says Fitz.

Sharon shuffles in a drawer, fumbles with the box.

"Don't you know where it is?" says Nigel.

"Hold on, I'm getting it."

"And two of bicarb," says Nigel.

Sharon opens the boxes with a slow deliberateness.

"One epi, two bicarb," says Nigel.

"Time?" asks Fitz.

"Twenty-eight," says Maria.

The four of them stand. Fitz pounds back and forth. He feels thirsty and also needs to urinate. He can never get away to pee, and then always more coffee, more coffee through the night. He feels the compressions in his bladder as he jolts forward again.

Maria bags. She says, "You guys want to call it?"

Nigel says, "Give it till thirty."

Fitz has locked his arms, and watches the monitor, the hill-like tracings that his compressions produce. *Just like little hills.* There is no atrial electricity, no actual conduction or repolarization. Just picking up the motion.

"Twenty-nine," says Fitz. Then, "Listen, I'm getting tired." The pressure on his bladder is insistent and angry now with the motion and strain.

"Thirty," says Nigel.

Let's call it already.

"Okay. Let's call it," says Nigel.

Fitz continues compressions for a few seconds, then ten seconds, then a bit longer until he says, "All right, I'm calling it." He stops.

———

As they leave the bed Nigel says, "Sorry for the disturbance, Mr. Singh. Are you all right?"

The man in the next bed nods, his sheets pulled up under his chin.

As they leave the room Fitz says, "What's his name?"

"Mr. Dizon."

"Who's going to phone?"

"Is there someone? Wife or something?"

Flipping through the chart. "Brother in Etobicoke."

"You ran the code," says Nigel.

"Sure. I'll phone. You write a note."

"I don't care. I can phone. I don't mind."

"No, I'll phone."

"Fine. When you're done, you write the note. I'll co-sign it."

As they leave the floor Fitz says, "You think it was ten minutes when the code blue was called?"

"Ten minutes, my ass. He was cold as a brick when we got there."

A LONG MIGRATION

—
—
—

MY GRANDFATHER WAS AN ORPHAN. EITHER HE never knew the identity of his biological parents, or he was never willing to reveal this information. For the Chinese, heritage is of great importance, but adoption forms a new and legitimate lineage. Thus my name, Chen, as a grandson descended of an orphan, is from my grandfather's adoptive merchant family in the province of Guangdong. At sixteen years of age, my grandfather suddenly left Guangdong for Vietnam. He said there was a plot against him that had to do with jealousy over grades at school. My uncle Will said he was told that my grandfather had an affair with the schoolmaster's young wife. Others said that the schoolmaster warned my grandfather to leave, because the concubine of a local warlord had eyes for him.

The family matriarch in Vietnam sent my grandfather to Hong Kong for school. My grandmother said that this was because he was a difficult person whom the matriarch didn't want to deal with, but my grandfather said that he pleaded with her, begged for a higher education until she sent him to Hong Kong.

In Hong Kong my grandfather, my Yeh Yeh, finished high school. He became a partner in a shipping venture. Yeh Yeh met my grandmother, my Ma Ma. The Japanese invaded Hong Kong, and Yeh Yeh said that he was persuaded to marry my Ma Ma in order to save her from the occupation. Yeh Yeh had papers that would allow him to return to Vietnam. Ma Ma asserted that he took advantage of this situation at a time when her family's power was thin, to induce her to marry. Both agreed that he was promising though not wealthy, and that she was the princess daughter of her father's dying empire. Ma Ma contended that Yeh Yeh thought she still had money and married her for this. Yeh Yeh said that he married her because he loved her. Also, he said, it was a gesture of goodwill toward her older brother, who had helped Yeh Yeh enter business and who was worried for Ma Ma's safety in Hong Kong.

I was sorting through these histories during that last winter in Brisbane. I had first met my grandfather when he was spending the last of his money touring North America. He was both the heroic and tragic figure of many family stories—at once shameful, legendary, and safely exiled in Brisbane. Now that I was to be Yeh Yeh's companion in the period preceding his anticipated death, I was anxious to find out what was true and what were the exaggerations of memory.

The accounts always changed a little depending upon who told them, and my Yeh Yeh's versions could shift from morning to evening. Rarely did a new version of a story require the old one to be untrue. Instead, it was as if the new telling washed the story in a different colour, filling in gaps and loose ends so as to invert my previous understanding of the plot.

During those months, Yeh Yeh pissed blood every morning. Sometimes it would be just a pink-tinged trickle, but often there would be flecks of clotted blood like red sequins swirling in the toilet bowl. Yeh Yeh had me inspect the toilet daily to give my opinion. One day it was red like ink.

This was the break after my first year of medical school. My family expected that I would use my wealth of clinical knowledge first to care for grandfather, and second, to alert them when things neared an end. I would pronounce his impending death, and this would set in motion a flurry of rushed phone calls to travel agents. On jets from around the world, my relatives would hurry to Australia to be with grandfather as he died. I felt obliged to forecast correctly. It would be awkward if all of Yeh Yeh's children flew to his bedside only to find him recovering from some brief crisis and not dying. Then they would wait, their workplaces would hound them, and they would finally be obliged to depart with grandfather still alive. Alternately, if I called too late, my aunts and uncles would make a frenetic dash hoping to witness grandfather's last living moments, and only be able to attend Yeh Yeh's funeral.

In my luggage, which was packed in Toronto, my grandmother sent an oblong wooden box that contained a series of small brown bottles held in felt indentations. Each thumb-sized bottle was capped with a tight cork, and tied around with string. There were two straight rows of these healing extracts. A paper label in Chinese was pasted on each bottle, and the strings were different colours. Each morning, after his urination, grandfather dressed himself while his tea was steeping. Always suspenders on last. He lifted this box from a drawer, removed the next in the series of bottles, and drank its contents. Then he poured a mug of tea for himself, and one for me. Yeh Yeh never said anything about this box of medicines. He was good at talking but had difficulty speaking about what was most important. My grandmother, Yeh Yeh's first wife, had divorced him forty-three years ago and now lived in Toronto, the geographical other side of the world. Yeh Yeh put the empty bottle back in its slot, and the box back in the drawer. He was quiet for a while as he drank his tea. Every morning he told me to thank my grandmother for this gift, as if forgetting that he had told me to do so the day before.

Seeing the toilet bowl dark with the red-ink urine, I said to my grandfather, "These things can happen. Let's see if it settles tomorrow. Drink lots of tea today." I wanted to sound knowledgeable about the issue of bloody pee.

The next morning, it was a happy rose-coloured stream with clots like coarse sand. I felt certain that I would forecast the end accurately. I gazed into it, looking deeply through the urine into the drain, asking the liquid what it foretold. I also peed into the toilet, and the red swirled up like an eddy. Alive for a moment. I flushed the toilet and it funnelled out almost clean, with a little bit of staining at the water line.

"You're very smart," said my grandfather. "It is better today."

Renal cell carcinoma. They had operated once. My Yeh Yeh had refused a second operation. Just as well, said Dr. Spiros, it would only prolong things.

My grandfather lived in a cottage at Glenn Hill Retirement Village. There was a long cinder-block building fronted by a watered lawn. This building was divided into individual units, all accessible from a walkway. These were called cottages. The residents of the cottages ate in the main dining room along with the residents of the dormitories. The main difference was that the cottage-dwellers were able to walk and dress themselves, while many of the dormitory residents were wheeled to meals. Yeh Yeh did not participate in conversation at Glenn Hill meals. If asked a direct question at the dinner table, he would pause, raise his head as if unsure that he had been addressed, and say with a sad wave of his hand, "No speakie Englis."

In Vietnam, Yeh Yeh had been the proprietor, headmaster, and star lecturer of the Percival Chen English Academy. Early in the morning, my uncle Will—who was finishing high school at that time—would find his father sleeping on the couch in the front room. Yeh Yeh would still be wearing his tuxedo from the previous night of drinking, gambling, and bedding prostitutes. My uncle would help his father upstairs into bed. Yeh Yeh would sleep in the morning, and look fresh again by afternoon to go to the school. He had no fixed teaching schedule, but would appear in classrooms intermittently. Star lectures. That's what the students paid for, to be in his school, to be taught by Percival Chen. Decades later, there were alumni reunions in California. Many credited my grandfather with teaching them both English and an attitude for success. At that time, the Americans were sending platoons and money into Vietnam. English was a language of opportunity. Yeh Yeh's fortune was made but never accumulated. It was quickly gambled, vigorously transformed into cognac, and enthusiastically given away in late night transactions. There was a plaque from the Saigon Rotary Club on the wall next to his mirror: *To Percival Chen—For Exemplary Generosity and Community Involvement.*

On the telephone to Canada, I asked my dad whether grandfather really had forgotten all his English, or whether he just pretended to have lost it. My father said that when they were children, they all thought their father was a master of this language. Yeh Yeh told me that he had always faked it, that at the British school in Hong Kong he had learned that the British display great confidence when they don't know something. Later, at his own school, when he couldn't spell something he was teaching, he simply avoided writing it down. He claimed that he never really spoke English properly, but had convinced people that he did. The hired teachers were Canadians, Brits, and Australians. These people corrected spelling mistakes for the students, so he didn't need to. I suspect my grandfather understood more English than he admitted, but that he could not take interest in conversations at Glenn Hill. *Aren't the potatoes salty today?* In his cottage, Yeh Yeh kept a bottle of Remy Martin XO cognac in the cupboard above the sink.

My grandmother claimed that grandfather had ruined her life by gambling and womanizing. She said that his behaviour led her to nag and fight him, and this created bitterness in her. It was this wound that had made her such an admittedly difficult woman, she said. Sometimes she explained this after yelling at me or another family member. My grandfather said my grandmother ruined his life, because early in their marriage her nagging and fighting compelled him to seek solace outside their home. For a Chinese man living in Saigon when Vietnam was still Indochine under the French, this meant mah-jong houses. They would bring hot dim sum late into the night, and smiling compliant women at any hour. There was nowhere else to go, he said. Yeh Yeh admitted that it was wrong of him to spend so much time and money in unfaithful ways. He recognized that this would anger any wife, but said that he sought these comforts initially because there was no peace at home. My father told me that although the school was lucrative, Yeh Yeh never had any money. The school fees went directly to loan sharks. Yeh Yeh bought a new Peugeot with push-button gears, but once the family had to sleep in the school for several months because they could not afford to rent a house.

In Brisbane, my grandfather had many friends. Enough of the Chinese in Vietnam had emigrated to Australia that he still had social standing in this new, hot, white country. We were often invited to dinner. One couple who took us out was younger than my grandfather, but older than my parents. Dr. Wong was a retired orthopaedic surgeon who had graduated from the Percival Chen English Academy before studying medicine in Glasgow. After retiring, Dr. Wong had become an Anglican minister. He and his wife, with Uncle Will's encouragement, were trying to convert my grandfather to Christianity before he died. Grandfather was a prime candidate. He was previously sinful and glamorous, now reduced to economic subsistence although still drinking XO cognac and gambling once a week (I had become the chauffeur for these outings, which my uncle was not to be told about). We were having a dinner of scallops, delicate oysters, and the lobsters without claws that they catch in Australia. My grandfather produced his flask and asked the waiter to fill a glass with ice. He poured cognac for himself and offered it around the table, but no one took any. The minister and his wife were teetotallers. Yeh Yeh poured some for me. We talked about Jesus.

My grandfather was receptive and interested, although during years of friendship with Dr. Wong he had politely and charismatically sidestepped the issue of faith. He questioned Dr. Wong about the parable of the sower. Yeh Yeh asked whether God would mind if he had sown seeds that lay ignored for a long time before sprouting. Dr. Wong said that it was all the same as long as there was faith at the time of judgment. I imagined my grandfather weighing the odds. Death was an awaiting certainty and beyond that the odds were unknown, but there was nothing to lose by laying a few bets on the Bible. What was in the past could be repented for, and the future was short.

They set a date for the baptism.

My grandfather didn't drink tea in restaurants, because he didn't want to fill his bladder and have to pee blood during dinner. He sipped cognac on ice. A great deal of food remained on the table when everyone stopped eating, mindful of their cholesterol and their diabetes. They counted on me to finish everything, which I tried to do.

After Ma Ma divorced Yeh Yeh, she married a man whose business was mostly in Taiwan. This was daring at that time, for a Chinese woman to divorce her husband and then remarry. It was in the newspapers. While reading in his garden one day, her new husband was assassinated. The bullet travelled expertly through the back of his neck and out his throat. He would not have suffered. He was thought to be a candidate for leading a Chinese secession movement. My father said this was a political ambition only imagined by others, and that his death was unfortunate because he had been kind to my grandmother. This had helped to calm her. She was still excitable, and that was the last point in her life when her beauty could, at least superficially, compensate for her temper and vindictiveness.

Yeh Yeh no longer had an excuse not to marry his mistress, and so he did. She became Second Wife. Second Wife did not get along with grandfather's new mistress, who became Third Wife—although they were never legally married. Both wives lived in the same household.

Third Wife was docile, and tried to submit to the will of Second Wife, who nonetheless continued to be unhappy with the situation. Second Wife tried to kill herself with a gun, but managed only to shatter her arm, which then had to be amputated. With the shame of the disabled upon her, my grandfather bought her a house and sent her money periodically. No one has been able to tell me what happened to her after that. Third Wife was kind to Fourth Wife. Fourth Wife was sixteen years old when she married my then middle-aged grandfather. Fourth Wife was more cunning than Third Wife, and insisted on a legal marriage. Soon after this, the Viet Cong changed Saigon to Ho Chi Minh City, the Americans were suddenly gone, and those who had links to the capitalist economy were being imprisoned or shot. My grandfather convinced the High Commission that he was a British subject by virtue of his having once lived in Hong Kong. When he fled Vietnam, Fourth Wife went with him because she had marriage papers, while Third Wife remained in Ho Chi Minh City with her child.

One day, my grandfather woke, peed in the toilet, and then went back to bed. He did not dress. He told me that he didn't want to get up that day. He felt tired, and the thing in his side was growing.

"Come and feel it. See what you think," he said in Cantonese.

His left flank bulged as if a balloon was being inflated under the skin.

"*Mo toong*," he said. There is no pain. He felt his side delicately, and pulled up his shirt so that I could see it. I pressed the tumour gently with the tips of my fingers. It was firm, hard like cold Plasticine. What did I think?

"*Ho choy mo toong*," I said. It was fortunate that it wasn't painful.

"*Hai*," he agreed.

Yeh Yeh explained that he always wore suspenders in these past few months. If he wore a belt, he pointed out, it would rub his side where the tumour was growing under the skin. His biggest fear was that the skin would split over the growing lump. He wore his pants slightly loose—held up by suspenders to avoid friction on this area. The thought of the cancer escaping from the confines of his body and making itself public in a wet, bloody way horrified him. He said he wouldn't be able to care for himself if the thing broke through. They would move him to the dormitories. Go look in the toilet, he told me.

I looked in the toilet. There was thick blood. It seemed to have a surface to it, clotting as if there was so much blood that it had become independent of the urine. Experimentally, I flushed and saw the thickness of it break up and swirl. It was not as viscous as it initially appeared, but this was a deep and serious tone of red.

"Yeh Yeh," I said. "We should go to the hospital."

"No hospital."

"But you look pale. You are weak. Dr. Spiros said this might happen, that you might lose blood and need a transfusion."

"No more hospital. Your grandfather dies here."

"Yes, but if we go to the hospital, they may be able to help you live longer. We'll come back here, and you won't have to go to the dormitories."

"Who needs hospitals? Besides, you're a doctor. You're here."

I was early in my training and wanted to pretend to be a doctor. I suggested that we call Dr. Spiros.

"Bring me my medicine," said grandfather. He wanted the box of little brown bottles. I went to get them. There were eight remaining. I pried the tight cork from a bottle, gave it to Yeh Yeh, and made him a cup of tea. In Toronto, I had gone with my grandmother to the herbalist on Dundas Street to buy these medicines. I had been surprised by her concern for Yeh Yeh's well-being, and her desire to purchase medicines. She had questioned the herbalist vigorously in purchasing these herbal concentrates, which were reputed to invigorate the kidneys. She had insisted that the medicines must be of the best quality—nothing fake, nothing second rate. Before buying them, she produced her trump card, telling the herbalist that I, her grandson, was a brilliant doctor and would smell each vial before she would buy them. The herbalist smiled obligingly, I sniffed them each in turn—their odour both bitter and heady—and told my grandmother that they smelled very strong. She was satisfied and paid for them.

Dr. Spiros was not in his office. His registrar was there, but said that he couldn't assess anything without seeing the patient. We should bring him to the emergency department, and if they wanted to involve urology, they would page them. Yeh Yeh refused to go. I called Dr. Wong, who came to the cottage and spoke to my grandfather. He felt the mass, and then told Yeh Yeh that as an orthopaedic surgeon he didn't have much expertise here. Yeh Yeh should see his specialist, he said. I realized that real physicians, when called upon in awkward family situations, try to pretend not to be doctors. Grandfather said he was ready to die. Dr. Wong said he could bring elders from the church for a bedside baptism. Yeh Yeh agreed.

The two of us strolled down the walkway in the bright warm afternoon of the Brisbane winter to Dr. Wong's car. He said to me, "You know he's going to die?"

"That's why I'm here."

"*Nay ho gwai,*" he said, patting my shoulder. You are very obedient and well-behaved. A Chinese compliment.

That night, I asked grandfather if he knew who his real parents were. He told me it didn't matter, that one always has to move forward, otherwise the past holds too much pain.

After two years in Hong Kong, my grandfather and Fourth Wife moved to Australia. Toward the end of the

Vietnam War, my aunts and uncles had been sent to different countries. The idea was that someone, somewhere, would land on their feet. Uncle Will went to Sydney, and later sponsored Yeh Yeh from Hong Kong. After several months, my aunt Alice told Uncle Will that if Yeh Yeh continued to live with them, she would leave. He was drinking and gambling heavily. Fourth Wife was younger than all of Yeh Yeh's children.

My uncle helped Yeh Yeh and Fourth Wife buy a house in Brisbane. Yeh Yeh told me he had never wanted to stay in Sydney. Too cold. Brisbane is tropical. Fourth Wife started a restaurant, and began an affair with the cook. She divorced my grandfather but continued to visit him weekly in the retirement home they found for him. That was twelve years before the cancer. He told me that it's understandable. A younger woman wants a younger man. Yeh Yeh relied on Fourth Wife to bring him cigarettes. While smoking these cigarettes, he spoke sadly about the early arguments, the poisoned misunderstandings he had with Ma Ma. At that time they were younger than I was now, he told me.

The next day, Yeh Yeh was too weak to stand. His forehead was pale and sweaty. The toilet bowl was thickly stained with blood. I had to lift him under his arms to get him to the washroom. He wouldn't eat. I called my aunt Alice and uncle Will to ask what I should do. Should I take him to the hospital? They asked me what they should do, should they fly from Sydney? Everyone else was in New York, Los Angeles, Toronto. With the time difference I didn't want to wake them. In the evening, against my grandfather's wishes, I called an ambulance. The spinning red siren lights turned on the wall of the cottage, making it look like it was in constant motion. They took him out, wrapped in an orange tube of blanket. I tried to be medical and tell the paramedics about his condition, but I couldn't remember any of the details.

Two days and eight units of transfused blood later, my grandfather was complaining to Dr. Spiros that he should be discharged. Dr. Wong had come to baptize him, and had brought fried noodles in white styrofoam boxes. The Wongs had a place on Stradbroke Island, and suggested that I go there for a rest. Grandfather was more stable now.

On Stradbroke, I stayed across from the headlands beach. In the morning I woke early to watch the humpback whales migrating north. As the sun streaked low across the water, their spouts were small torches in the grey shadowless tide. The light became full and round. I saw dolphins diving out of the crests of waves to hunt the fish that were driven into the cove. The sun lifted higher and burned through the day. From the pay phone at the side of the road, I called grandfather at the hospital. He was doing all right, he said. He had sent Dr. Wong to the cottage for the bottles of Chinese medicine. There were two bottles left, he said. I should stay at the beach and enjoy myself, and see whether they had fresh crab in the restaurants. Yeh Yeh advised me to have them sauté it in cognac, that's what he would do. He said that I should remember always to move forward, to not allow the past to become hurtful. He advised me that this was sometimes a difficult thing to do. Yeh Yeh reminded me to thank my grandmother for the medicines, when I would soon return home and speak with her.

WINSTON

———
———
———

IN THE BLACK PART OF THE MORNING OF November 6, Winston manages to sleep for the first time since Halloween. He wakes with a sudden, clear memory of the event, and decides to seek help. It has been years since Winston has seen a doctor, but now he desperately needs one. He walks to the nearby clinic, and stands outside for a while, wondering if this is the right thing to do. After all, some people say that doctors dispense poison. Winston decides that he must take this risk, and goes in.

For fifty-six minutes, Winston sits in the waiting room, where the receptionist stares at him because she can see everything about him and Adrienne and the grates and the whispering. For six minutes, Winston sits in the examining room waiting for Dr. Sri. When the doctor enters, he is too young, too friendly, and he moves too quickly—all of this is suspicious. Nonetheless, Winston explains (almost) every relevant detail, and after he has made himself perfectly clear, Dr. Sri—instead of running for the antidote, the syringe, the shot, the emergency cure—just sits there and says to Winston, "Let's be sure I understand: you feel that the reason you've been having these experiences, these feelings, is that you've been poisoned."

Winston says, "Primarily, I want to believe that you can help. Otherwise, I am permanently injured. But I have my doubts, suspicions even." His hands wrestle snakes on his lap. He looks down and says, "No, I've got to trust someone." He looks up. "Who else to trust but you, doctor? It's just doubts then. We won't say suspicions. That would be the wrong footing. Isn't it enough to say I'm on the verge of being destroyed?" His wiry frame leans far ahead, somewhere between a bow and a pounce.

"Tell me——" says Sri.

"So just fix me, basically. Wield your tests, potions, cures, et cetera. The evil in my bloodstream fizzes my brain, makes neurons swell and pop. That blue drink— I knew something was funny, not the funny colour, not ha-ha funny, but *funny*. Put down the glass, don't even sip, said my inner voice, but I didn't listen. I was wearing this ghost costume, and it was such a nice party and everyone seemed so nice and I really wanted everyone to like me. Adrienne said they loved me, it was a classic costume. But then she poisoned me." Suddenly, Winston looks like he might cry.

"What did—"

"I can't think, can't sleep. Or maybe I can't sleep *therefore* I can't think. Doctor, give me a sign to trust you."

Sri unclips his laminated name tag, holds it in front of himself like a talisman. It reads *Dr. Sri. Resident Physician, PGY-1.*

"That looks serious," says Winston. Sri is about to clip the tag back on the pocket of his shirt, but Winston reaches for it. "Let me see."

"Sure."

Winston takes it, turns it over to look at the bulge of the magnetic-coded backing, runs his finger along the edge that is worn from card-readers, holds it up next to Sri and compares the faces.

"Smile," he says.

Sri imitates a smile, and only once he has done so does he see that his patient might be making fun of him, might be taking advantage of him and will at any moment laugh at the humour in a momentary tilt of the balance of power. But Winston regards him studiously in a quick moment and then hands the card back.

Sri says, "When did this problem begin?"

"The drink, like I *said*, the blue drink."

"You said you remembered the poison. As if you didn't know right away."

"This morning. That is the *ethos* of poison: that the victim does not immediately realize. You know this drug, of course? Bad stuff?"

Sri says, "We sometimes see the mind affected in this way—even in illness, and some think of illness as a kind of poison."

"Exactly, doctor, the poison has made me ill."

"Sometimes, we don't find a poison, and illness itself is the issue."

"I thought of that. See, even *you* think I'm talking crazy, right? Thought of it already, that people would think I'm going nuts, and that's why you, being a doctor and everything, have to treat the poison because this stuff is making me *sound cuckoo*. You've got to fix it before it *does* make me nuts."

Winston smeared peanut butter on a banana. As he ate, he wrote.

November 3

Morning. Is it really? Yes, of course.

Sheep, they say. Counting.

So bright. Upstairs—if only Claude and Adrienne would be quiet.

Sheep: how many does it take?

I should complain. No, that's not right, neighbours and all. I could speak to them about the noise. But Claude has a temper. Why not complain? It's not right. That would be dangerous. Why? No.

Winston sat sideways at the kitchen table, hunched on the chrome-legged chair. He had not slept since the night of Halloween. He heard the downhill thumping of feet from the third floor to the second. A slight pause at the second floor, at his own door? Maybe not. Or maybe a pause, but perhaps it was because Claude had an untucked shirt, or a coat to zip up. Maybe nothing to do with me, he thought. Maybe no pause—he was not certain. The feet drummed down to the first floor. The scrape open, then clunk closed of the solid door, and then the secretive click of the bolt thrown shut. The screen door made a metal whine, then a wire smashing sound. From his square-framed kitchen window, Winston watched his upstairs neighbour Claude walk through the first-frost mist of the shared backyard and climb into his small red car. Winston felt relief, and wondered if he would now be able to sleep. The red car whined, its headlights shone pillars in the mist, it backed out and roared down the laneway.

Winston heard soft, shuffling footsteps above him. He crouched to the ventilation grate. Big, slanted vents angled slightly upward from the tall baseboard. The floor undulated from side to side; the dark wood strips foot-worn in some places and warped in others. The shape of the grate was soft, blurred by successive layers of thick white paint, and this same paint had jammed the grates open so that he could not avoid, he told himself, hearing Adrienne hum softly to herself, running her bath. Winston remained crouched to the ground, heard the *plunk* like the sound of his own swallowing as she entered the water. He imagined the moment that preceded this—the robe slipping off her shoulders— perhaps the white silk housecoat he has seen fluttering in the backyard. He lay with his ear against the jammed-open grate, reassured himself that he could not avoid hearing the splashing noises of Adrienne's bath. Later, the water drained with a funnel sound that went through his whole apartment. She must be drying herself, he thought. One of the big, fluffy purple towels that Winston has seen her pin on the laundry line in the backyard—Adrienne waved whenever she saw him watching from his window.

The day glared brightly.

Then came night—illuminated by the conversations from the third-floor apartment.

Dr. Miniadis, the supervising physician, is in the observation room reading journals and listening to Smetana's *Moldau.* When Sri enters, she removes her headset.

He says, "Were you watching, Dr. Miniadis?" On one of the row of screens, Winston swings his foot.

"Unfortunately, I was not," she says, and smiles brilliantly at Sri. "Please." She removes a handful of charts from a chair, waves at it beneficently. "Go ahead."

Sri sits, centres his notes on his lap, and says, "Winston is a twenty-two-year-old man with no previous psychiatric history who believes that he was poisoned by his upstairs neighbour Adrienne. He believes that after secretly administering a drug to him in a blue-coloured beverage, she seduced him at a Halloween party. He is sexually and romantically obsessed with her, feels that she is secretly in love with him and that she wants to abandon her husband, Claude. Winston believes that the drug produced a temporary amnesia and also has caused his profound sleep disturbance." Sri moves his mouth to wet his tongue. He continues, "The patient reports multiple somatic complaints, a sense of hyper-vigilance, and has paranoid ideation concerning this woman and her husband. There is a suggestion of auditory hallucination—whispers heard in the night—and perhaps of thought implantation. Winston is paranoid, with some morbid thoughts, but has no homicidal or suicidal ideation. His thought process is at times tangential, his speech borders on being pressured, and my overall impression is one of a first-break psychosis."

Dr. Miniadis's upper body, clad in a multicoloured striped sweater, sways a little with the rushing up and down of the *Moldau*, which emerges, constricted and tinny, from her headphones.

She says, "Wonderful," and beams at Sri. Her eyes, magnified by teacup-sized reading glasses, seem to float in front of her.

"Of course . . . well, he has no active homicidal or suicidal ideation so I suppose that is wonderful . . . in its own way. My differential diagnosis includes thyrotoxicosis, and a poisoning syndrome."

"Marvellous case presentation. I am *pleased*, Dr. Sri. Very pleased. You paint a good picture: a descriptive summary, appropriate inclusion of diagnostic impressions, and just enough detail to make it alive."

"Toxicology is not my strength."

"Hmm."

"But I can't think of an agent that would produce these symptoms."

"Agent? Ah, the poison issue. Dr. Sri, I admire your open-mindedness. Youth, with the magical new experience of clinical pathology. You've heard that the sound of hoofbeats implies the presence of horses? It is true that we must look carefully for zebras, but for the most part we expect to find horses." A grand smile.

"So . . . what should I do?"

"What, indeed? You are fortunate. A fine, fine case. Fascinating. You could wait years to see such a rich, exciting clinical picture. The mind—a force to behold. And so. What should you do? Examine carefully. Drink it in! Take full advantage of this educational opportunity."

"It seems like a psychosis, then?"

"Amazing, isn't it?" says Dr. Miniadis.

"Should I consider neuroleptics?"

"Remarkable drugs. Read up on the atypicals." Dr. Miniadis taps the journal in front of her.

"What about. . . . Well, the patient insists we test him for poisoning."

"Naturally. Zebras. Always, people are drawn to zebras." She taps her fingers on the headphones.

"Then I'll send for a TSH, lytes, and a tox screen? The patient insists," says Sri, almost apologetic. "It will satisfy his questions, and build trust."

"This is the dilemma, to build a rapport, to allow the legitimacy of experience, but never to speak of what is *not* real as if it were."

Sri is hesitant, sheepish in asking, "Dr. Miniadis, is there a drug that causes this?"

"Causes what?"

"What this patient has experienced—the temporary amnesia, the sleep disturbance. A new synthetic substance, maybe?" Winston had pressed Sri on this point, and because Sri was not certain in an absolute way, he had deferred the question, saying that he would ask his supervisor. "It is striking that the patient has insight into the disrupted nature of his thought process, but believes it is the result of poisoning."

She smiles, raises her hands as if to frame her face like flowers in a vase, and says, "Our world is mysterious. You're doing well, Dr. Sri." She places the headset on her ears, leaving Sri no choice but to exit the room.

Morning crept up slowly, sneaky, until suddenly it was day.

Winston had not slept since Halloween. He wrote in a scrawling, angry hand.

November 4

Claude goes to work so early? So chipper! Energetic!

He drinks coffee, maybe. Coffee from grounds, grounds from beans. The beans are red before roasting, who told me that?

That's it, coffee. Shall you drink coffee?

No, I need sleep. No coffee for me.

Cigarettes, the calm. You're out. Their noise, all night. Chitter chatter chipper chapper.

The red car left a snake-trail of exhaust in the lane, which slithered its belly into the ground. Winston felt the shocking cold of the chair leg on his ankle. He curled his foot around the metal.

The sheep jumping, that's what I forgot. The jumping part. You forgot the jumping. Each part is crucial, evidently. So what if I sleep? Then what? So what?

It's not safe.

THAT's why I haven't been sleeping, because it's NOT safe.

Sleep is an illusion of the happy, vulnerable people.

Listen to those feelings, the inner leading voice.

No. No. No. It's perfectly safe, sleep is the safest thing, what am I thinking?

It's NOT safe.

Who put that thought into my mind?

It's just NOT safe.

No, it's safe, who put that thought there?

Where has slumber gone?
Sleep is the escape that has escaped.

Adrienne hummed. These soft morning throat-sounds were as close as if his ear were against her neck. Instead, they came through the ventilation grate. Winston crawled across the floor, heard Adrienne twist one knob of the faucet and then the other, the water rushing circles around the tub. He heard the shuffled *thump-slap, thump-slap, thump-slap* of her heel touching, followed closely by the ball of her foot. He crawled to the couch, took a pillow, placed it silently next to the grate, and lay there with his ear against the layered paint that smelled like rain falling on dust. Winston decided that it was okay, that there was nothing wrong with it, that he had been kept awake by Claude and Adrienne all night for three nights, and so there was nothing at all wrong with what was essentially the private pleasure of listening to her bath.

In the clinic washroom, Winston produces urine for the drug screen, tucks himself in, and zips. The vial is warm in his fingers, his arm hot-achy from the bloodletting, staunched by a tightly taped cotton ball. The sign says 1: OPEN DOOR, 2: PLACE SAMPLE ON TRAY, 3: CLOSE DOOR SECURELY. This little square door in the wall is just big enough to allow a hand to enter. Winston opens the door. In the passage, there is a small plastic tray for the urine sample. Winston sees the latch of the door on the other side of the wall, and wonders whether the door was closed before he pissed, or whether he might have heard this little door open while he was pissing. Could someone peer through here? He should have watched the actual door while he was standing, legs apart, in front of the toilet, though aim would have been an issue. The latch could probably be popped from the other side with a strong thumb. Clever, how they put it behind where a person stands, so you don't necessarily see if someone peeks. He could try to open it from this side, but then they would see him checking it out, and if someone had peeked, they would know that he knew. The thing to do is to pour. Yes, to use the sample vial to pour a thin stream into the toilet and see if, at the moment when someone might presume that he is turned to face the toilet, the door clicks open. Winston thinks of opening the vial, of pouring his urine into the toilet while watching the door. Except his bladder is now empty; they will be suspicious if he is too long in the bathroom, and maybe it is safer to play along. He places his vial on the tray. Closes the latch. Goes back to the doctor's room, sits nonchalantly as if everything is just fine and above suspicion, waits for Dr. Sri to return.

Winston had not slept since Halloween, and with the desperate, grating morning came the shamed anticipation of Adrienne's bath, a further embarrassment. Claude's feet descended the two flights of stairs, accelerating in a drum roll. Winston wrote.

November 5

I confront them today.

This may be deliberate.

They must know that I hear.

Last night, their sounds were strange. The baths: Adrienne hears me listening. She knows. Should I speak to Claude? Maybe Claude, but if she heard me and she told him, then he will kill me. It's just bathing sounds. The sound of water soothes me, I'll tell them.

He is bigger than me.

They're talking. They know.

Winston sat at the kitchen table, which was covered in a green faux-marble surface and rimmed by a gleaming chrome band. It, and the chairs, were part of a set. Winston watched the departure of the red car. The window was rolled down and Claude's left elbow was perched on the door.

It should be Claude that I speak to. No. Better to speak to Adrienne. She knows, of course. What will she say?

How would she know?

Know about the talking or about the baths? Maybe she wants me to hear the bath, could that be? No, NO! That would make it wrong, make her ugly. This is about the talking. You need to discuss. Focus and discuss. Talk about the noise. Yes, thank you, talk about the noise at night. Really, it's a noise issue. The bath is separate, but if she knows I hear the talking she will know about the bath, but that is nothing.

Yes.

It's a shared house, which should be quiet. A noise issue, yes—primarily one of late-night quiet. Crucial for sleep.

Later that morning, on the third floor where there is no landing but only the stairs leading abruptly up to the apartment, Adrienne opened the door.

"Hi, Winston, come on in."

"I shouldn't."

"You're going to stand there?"

"It's just something, a little thought I wanted to sort of mention quickly, so I shouldn't come in."

"What is it?" she smiled, which made him feel very badly but also glad and a little bit hopeful about lying there next to the ventilation grate each morning.

"It's about the house really, it being an old house and everything and you know how old houses weren't really designed to be separate apartments so some things are a bit wonky and haphazard like the air ducts and noises and plumbing and I'm a light sleeper so if noises are an issue it's really an issue, so I—"

"Step inside? I made tea. It's steeping, and there's a cup with your name on it."

"Sure."

Adrienne brought Winston's tea the way he liked it—a drop of cream and three sugars. They sat across from each other in the living room, and Winston had the anxiety of desiring comfort, of knowing that Adrienne was one of only three people in the world who knew how he liked his tea, the others being his mother and himself.

Adrienne looked at him as she did whenever he dropped in, which was as if she had known all along that he was coming, and she saw exactly what was in his mind, and she understood precisely what would make him happy but was forbidden from telling him because to do so would deprive him of an important challenge.

"Did you have a good time, the other night?" she asked.

"What?" he said, always startled when she asked an opinion of him. It was his favourite tea—Earl Grey. She must have known that he would be coming upstairs.

"Halloween—ghosts are so *classic*. Especially with flowery bedsheets." She raised her teacup slightly to Winston in salutation of his superb costume choice, blew the top layer with a long breath, and sipped.

"I had a great time. Thank you."

"Everyone said you were so funny. You were all right in the morning? I guess you don't normally drink that much, but there're nasty drunks and there're funny drunks, and everyone loved you, said that you are definitely in the funny category. How did you feel the next day?"

"About the same." Winston remembered the first drinks, the pitcher of blue fluid with cherries floating in it, and then the next morning waking up in his own bed. He wished he remembered being funny and loved, just like she said.

"You had to be put into your bed, hope you didn't mind."

Winston was about to ask who had tucked him in. Was it her? Or her and Claude? Or the partygoers as a group? Or Claude alone? Or her alone? Instead he said, "I've had difficulty sleeping." He now suspected that she had noticed that he had observed that she was not wearing a brassiere. Perhaps she saw that he had reddened, or at least he presumed this from the heat on his cheeks. She didn't cross her arms or turn to the side despite any attention of his that she may have become aware of. He looked into his tea.

He sipped. The tea was perfect.

"I used to have that," said Adrienne. "Is it because you're excited about something, or you just can't let go?"

"Neither." Now Winston realized that he could not blurt out that his state of insomnia was fuelled by her and Claude talking through the night. Sheep or no sheep. Perhaps he had heard facts that he should not know, ideas that would be dangerous. He had not been able to detect the actual words. He did not understand why he could not make out the words, but he couldn't, so maybe there was no danger? However, they spoke softly, mumbling-like, certainly of dark secrets next to which his life would be of little comparative value. He had come very close, too close to revealing himself, and with a sudden panic he jumped, spilled tea on his knee. "Something urgent. Important. I remembered. Have to go."

"Are you all right, Winston?" she asked.

He tumbled downstairs, locked the door of his apartment behind him. Sat behind the door, a narrow escape. Could not remember if he'd put the teacup down, or if he'd spilled it on the floor and owed an apology.

Sri pauses outside the door of the examining room. Of course Dr. Miniadis is right, he assures himself. Horses. Winston jumps when Sri enters the room, and Sri is unsure whether this is a startle of suspicion or optimistic anticipation. Sri sits, wonders if he should have googled "recreational amnestic." He becomes aware that Winston is waiting for him to speak.

"You should come into hospital," says Sri. "A specialist will take care of you."

"A poisoning expert?"

"An expert in your type of situation."

"In poisoning," says Winston, satisfied.

"Your kind of experience . . . we find is best addressed on the psychiatry ward. They are concerned not only with poison but with the mind."

This is unnecessary, says Winston in a rush. With the test results, can't they simply administer the antidote? The poison, he says, keeps him from sleep, slows the mind, disrupts the form of his thoughts. Sri chooses his words carefully, speaking in the third person. He explains that situations similar to Winston's are carefully examined on the psychiatry wards. Winston says that he is not crazy, not loony, not bonkers, not asking for a miracle but only for a cure, which is what any poisoning victim wants. Sri speaks in low, measured tones, asks him if he will take a medication. Sri feels his own heart pounding, remembers that they are taught to speak in the mood they wish the patient to absorb. Winston says that this, at long last, is what he has come for: the antidote. Sri writes on a prescription pad. He tears off the prescription, holds it in front of himself like a peace offering.

Before Sri can explain the prescription, Winston says, "That little door in the bathroom: the inside door opens from the outside, right? Who watched me take a leak?"

"What door?"

"I'm not saying you, or any specific person specifically, although if you did need to watch me pee for a bona fide medical reason I suppose that's cool but you should let me know about it. I'm not freaking out or anything—I'm just telling you I don't appreciate it."

"Didn't you close the door, Winston?"

"Don't play dumb. The cubbyhole door, where you put the pee."

"The passageway for the urine sample?"

"Naturally, it concerns me, as it would concern anyone, that someone watched my urination."

"No one watched you, Winston."

"I'm trying to be polite about this."

"What would you do if you found out someone were watching you?" asked Sri. He thought of the criteria for admitting someone to hospital against their will: danger to self, danger to others, failure to care for self. "Do you feel so frightened that you might do something . . . physical . . . to protect yourself, for instance?"

"I need to protect myself?" says Winston. "Am I being watched all the time?"

"I'm not saying that. I'm asking if you feel a need for self-defence?"

"How should I defend myself?" says Winston.

"That's not what I'm suggesting, but have you thought of it?"

"You know, Claude and Adrienne live just upstairs."

"I know," says Sri. "Do you think they watch you? Would you defend yourself against them?"

Sri listens for a clue, some indication of an impending debacle which will allow him to keep Winston involuntarily. He feels guilty, as if he is circling Winston with a lasso.

"So I am watched, then."

"I want to know what you would do if you were really convinced that someone *was* watching you."

But then, what does one do with a horse that thinks it is a zebra? Sri throws the lasso wildly, saying, "Are you so scared that you would try to kill yourself, or maybe someone else?"

"Kill myself?" says Winston, alarmed. "Are you

crazy? The surveillance is worse than I thought. So just tell me, what's the big deal about seeing how I pee?"

"I can attest that no one watched you in the bathroom, but—" and he thinks of leaving aside the issue of the cameras, but to hide something now could lead to problems later. "Someone is viewing us right now, of course, but that's different. We have a camera system . . . anyhow, you know about that, don't you?"

"What?"

"Cameras. Not in the bathroom, but all these rooms are, let's not say watched, let's say monitored."

Winston looks around quickly, realizes that he is seated far from the door, that they are on the third floor, that it is too high to jump out the window, that the architecture has trapped him, and that he is correct. He knew that he was being watched.

"Then I have to be careful," he says, whispering to Sri, already half-standing to leave.

"Didn't you read the signs in the waiting room? This is a teaching facility, so there're cameras running. But it's not someone 'watching' you in the sneaky way you feel that someone is watching. It's a routine, normal part of our teaching institution. It's a person, a *real* person. Dr. Miniadis is the supervising physician today, so she can see all the rooms. There's the camera." Sri points at the one-way mirror that shields the lens. "It's a physical camera, with wires, and it's *really there,* but not the way you think someone is *watching you.* You know what I mean?"

"That's exactly what I feel, that someone is really watching me."

"Now, to be honest, often Dr. Miniadis doesn't watch." Sri says this in complete confidence that she never turns away from her headphones and her music, and therefore does not hear him give this explanation.

"Now I'm confused. So then who's watching?"

"Really, no one. She's there in the monitoring room but I'm sure that she's not paying attention. In a true sense, no one sees us. But you asked and so I just want to be honest and let you know that these cameras are running."

"Wow," says Winston, reclining slightly and considering this information. He leans forward and whispers, "The poison gives me special power, so that I *know* when I'm being watched, like an extra sense. See, before you said it, I already *knew* that we were being watched. I told you. You heard it. I *already knew*."

Having fled downstairs, Winston sat with his back to the door of his apartment, the tea stain cooling on his leg. The Halloween party that he had not thought of for days now emerged in detailed memory.

The pitcher of blue fluid, maraschino cherries bobbing like eyes. Adrienne a harem girl, Claude the sultan. Three Viking brothers with daggers charged at Winston—he screamed until the rubber swords collapsed instead of impaling him. "Are you happy, Winston?" said the harem girl as she shimmied her hips. "What is your pleasure?" Tigger called him Winnie, and handed him a drink. He tore a wider mouth-hole in the bedsheet that made him a ghost, and gulped at the air in fear of the pressing, dancing, shouting crush of people. A tiny female jockey on her strong-haunched stallion charged around the living room, yelled "Giddy-up! Giddy-up!" The horse reared in front of Winston, whinnied, shook its head, almost threw off its glasses. "Silver is spooked by ghosts," the jockey said. Claude toasted Winston, who said that he was not feeling well, that this was too much for him. Claude said, "I am the Sultan, and I command you to party!" and handed him a tumbler of the blue cocktail that was named Red Sky at Night. With his third drink, Winston began a ghost howl. Phantoms pursued him, and he chased them in return. All around him was the murmur of plotted conspiracy and special powers, and Winston told them of his knowledge that people watched him and yet could see right through him, that he could hear their thoughts even when he didn't want to, and that he wished people would stop inserting words into his mind. Laughter confirmed and mocked him. Joan of Arc sympathized, said that she had never realized that being a ghost was so trying, but asked him if he had ever tried to go into battle as a woman pretending to be a man. After Winston fell, the harem girl helped him to his feet, shooed people from the stairs to bring the ghost to his apartment, steadied him until he was in bed. "You overdid it, little ghost," said the harem girl. "I know your thoughts," said Winston. "And you'll drift through my room at night, right? Let me get you some water." The harem girl sat as he sipped the water, watched him drink it all. Only after swallowing did he realize that it had been unusually blue, just like the Red Sky at Night. Then came the harem girl's dance—perhaps she didn't realize it was his first time. He was unsure if he wanted her to know how glad he was that his first time was with her, or if he wanted to conceal his inexperience.

Yet now, the details of the harem girl's dance were blurred. Winston achingly, importantly, wanted to remember the texture of skin, the scent of neck, the drift of veil, but all this was fuzzy. What clearly remained was that Adrienne had ignored the aftermath of seduction in the banality of innocent tea preparation, that she had poisoned him to do this, and that the poison had made him forget but now he remembered. What else would the poison do? The mind's implosion? Explosion? Possibly, this was not true love. He had to get help, to find the antidote.

Sri says, "You said that Claude and Adrienne have been your friends for a long time."

"Best friends," says Winston.

"You wouldn't hurt your best friends, then."

He looks away from the camera, at Sri. "Adrienne wants to be with me. That would make her happy, though I suspect it would upset Claude. Yet, I'm wary of a woman who poisons me to sleep with me."

"What will you do?"

"I must wait, and listen." He stares straight into the shielded camera lens.

"And?"

"And be vigilant."

Sri decides that there will be no spoken clue that will allow him to confine Winston against his will. He turns to his backup plan and says, "Also, you need to take pills that I will prescribe. One a day. And come back in three days."

Winston says, "This is the antidote."

"It may help you."

"And the tests?"

"Takes a while for the results. We need to make a deal. If you start to think about hurting anyone, or hurting yourself, you call us first. Can you commit to that?"

"And you'll help me?"

"Yes, and you must come back in three days."

"Three days, the magic triad."

"To see how the pills are working," says Sri. "Before you do anything that might . . . hurt anyone, you have to commit that you will call us and we will help you. Have we got a deal?"

Winston nods slowly.

Sri gives Winston the prescription.

—

Winston sits cross-legged at the kitchen table, facing the door of his apartment, next to which stands a narrow green bookcase with a stencilled frieze of red flowers. He watches the bookcase, has already smoked half of the pack of cigarettes that he bought. The butts hiss briefly as he pushes them into the moist soil of the potted gardenia on the windowsill. In the backyard, no red car. On the third shelf of the bookcase is an orange glass dish whose surface is bubbles of thin cold membrane—*molten sand cooled,* he thinks. In this dish are Winston's keys, and his wallet, and a small, secretive paper bag that would be too slim to hold even a thin sandwich. Inside the paper bag, whose folded mouth the girl at the pharmacy had stapled carefully as she smiled at him (too prolonged a smile, he immediately realized), there is a yellow plastic canister. He saw her put it in, this canister with its push-down-turn-counter-clockwise-childproof top and the printed label fixed to its side, brimming with green and white capsules. Green and white capsules, the kind with the little ridge through the middle that are slippery once in your mouth—easy to swallow. Now, Winston tries to remember: *Did Dr. Sri say it was a cure? Or an antidote? And how long have I known Dr. Sri? But he would have prescribed the right thing, because I told him about the poison. Unless he's a poisoner himself.*

The red car.

The red car is in the backyard. *Parked sloppy.* The gate ajar. *Why parked so sloppy? In a rush? Is Claude in a rush because he has discovered about us?* The methodical bump, bump, bump of feet climbing upstairs. Every poison has a remedy—that much is common knowledge.

"Hi, honey," Adrienne's voice leaks down the stairs and through Winston's door.

So the thing is: eating the green capsules? Green and white bullets that must be a cure, or antidote. Cure or antidote? What's the difference? Will either really do? Why would a woman who loves me poison me? From her own fear, perhaps, but wouldn't she know that this could sabotage everything between us? Unless she doesn't really care, is using me. Winston tilts the cigarette into the planter, exhales. *Are the capsules part of the deal? The doctor made me make a deal, something about three days, about doing something or other, calling before doing something else. Before doing some particular thing, I am to call someone, and take something.* He wants to remember the harem girl's dance, that part so horribly, tragically fuzzy.

Why should I have to eat pills? Why not an injection, a surgical procedure? This is a perfect way to make me take something, to make it look like I wanted to take it. Is that the deal? The capsules are in the childproof yellow canister with the white lid stapled into the brown paper bag on the orange glass dish upon the green bookshelf next to the door right where they should be. *One a night, the doctor said.* From where he sits, Winston can see the edge of the bag.

The sound of an explosion, of a grenade launcher, of a malicious rocket; the door being knocked.

"Winston?" says Claude.

The roar of a building collapsing, of a crumbling rock face, of an iceberg splitting; the door being knocked.

"Winston?" says Claude. "Are you home?"

"Oh. Hi, Claude."

"Hey buddy. Adrienne said you came by yesterday, that you aren't feeling well. You okay?"

"Never better, Claude. Million bucks."

"Adrienne's making her chow mein. You're welcome to come up. She's making too much, as always."

The throbbing of an April river, of fingers in the cold, of stop-and-go traffic; his heart. He says, "Sure. Sure. Maybe later, for sure."

Then the whispering. He dares not move. *I should take the antidote now.* They will know if he has taken it, because they hear him walk across the room just as he hears them back and forth in their kitchen. Winston follows their footsteps from fridge to counter, counter to table, table to stove. *Strange. So much movement for chow mein? Why the laugh?* It is about him, her giggling. Such a cruel woman: to poison, then love, then laugh. Claude laughs too. Perhaps Adrienne has let him in on it. All a big joke. *I'm a big joke. They may kill me tonight. Why don't they let me sleep? Die painlessly?*

Fifteen minutes later, a machine gun, a tooth whacked out; the door being knocked.

"Dinner's on, Winston. I put snow peas in it," says Adrienne.

She does love me.

"Are you okay in there?"

"Fine."

"You didn't seem well yesterday."

"Just fine."

"If you're not feeling well, you should see a doctor."

"I saw a doctor." *Why did you say that?*

Claude's voice now: "You're okay, then? They didn't slice you open? Good for you. Noodles are hot, buddy. Come on out." *He said* buddy *in a homicidal voice. Slice me open. Why would I be sliced open?*

Adrienne's voice: "Ignore Claude. He's being stupid. Did you get some pills or something?"

"Yes." *That was a mistake, dummy.*

"What kind of pills are they?"

"What pills?"

"The pills you got from the doctor."

"No, there's no pills." *That's better.*

"If you got some medicines, you should take them, Winston," says Adrienne. *The witch who loves me casts spells through the door.*

"I said yes but I meant no, because I don't need pills. The doctor said I don't need anything."

"You want some noodles?" she asks.

"I ate."

"He ate," Claude says to Adrienne. "Let's go."

"I ate!"

"Gotcha, buddy," says Claude through the door.

As they go up the stairs, Claude whispers to Adrienne.

The reply comes in her higher-pitched hiss: "Be nice, Claude." Their door shuts with the clang of a manhole cover.

Winston watches television, allows the sitcoms, infomercials, and reality TV to speak their special messages to him. Three hours later, he writes.

November 7, 1 a.m.

Was about to take pills. Now see, just in time. So clever—green & white & poison. Pharmacy girl smiling, just smiling away.

Obvious.

Adrienne said about doctor. Wanted me to go to the doctor, she knew, knew the doctor. Part of it.

It is dark. Winston debates whether to make a run for it. But where to? And Claude has a car. He could steal the car, but it is booby-trapped, wired with explosives. He should call his mother, but the phone is tapped. Winston pulls out the gardenia, holds the stalk and lifts out the pot-shaped mould of dirt, empties half the pills into the flowerpot, leaves the yellow plastic canister open on the table—casual, no, he moves it three centimetres to the right where it appears even more casual. He slides it a centimetre to the left. *What time of night is it? Are we headed away from light, or toward it? But maybe if I don't take the pills they will kill me anyway. They will know that I know too much.* Winston picks up the telephone and dials the emergency number that Dr. Sri gave him.

"Dr. Sri? I have crucial information to transmit."

"This is Allied Paging," says the chipper female voice.

"Calling Dr. Sri."

"I can page him. Is this a medical emergency?" Her voice bobs up and down in a xylophonic manner.

"Yes."

"Your number?"

"My what?"

"Phone number, please."

"I'm not giving you my phone number."

"Dr. Sri will need it to call you, sir."

"Would you give your phone number to just anyone?"

"I'm sorry, sir, but I could send a text message if you prefer."

"Answer me. Someone calls you and asks for your phone number. Would you just give it?" says Winston.

"But sir . . . if someone called you, they already have your phone number."

"Your point?"

"Also, sir, I didn't call you, so there's no need to be alarmed. You called us."

"That's why you don't have my number."

"I'm not sure I can help you," says the female voice, bouncing octaves up and down.

"Doesn't Dr. Sri have my phone number?" asks Winston, seeing that this woman (too cheerful) is also part of the string bag drawing tight around him.

The woman says, "I doubt he has your phone number handy."

He will outsmart them. "Send a text message."

"Thank you, sir, go ahead."

"Say that Winston is taking his pills, and doing very well."

"Thank you, sir, good night."

A narrow miss.

He smokes.

Winston inhales the buzz and the calm, smokes the cigarettes down to the filters, holds one until it smoulders and singes a brown line on his index and middle fingers. Lights another. Each cigarette more jittery, more tight, each puff fails more and more to soothe.

He opens the window, feels the damp, cool air in the circles around his eyes.

A meowing sound, the private moan. Winston wants to listen, then thinks that he should not. Then the creaking, the flexing of his ceiling, their floor—the dry wood fibres made to twist. Claude's low grumble, the warp of him into her, the soft slapping sound—at this distance like the clock ticking—again Adrienne's insistent cry like something being pulled from her. Winston decides that he should not listen. *They want to see if I'll listen, see if I'm guilty enough to kill me.*

He wants to listen.

Ultimately it is habit, the habit of pleasure, of cigarettes, of inhaling and exhaling the promise of alertness and calm, that overcomes his panicked resistance, that wins him over so that, in habit, he crouches and then lies down next to the jammed-open, painted-over ventilation grate that it is not his fault he cannot close, listens to the growing noise of their fuck.

He unzips his pants.

Afterwards, Winston wipes his lower belly with a tea towel but the skin remains sticky. Their animal time has faded into jungle breathing, and he smokes the last cigarette in guilty panic. *Now I'm dead.*

He writes.

November 7, 3 a.m.
Soon, will be over soon.
Eluded green and white pill poison, but the tea poison is in me. No sleep. Super neurotoxic drug enhances my super hearing. The voices clear now, the plan. Pack my suitcase. Hope. We may kill Claude.

Adrienne says, "Don't eat all the chow mein. Leave some for Winston."

Claude says, "He spies on us."

"You only know that because you listen to *him.* Claude, I love him. I'm sorry, but the other night, the party, I poisoned him to be with him."

"Tomorrow I slice him open. Stem to stern."

"Maybe I'll kill you to be with him. Don't eat it all. Winston will be hungry."

Winston's mother says, "You think I don't feed him?"

"You're his mother. I should tell you that tomorrow either I'll kill Claude or we'll kill Winston. Depends how I sleep."

Claude says, "I listen to him because he's spying on us. Right now."

"He used to listen to his father and me," says Winston's mother. "We knew."

"He'll be hungry. Stop eating like that, Claude. You're full."

"I feed him, you know," says Winston's mother.

Adrienne says, "He's taking his pills. He's a good boy, and I love him."

"He never used to take his pills," says Winston's mother. "Used to hide them in plants."

Claude says, "That flower."

"Winston," says Adrienne, "take your pills. Do you know that I love you? If I kill Claude, I'll need you to hold him. Wasn't the other night wonderful? We may kill you though, then you'll have to hold still."

"Will you keep on poisoning me?"

"Take the pills, my love."

"When will you decide who should die?"

"Oh, it depends how I sleep, dear."

"Will you keep on poisoning me?"

This conversation repeats three times, four times, five times, again.

—

All night they talk. Later, Adrienne admits that, yes, it is her poison that has made his hearing so sensitive.

In the morning, Sri arrives at the clinic an hour before the first patients are scheduled. He writes missing details on the call forms, the records of his nighttime conversations. The forms are relatively complete until around midnight, and after that consist of dates of birth, jotted thoughts, a few phone numbers, words that seemed striking at the time. On one sheet he has written, *Right ear pain.* On another, he has scrawled, *Child screams twenty minutes then settles.* The call forms must be completed. There must be a record of the nighttime fears, of the questions that come in the dark. A woman called to ask the correct temperature of bathwater. A man called on his Toronto cellphone, while on a business trip in Texas. He wanted a prescription faxed to him in his Austin hotel room, was angry that Sri refused.

Sri scrolls through the text-pager, sees the unanswered message.

WINSTON> IS TAKING PILLS> DOING WELL>

Sri brings up Winston's number on the clinic computer. He didn't have the number at home, last night. He calls. It rings for a long time. He puts the phone down. Sri finds Dr. Miniadis in the observation room with her morning coffee. *Tosca.* In the mornings, it is usually opera.

She says, "Ah, the fine, young Dr. Sri. How did the night treat you?"

At this question, it is always possible to answer with respect to the events of the night, or the responses to them, or neither. Sri says, "It was long. Shall I review the calls with you?" Sri summarizes the calls, describes them the way one writes captions for cartoons. Dr. Miniadis nods absently. She asks occasional, leisurely, clarifying questions in the manner of the well rested. Once they are finished, Sri hands over the records for Dr. Miniadis to leaf through and sign. He says, "There was a text message with no phone number. Winston—the first-break psychosis. I tried to call this morning, but no answer."

"The poisoning, seductive neighbour, et cetera," says Dr. Miniadis.

"I did a med-line search last night, tried to find any case reports of such a toxidrome. I wondered, maybe a new rave drug?"

"And?"

"No such description." He feels satisfied that he looked, and that he did not find what he had looked for.

"Tell me, Dr. Sri, if you woke up one day and saw a purple bird in your room, what would you think?"

"Excuse me?"

"A purple bird. Even a little one. We won't say a parrot or a vulture, but just a tiny purple bird sitting and chirping at your bedside. What would you think?"

"I would wonder how it got there."

"And how might it have gotten there?"

"I would check the windows, the doors, and any-where else a bird could have flown in."

"What if you called someone to help you with the bird—to remove it—but then it was gone. What would they think?"

"That would depend on their sense of humour."

"There are no purple birds native to Toronto," says Dr. Miniadis. "But despite that, you would be left with the spectre of a flying, tweeting creature having appeared in your room. Do you think this will happen to you today? You will go home to sleep, yes? Will you wake to find a bird?"

"I sleep with the windows closed," says Sri. "Even if a bird escaped from a pet shop, or the zoo, it couldn't get in." He imagines Dr. Miniadis creeping outside his window, birdcage in hand. "At least, I don't think it could."

"What if one morning, despite your fastidious window-closing, despite the lack of such creatures in the city of Toronto, you woke up and there was a purple bird? At the very least, you would check the window, perhaps buy a birdwatcher's guide. It doesn't make sense, but your mind would want it to, might even contort in order to explain it." She stirs her coffee. "Right now, it's still early in the morning. Perhaps your Winston is asleep."

"He was having difficulty sleeping."

"There you go, an explanation. You see how the mind needs to make sense of things."

Sri thinks of Dr. Miniadis outside his bedroom, propping up the window, releasing the bird into his dreams.

He says, "Shall I call Winston again?"

Winston writes.

November 7, day break

Didn't sleep. Talking all night, my mother especially won't shut up. More frightening to hear. Wish I couldn't. Adrienne woke. Heard the bath. Claude drove off this morning, like he always does. At least it looked like he did. A trick. He might be upstairs. I didn't hear the decision, whether they will murder me or whether I will have to help kill Claude. Scared of blood. Phone rings. I know not to pick it up. Out of cigarettes, should have got two packs.

Sri tries to phone Winston again before leaving the clinic, wishing to erase the jitteriness of unfinished business. No answer. He goes home and calls Winston from there. Today he is off, because he was on call last night. In the steam of the shower, Sri tells himself that this is clearly a psychosis. His gut whispers, *Zebras do exist.* But he is a physician, he tells himself sternly, who should deal not in gut feelings but in facts.

The facts:

Fact 1: an upstairs neighbour.
Fact 2: a sleep-deprived man.

What else does he know? And why does he care? No, stick to the first question: what are the facts?

Fact 3: tension and fog can appear between neighbours.
Fact 4: the presumption of physicians.
Fact 5: recreational chemists are constant innovators.

When Sri steps out of the shower, his face suddenly feels cool, clear, and alarmed. Is he now inventing so-called facts? He pushes away this possible slip. Sri calls Winston before going to sleep. Ringing, ringing, more ringing. Sri goes to bed—the grateful sleep of having the pager turned off. He falls asleep nervous that he might dream of birds, but it is a dreamless blank sleep.

Sri wakes into a light that has the melon colour of afternoon. He is somewhat fresher for a few hours' rest, but he did not have the dense post-call sleep that sometimes permits a new day to begin. He realizes that what underlies his fitful rest is the situation both having an uncertain reality and now being out of control. Either of these alone would be acceptable, almost normal, but the combination bothers him. Winston is not admitted, not observed, not reliably medicated, and not answering the phone. The situation has slipped out of his grasp, and Sri decides to place his hands on it, to find out what is real and what is not. This would help, whatever the facts may be. He is awake in the clear-eyed yellow light. There is no purple bird, he notes.

Sri calls the clinic and asks about Winston's drug screen, which the receptionist locates and says has come back clean. So it's clean. Sri asks for Winston's address. Crawford Street is not far, a short sunny walk. Sri pulls on a jacket, goes out. The trees are angular frames, and some of the fallen leaves press like mortar into the corners between buildings and sidewalks. The alert bite of the breeze signifies that first snow will come soon. Most of the leaves have faded to grey, although some still show bursts of yellow and orange when blown suddenly across the road. Tomorrow, or maybe the next day, will come the snow but today the sky is the pure, amazing blue that is the colour of promises. Sri follows the numbers, finds the house just north of Queen.

Just before walking up the steps, he wonders why he is here. Well, no point thinking about that now, he decides, and goes up to the porch.

Three buzzers, three mailboxes. The house is tall and narrow as if it had stood on tiptoes and then turned sideways. Sri rings the middle buzzer, the second floor. He hears it sound, he thinks, upstairs. It could be a different button. Sometimes the wiring and the buttons are not what one would expect. Sri looks up at the windows, at the two colours of brick, the lighter brick in modest geometrical patterns around the tall windows and the skinny door. He rings again and backs up, shields his eyes against the glare on the windows. Sri sees a shiver of the window shade and waves. Was it Winston? Did the shade actually move? Now, its fabric looks still. Certainly there is no face. Maybe the suggestion of movement was a trick of light on glass.

Counter-transference, thinks Sri. That's the word that's been tickling at him. They have been taught to beware of counter-transference, the emotions a physician has in reaction to the patient. No, not to beware. They are taught to be aware. He can almost hear Dr. Miniadis saying, It cannot be avoided, but must be channelled.

The top buzzer. There is the third floor, the alleged poisoners. Sri presses the top button. It is a fine day on Crawford Street, which opens into Trinity Bellwoods Park, a park that has its quiet heart low down, tucked into a ravine. Sri decides that if no one answers the door, he shall not magnify his concern, but will urge himself to feel relief, and will walk down the pathway toward the ravine, stirring leaves with his feet. He will have the freedom of having followed his uneasy feelings about Winston, of having tried every reasonable method to return the numberless page, and of having completely discharged his duties without any answer at the phone or the home. Sri tells himself, with a firmness to counter his sense of worry, that if no one answers, he will not pursue Winston any further than this doorstep, and he will simply wait for the situation to come to him again, if it does.

He is about to turn when he sees a woman's face at the door. She hesitates. The door makes a hollow sound as it opens.

"Can I help you?"

"I'm Dr. Sri," he says. In such situations, it is important to use the title. "Winston's doctor."

"Come in." But she doesn't move. She leans forward to Sri and whispers, "He's been talking to himself all day."

"You are his . . ."

"Upstairs neighbour. Adrienne. These old houses, you can hear everything. Did Winston call?"

"In a way." So there's an Adrienne.

Still whispering, "Winston keeps to himself. Past few days, he's acting strange. What's wrong with him?"

"It's hard for me to say."

"What do you think?"

Sri whispers, "I can't tell you. Doctor-patient confidentiality."

Adrienne looks slightly offended, and then unsure whether she herself has given offence.

Sri says, "I understand you had a party." He tries to say it casually, socially, the way one says, *Oh, a party—how nice!* but it feels unfair to ask a question after saying that he can give no answers.

"Yes, there was a big party."

So there was a party.

She says, "I've been out of town."

"Halloween?"

"I was in Montreal. But I think the first-floor apartment had some people over. The recycling bin was full."

"May I come up?" Was there a harem girl? he wants to ask.

Up the stairs, dark inside. Both of them stand at the second-floor landing. Sri knocks.

He says, "Winston? Winston?"

Behind the door, silence.

Adrienne says, "It's the doctor. Your nice doctor here to see you."

Sri says, "I got your page, but I couldn't call you back because I didn't have the phone number. I tried to call, but you didn't pick up. And I was in the neighbourhood, so I thought I'd drop in." Sri feels obligated to fill in this picture, to justify the steps by which he has arrived at this second-floor landing with Winston's upstairs neighbour. "Good news. Your drug tests are negative."

Winston says through the door, "Why did you decide to kill me, Adrienne?"

Adrienne's expression is completely unchanged— the way that someone who is really shocked often does not have it within their repertoire to actually twist even the smallest facial muscle, or is it the way that someone who is not surprised is simply not surprised?

Should he ask how she went to Montreal? Car? Train? Maybe catch her out. That's going too far, Sri decides.

Sri says, "No one wants to kill you, Winston."

"You're in on it, doc. I thought you would pick me, Adrienne. Didn't want to murder Claude, but if that's what you want, I'd do it. Really would do it. But why do you have to kill me? Forget the whole thing. I'm sorry for listening. Honestly very sorry."

"Are you taking those pills, Winston?" asks Sri.

"Oh, very nice. Your poison. The blue-drink poison, and the tea poison, and the pill poison. You think you'll get me somehow."

"Can we come in?" says Sri.

"Stay away!" he screams.

"Who's Claude?" whispers Adrienne.

"Claude isn't your husband?"

"I have a roommate, Claudia. I barely see her, I work nights."

Does she have a harem girl costume? Or maybe is she sort of . . . masculine? Sri wants to ask, but stops himself. The facts are shadows of themselves. Behind the door, Winston is howling.

Sri says to the door, "You paged me, and usually when people page me, that means they need help."

They hear scraping, and a thump against the door. Scrape, thump.

Sri whispers, "He's barricading the door."

Adrienne says, "Don't do that, Winston. If you scratch the floor, Mrs. Brooks will make you pay. You know how picky she is."

"We could have had something together, but then the poison. Did you think I'd trust you after the poison?"

Sri asks Adrienne, "Can I use your phone?"

Sri tells the police that his patient is psychotic and has been having thoughts of murder. He is aware that Adrienne hears him, and it only seems fair that she know something about the situation. They will send a squad car, they say. Sri calls Dr. Miniadis, who seems unsurprised to hear that her resident is calling from the upstairs apartment of the alleged poisoners of their psychotic patient.

Adrienne appears with a tray. "Tea?"

"No thanks."

"Freshly steeped."

"I'm good, really."

She pours tea for herself. A little cream, three sugars. There is an empty cup. Crashes and howls shake upward through the floor.

Adrienne says, "You like being a doctor?"

"It's great."

Teacups and saucers sound so dry, clicking on each other.

"I can make herbal if you prefer. Mint, rosehip, or camomile."

"Really, I'm fine. I had a cup just earlier," he lies.

They sit in the sunny front room, which is all plants and books and light. No siren, no slam of car door or chatter of police scanner. It is a beautiful and quiet day, except that Winston has begun to scream,

"Don't! Don't! Don't!" pierces the house.

Sri thinks that he should have emphasized the unpredictable nature of his patient, the possibility of sudden calamity, the need for the immediate appearance of officers. Despite the screaming and smashing from below, Sri feels much better now that he has decided that Winston is psychotic, and at least Winston is still alive and has done no one else any harm. Sri wishes to go for a walk in the park, and then feels guilty at this thought, which competes for mental space with his feeling badly for his patient. Adrienne pours herself another cup.

"Are you sure?" She gestures at the empty teacup, saying, "It's *not* poisoned, you know." This is meant as a joke, and Sri smiles as if complicit. Then he feels that his poor reciprocity of humour makes the subsequent silence, and the dull clinking of the spoon in her cup, more acute. She pours tea in front of Sri. He can see why Winston finds her attractive.

A cup of tea would be ideal on this afternoon before the onset of snow. No, better not. He reminds himself that if he believes it to be truly not poisoned, and he feels like having tea, why should he not take a sip? Can he not see that Winston is psychotic?

The teacup handle is warm, and the porcelain body of the cup scalding. A steaming sip, perfect. It is at this moment that he sees it. Very briefly, but long enough to make a definite impression on his retina. It is outside the window, and pauses for a moment on the brick ledge, pecks at a strand of ivy, seems to hunch (if birds actually hunch), then darts upward into the air. Adrienne sips with the self-consciousness of a host to strangers.

Sri says, "Um . . . was that a purple bird? Just out the window."

"I didn't see it."

Are there purple birds? Here? Maybe a nest. He has never heard of a purple bird. Maybe from a pet store. That happens all the time, tropical creatures escaping and living in sewers and eating cats. Sri reminds himself that birds do not live in sewers or eat cats. Downstairs, there is screaming and the creak of wood breaking, thud thud thud as Winston thrashes.

"I was just imagining things. A strange light." Sri smiles hesitantly, offers a pleading grin as if they should both be accomplices in this little joke. He tells himself, firmly, that there are no purple birds in Toronto. The tea has a wonderful aroma but he resolves to ignore the scent, and places the cup delicately but securely on the saucer.

ELI

—
—
—

THE POLICE HAD THE MAN IN CUFFS. WRISTS BEHIND his back, arms twisted high between his shoulder blades. He cursed them.

"Behave," said the female officer.

Blood ran down his face. Thick, opaque over his neck, it soaked his shirt collar.

"Hey doc, how long?" called out the male officer. They were in the hallway, waiting to have their prisoner registered at the front desk.

"Lot of people here. Up to the triage nurse," I said,

not breaking stride. Wait your turn, I thought.

The officers, one short man, one tall woman, were speaking to the emergency triage nurse. I knew what they would be saying: We're short staffed tonight, we're stretched thin, tons of calls, help us get this done. The nurse would be saying: We've got chest pains, belly pains that have been waiting for hours. The police wanted to get in quick. In and out. Feet are built to move and standing is more tiring.

Volumes were rising at this time just after dinner, a few hours before midnight. We speak of volume as numbers of patients, the way they fill our fixed space. It is also the volume of noise that we actually hear. The crying of the child, the belligerence of drunkenness, the thin whine of a failed suicide. The noise and presence fills the waiting room, a condensation of the city's private screaming made public.

Several minutes later the triage nurse asked me, "Doctor Fitzgerald, can you see this patient?"

"The one with the cops? You want me to see him first?"

"He'll be a quickie," she said. "He's in the quiet room."

The quiet room—our euphemism for the screaming, struggling, calm-down-or-we-tie-you-down room; also the actual name of the room.

The two police were standing outside the wired safety glass door, which could be locked and unlocked from a control at the central desk. Inside that room was a panic button on the wall that triggered a silent alarm.

"Got a live one for you, doc," said the male officer, badge 1483.

"Glad he's alive," I said. Through the glass, I could see the man twisting on the stretcher. "This your prisoner? You got him in quick."

"Thanks for seeing us fast," said the male officer. "We only got three cars on the road."

"We've got thirty in the waiting room," I said. "Funny night."

"Well, you've got to know how to laugh," said the female officer, badge 6982.

Police stand and talk and lean on things as if they belong anywhere. For most people, there's a distinction between a place that is theirs and one they are visiting. Cops—you see them with their sidearms jutting out, their elbows resting on diner counters, parked in no-parking zones, using the staff washrooms in the hospital. Their hats hold in their hair, tidy.

"Tell me about your man here," I said. The bed rattled as he lunged though held down by cuffs.

"Not much to tell," said the male officer. "Fell, cut his head open. We need him fixed." Some fall. Forehead split open, bleeding a red curtain. He shouted obscenities, shook his head. Not even a scrape on his hands. People put their hands in front of them when they fall.

"Fell, huh? Clumsy guy," I said.

"Eli has very poor coordination," said officer 6982.

"What made him so clumsy?"

"You see, Eli is a bad man, and we find that many such people are accident prone," said officer 1483.

The game is supposed to go like this. The police give the precis: Look doc, this guy did such-and-such, and we caught him, and now this-and-that has happened so we brought him to hospital. Maybe they say what they think the diagnosis will be. The officers usually imply what they think should happen to the prisoner. They can't say it outright—'course, you're the doctor, they must say in conclusion, as per protocol. Then the physician can respond to this play: Well, officers, I need to do test A, procedure B, and check for problem C. If A turns up normal, B works out well, and C is absent, I'll pronounce your prisoner, my patient, healthy and you're good to go. All with a wink and a nod.

I was irritated that these officers seemed to want to play a modified version of the game: You do your thing and we'll do ours. This is sometimes the case with more serious charges, and all the more reason for me to play carefully. Cops and robbers and doctors. It's a game where mostly everyone can be happy if we all play nice. The police are surprisingly kind to the prisoners, as long as they're docile. They treat them like younger siblings, showing them where to sit and filling in forms for them. Just like an older brother, the police turn nasty in an instant if the prisoner becomes difficult. *You better settle down.* Benevolence and cruelty are separated only by a veneer of whim which, in medicine, we understand.

I opened the door, went in. His smell grabbed me and twisted my stomach so I had to force down the urge to vomit.

"Hi Eli," I said.

"Get me out of these," he said.

"I'm Dr. Fitzgerald, the emergency doctor. What happened?"

"They're fuckin' nuts. Get me out."

"I am Dr. Fitzgerald," I repeated. In medicine we pretend that our names may be enough to control a situation.

"Breathe," I said. I sat on the edge of the stretcher, next to Eli's cuffed ankle. *Always sit down with the patient,* I was taught. *It makes it seem like you've spent more time and that you care.* In a chair, on the stretcher. *If you give this impression* (this is the subtext) *then the patients will do what you say and leave quickly.* I liked the stretcher, since sitting on the edge of the bed is what everyone's parents once did. *Where is it sore, dear?* "Speak—slowly. How—did—you—cut—your—head?" *Speaking slowly and loudly transcends both agitation and language barriers.* Another clinical pearl.

"Set-up. It was a set-up." He pulled and rattled at the metal bands tight on both wrists.

It was nauseating to breathe, with the closed-in smell of piss and sweet-sour human stench. I pulled on gloves, flexed and extended my fingers so that the latex was tight on my skin.

"Pain anywhere?" I asked. I felt inside Eli's split-open forehead, ran my finger over the warm smoothness of skull. It was a straight gash from the hairline to the top of the nose. The blood flowed hot, an anxious stream. A man can bleed to death from the scalp, but not the forehead. Cuts in the face look worse than they are. I explored with my finger, to feel for smashed fragments of bone.

"Shit man, stop that," said Eli. He swung his head.

"They say you're clumsy."

"Fuckin' cops playin' drums with my head say I'm a killer gonna make me pay some shit." Eli kicked against the cuffs on his ankles, which rang out on the stretcher's chrome frame. I stood. "Fine bitch cop there, huh?" said Eli. He winked at the female officer through the window. Her expression did not change, but she enclosed her right fist in her left hand while looking at Eli.

I left the room, took a big breath of clean air. The clatter of Eli's rage drifted through the wire-strung windows. The child in the next stall was crying.

"What's the deal here?" I said to the two police, who were leaning on the nurses' counter.

"We need him fixed," said officer 6982.

"Right," I said, and did not move.

"That's the deal," said officer 1483. He turned toward the quiet room and smiled at Eli. Officer 1483 had a fresh haircut. The nape of his neck was raw from a razor.

"And his head split open? Like that when you got him?"

"Fell. And banged his head getting into the cruiser," said officer 1483. "Already filled out an incident report."

"Did he pass out?"

"Nope."

"Vomit?"

"Nah."

"Something about being a killer," I said.

"When you're done, we'll take him to the station," said officer 6982. "Get him out of your hair."

Cops. They want to get seen first. Put them at the front of the line but then they won't talk. None of my business, they figure. They were responsible for his legal ailments, but I was now liable for his medical misdemeanours. It would be awkward for me at the inquest if the Crown said, Doctor, tell us a little more about the head injury that led to Mr. Eli's demise. The police records state that all circumstances were explained to you. The doc holding the chart last has to explain everything.

Maybe Eli needed to see a psychiatrist—a name after mine on the chart. Was Eli psychotic? Could be. I'd better find out. Police inquests are tedious, nitpicky, and it's lonely being the only physician on the stand. I went back into the room, into the thick piss smell. His pants were dark. Can't blame a man for that when he's scared and cuffed. Acid—that's what it must smell like inside a pelvis.

"Listen to—"

"Get me out doc get me out I gotta get out."

"Shut up. Listen to—"

"Ya fucking, you're not a doctor, ya fuck."

Now both of us shouting: "Listen to me. I am your

"Last month I'm minding my own business, this guy

doctor. Are you hearing voices? Are you seeing things

comes up he says he's gonna shoot my dog unless I give

that other people don't see? Is someone out to get you?

him some names. See, I love my dog, she's all I got, and

Are you receiving radio or telephone messages? Do you

I don't got the names he wanted so things got a little

want to hurt someone? Do you have a psychiatrist?

outta hand and anyhow how's I to know he's a cop? He

What medications are you taking? Do you feel that

hit me first, sucker punch. I hit him back. Betcha he's

people are plotting against you, out to get you, that

banging that bitch cop there. Fuckers they said my

there's a conspiracy of some kind?"

time's up now they got me."

Then both of us stopped talking. In the sudden quiet, I stepped back and wrote in the chart for a little while. Then, "What can I do for you, Eli?"

Eli paused to consider his situation, and then said, "Why don't you suck my cock?"

I tried to breathe shallow, but the urine smell was so insistent I thought I could taste it. Outside the window, the officers watched and grinned. The female officer said something to the male officer, who laughed. When he saw me looking, he turned the other way.

"You're right," I said to Eli. "They really are fuckers—just like you."

I went into the hallway. "What's so funny?"

"Talking about something else," said officer 6982, smiling.

"You seem to think me and your prisoner are pretty funny." Cops, backwards garbagemen, always bringing *in* the trash.

"There's something I don't understand here."

"You should watch yourself," officer 6982 said.

"That a threat?" I asked. If these cops wouldn't play the game right, I'd look for a new game. I wasn't going to be the last doc signing the chart.

"Watch yourself with Eli," she said. "He's quick. Watch yourself."

"And he's mentally ill. We'll keep him here."

"Whaddya mean?" she asked, her voice now less relaxed. "We gotta get him back and book him."

"After our psychiatrist sees him."

"When's that?"

"Tomorrow morning." It was ten at night.

"What makes you think he's nuts?"

"Eli told me about someone threatening to shoot his dog, trying to get information from him, punching him," I said, and felt the first nervousness of enjoying this. "It's funny, he said it was a cop. That would be coercion, police brutality. Can't be true. So, Eli must be paranoid. Psychotic."

"You can't believe these things," she said.

"Not for a second, but I have to document what he told me, right here on the medical record," I said. I showed her the chart on which I had transcribed Eli's statements. "Must be delusions, poor Eli. He must be imagining the police punching him and so forth. Although I guess he's not psychotic if it's all true. You know anything about this stuff?"

"Can't say," she said.

"'Course not. Mental illness. Tragic. He needs help. I'll fix his cut after we scan his head." I was looking forward to finishing my shift, to saying goodbye to the officers as I left. They would be here all night unless someone relieved them. We all have our quiet ways of asserting ourselves.

Two hours later.

The CT scan showed no intracerebral blood, but an old broken nose. Eli was quiet. The officers had already called the station and requested relief, but no one had arrived. They were no longer jovial, but they still wore their blue-banded caps and sat up straight. I put on a surgical mask to breathe through.

"We're gonna fix you now," I said as I wheeled the suture cart into the quiet room. I scrubbed Eli's face and the side of his head with saline-soaked gauze. I poured salt water over his head through curses.

Eli said, "Fuck off."

"Listen to me carefully. Have you ever seen a psychiatrist?"

"No ya fuckin'—howdya like my face, huh, doc?" With the jellied blood washed away, I could see the cut was four centimetres long. A forehead bleeds more than you would think for that length.

"I got a good face?"

"You hearing voices?" I couldn't tell him to act psychotic. "Seeing things that other people don't see?" But a little fishing never hurt.

"Ya better fuckin' make it look good."

"Anyone out to get you?" With the otoscope I peered inside his ears. No blood behind the drums. The cut had a neat, straight edge. "You want to look good? Better hold still." This fish needed bait. "Eli, I'm worried about your mental health. Crazy people have to stay in hospital."

I drew lidocaine into the syringe. The anaesthetic swirled into the graduated barrel. I flicked with my finger, clearing the bubbles toward the needle, and expelled the air like a sneeze with a quick motion of the plunger.

"I don't want it to hurt," he said.

"It's gonna hurt."

"I'm hearing fuckin' spooky voices and seeing pink dinosaurs and shit," said Eli. He began to giggle.

"Thought so."

"I don't wanna feel nothin', man."

"It's gonna sting when I freeze you. You won't feel it when I'm stitching."

The syringe was between my index and middle

fingers. My thumb was on the plunger. With my other hand, I held open the end of the cut. I slipped the needle under the edge of skin, and my thumb eased down on the plunger. The tissue swelled and turned white at the injection.

Eli swung his head. "Hey that fuckin' hurts."

I held the syringe pointed into the air the way a cowboy raises his pistol to fire a warning shot.

"Don't move," I said. Sharps were open, syringes and needles. *A physician should be morally opposed to cutting himself,* I was taught. These instruments were for piercing patients, opening their skin. Sudden movements cause accidents, and it is a sinful violence to cut oneself. "Be absolutely still, Eli."

"Yo. It hurts."

"It'll hurt more if you move. One more chance, then the officers hold you." I didn't look up. I could feel the police watching through the window. Enjoying the show. I didn't want to need them. One more try. Again, I slipped the steel sliver through the edge of the cut, ran it under the skin's surface. Again, upon injection, he bucked. "All right, we'll get your friends in here."

I opened the door. They sat there grinning. "Come on in here. Hold your boy."

"Like we said, we just want him fixed," said officer 1483. "This sure is getting complicated."

The two officers clattered into the room, pulled on thick blue latex gloves, snapping them at the wrists.

"One at the head, one on the legs," I said.

Then it was a tumbling, struggling effort as Eli flailed and kicked. *Restraining people is an ironic task.* The more you restrain them the more they resist and the harder you must hold them still, strap them in, beat them down until a certain point is reached, until there's no point resisting. *Once they know who's boss, it's done. Like breaking a horse,* I was taught. *A show of force is best. A hand on each limb—make them see who's in charge, because then they won't resist anymore.* More limb jerking. Eli cursed, grabbed, pushed, and through this the officers shouted at him until they got him down. Now I was on him with the needle, injecting. Mostly for show now. The record would not state that I hadn't provided anaesthesia. I jabbed the needle in a few times as Eli bucked his head. I tossed sterile drapes over him, over the hands of the female officer who gripped his head securely between both palms and out-stretched fingers. Now the thread and needle; the thorn in my needle driver. The sewing is easy, it's getting the head to hold still that is difficult. The needle pierced skin, the black line pulled through, a one-handed knot. I couldn't tell whether he felt it or not, with all the roaring and thrashing. Maybe he really was psychotic. Then a flashing surge of movement, and the drape shook off as Eli lunged quickly and officer 6982 jumped back. There was red on the back of my hand, and wetness, and a gash in my glove from the new cut.

Upon seeing it, I felt the pain. It was a bloody hurt that dripped into the fingers of the glove.

"You piece of shit," I said to Eli. My tired annoyance was suddenly eclipsed by panic, my heart pounding, pushing the blood from the back of my hand.

"Told you to watch yourself," said officer 6982.

I ripped off my glove. "Why'd you let go?" I said, my own blood hot and running.

"Slipped."

"Your boy too strong for you? Get a good hold of him." I pointed the needle at her. She didn't know that needles are our pistols, because she calmly put on new blue latex gloves, and then the leather gloves that flopped out of her back pocket. I stuck my hand in the sink, and poured a litre of saline over it. I told myself to slow my breathing.

"Too quick for you," said Eli with a giggle.

Officer 6982 grabbed his head from underneath and at the sides, pinched his ears under her thumbs.

"Time to fix you, Eli," I said. I poured another litre of saline over my hand, tossed the empty plastic bottle into the corner of the room, and flexed my fingers. No tendon damage. Just skinned. I pulled on fresh gloves, then a second pair over the first. Breathing hard.

I reached over to the suture cart and grabbed a stapler. Usually we staple scalps and sometimes legs. It's less accurate, and when the staples come out they leave little marks like train tracks. I squeezed Eli's forehead, not paying attention to the alignment. *Thunk thunk*, in went the staples. The male officer forced down Eli's knees as he bucked at the hips. *Thunk thunk.*

"Aw fuck! That hurts, man."

"Shut up, you piece of shit," I whispered. I leaned the sharp corner of my elbow on his sternum. This leaves no bruises, and we use the pain of this spot to wake the comatose. I rolled my elbow over his chest, could see the blood smudging over my gloved hand. *Thunk thunk*, I put in a few extra just for the sting. "Don't bite the doctor." My fingers were sticky with blood inside the glove.

"Didn't mean to bite *you*, man," Eli laughed. "Trynna taste that sweet police meat."

"Watch your mouth," said officer 6982.

Had Eli been trying to bite the cop, or me? It's hard to know what occurs mentally in a lunge, in a movement. Maybe the motivations of an instant are most true. Did officer 6982 feel him slip, or did she let go? Did she sense he was going for a bite, and then pull herself out of the way? Had he intended me instead of her? Did motive matter now that my skin was ripped open? Anger needs to lay blame.

"Who ya trying to bite?" said officer 1483 from where he leaned over the knees.

"Yummy yummy," said Eli. His shirt had been pulled open in the struggle, and his belly shook as he laughed. Eli wiggled his tongue at the female officer. I saw her forearms flex as she compressed the sides of his head. Her expression did not change.

"Aiee!" said Eli, squeezing his eyes together.

Thunk thunk.

"I'm done." I threw the stapler across the room, clanging into the trash can. I peeled off my gloves and opened another bottle of saline, poured it in a steady stream. It ran clear onto the translucent flesh of my hand, and red streaming down into the sink. "Send in one of the nurses, will you?"

The police left. A nurse entered.

"Fiona, can you draw blood for hepatitis B and C, and HIV 1 and 2."

Fiona was calm. She told Eli she was going to take some blood. I stood with my cut hand on his forearm, in case he bucked. He flinched as the needle plunged under his skin. Dry. She rolled the skin under her white latex fingers. *Blood bears the curse of human malice. This life fluid may conceal destruction, the way words and thoughts can kill unseen. Within blood the idea of death can flow.* The blood from Eli's forehead had stopped, and now we sought to pull it from his arm.

"He doesn't have much left here," said Fiona, probing the network of old punctures and thickened scars for a suitable vessel. Eli tried to pull his arm away. I dug in my nails and he stopped moving, Fiona readjusted. Then the gush. The vacuum in the tube pulled up his blood squirting thin, safe, within the sealed glass walls. Fiona left the room with the blood in the tubes, like little glass torpedoes.

On my wrist were two jagged abrasions adjacent to my metal watchband, leaking red. The skin was peeled back, but not deep. Was it teeth? The cuff of my lab coat was ripped sideways. Did his teeth tear the coat? Was it teeth through the coat cutting my wrist? Or was it teeth pulling my watch, with the rungs of the watch-band scraping my skin off? I removed the watch, turned it over. The watch was perfect, unmarked. The human bite is the dirtiest, the most foul, and destined for infection. Worse than dogs or cats, because the human mouth is full of filth.

I sat down on the edge of the stretcher where Eli was handcuffed. He was tired from his efforts and lay quietly, eyes open, breathing hard. The staples in his forehead were haphazard and excessive in number. The wound did not bleed anymore.

"Eli. Why did you do that?" Until now, I had been mostly interested in creating clean paperwork, deriving a mild pleasure from inconveniencing the police. This no longer felt like quite enough, and I knew that I would feel cheated if I left it at that.

"Yo man, they fucked with me."

"Did I fuck with you?" I said softly. Now, I told myself, let it go if Eli makes a nice apology. The right apology. I made a deal—Fitz, you'll be nice now for the right apology, if he says something close to begging.

Eli shrugged.

"Is that what you say after you bite someone?" I asked in a very sweet way, knowing now that there would be no apology.

"Go to fucking hell."

"Open your mouth."

He half-opened his mouth, and I didn't see any blood. None from him, none from me. With a tongue depressor I lifted his lips, the way you lift the lips to see a horse's teeth. Gums intact. Saliva, though. *Saliva, clear and innocent, but sometimes it carries infections and curses like the words it lubricates.* I was angry at Eli for taking a bite, I was angry at officer 6982 for letting go, or slipping, or losing whatever balance lies between a head held and released. I darted the stick further into his mouth, gagged him hard—against the tongue only so as to leave no marks—and let him retch, grunting against the tongue depressor for a while, until I started to feel better.

"You're going with the police now." I turned away.

"Hey, I'm seeing shit. Dancing elephants and shit."

"Never heard you say it."

I plucked the suture off the tray and dropped it into the sharps disposal box. I placed the forceps and needle driver in the silver k-basin. Officers 6982 and 1483 stood outside the room, wrote on their pads. Eli watched them. No one's eyes were on the quiet room. I placed the scissors on the stretcher within reach of Eli's cuffed right hand. *The evil of blood is like a malevolent thought. Once it touches, the very suspicion of its presence causes it to grow, to distort motive and action, and to propagate its own dark, spreading reach.* Then I wrapped the light blue covers over the rest of the tray and picked it up, left the room. Eli's right hand lay on his side away from the window, and could not be seen from where the officers sat.

Outside the room, eight charts on the rack. Last time I checked we were three hours behind. I pressed gauze onto my cut.

"Sorry I lost my grip there," said officer 6982.

The child in the next room was still crying, the sound of a child who knows he's being ignored. The fact of being ignored made the waiting painful.

"Need some stitches, doc?" said the male officer, smiling. I felt the anger rising inside me—a heat that filled my chest. I exhaled. I felt the relief of justification about the scissors. I wrote in the chart that after being bitten, I had closed the patient's laceration with staples, and that the wound edges were well apposed.

"Bad stuff happens," I said, looking up. "You guys see it all the time. I've got to get a bandage. Then I need to speak to one of you."

At the nursing station, the father of the child in the next stall asked how long for the tests to come back. They paged me in the resuscitation room to reassess two patients, and announced overhead that there was a call for me on line six from a pharmacist. I gestured to Fiona, stepped into the drug dispensing room, and sat among the racks and drawers.

"How's your wrist?" asked Fiona.

"It's nothing. A scrape." I tried to sound convincing. "We have to send mine, too." I rolled up my sleeve. The Potential HIV Exposure kits were in paper bags on the left. Lots of pills. Yellow and black ones. Red and white ones. They made everyone so sick that no one ever finished taking the full course of precautionary anti-retrovirals. My sleeve was up, and Fiona's white latexed fingers directed the cool sharp rush of the needle. Seeing my own blood flow freely and thick, the texture of boiled milk, lulled me for a moment. I sat still. She pulled out the syringe with a quick withdrawal that was like the same pain in reverse. This blood wouldn't show anything. This was innocence blood, to show I was clean today in case I seroconverted later. My disability policy would pay for occupational HIV, but not if I got it a month previously from a hooker.

"Make sure it's labelled properly, Fiona. It's insurance blood."

"You okay?" she asked. "You better start the pills."

"No. No. Low risk, just a scratch. Maybe my watch, maybe not even his teeth."

"The pills make you sick, don't they? But he's got tracks all over."

"Sick like anything. I feel sick enough." I remembered his puncture-scarred arms, his smell of life in decay. "Maybe I should take the prophylaxis. Yeah, sign one out to me. Tell resusc I'm going to be a minute. Ask that woman officer to come in." I took one of the paper bags, shoved it in a pocket.

In the dispensing room there was a soft light that glowed from under the edges of the cupboards. This was to make it easier to count pills. I liked this room. You could see everything you needed to see. There was a knock.

The woman officer said, "Hi doc. Problem?"

"No problem. You know what? I don't think he's so crazy. He can go with you tonight."

"But what about . . ." she said, unsure how to phrase her concern.

"What, about coercion and police brutality, all that stuff? About that stuff?"

"Yeah, that."

"I wrote here in the chart that his account of the events changed from time to time and was inconsistent." I showed it the officer. "I'm sure a judge would find you more credible than your prisoner. If he has the chance to tell a judge."

"I'm sorry about the mess."

"The bite," I said. I smiled. "Like you said, gotta watch yourself. We both work with occupational hazards."

"All the time."

"About his head, I guess he fell on the car door, huh? That's what I'll write down, that he fell on the door of the cruiser while he was getting in. Clumsy."

"That's exactly what we wrote. Exactly what happened."

"You know what else? You may not have noticed this yet, but he's got multiple bruises on his limbs and torso. He was flailing around at some point. Hurt himself."

"No, I hadn't noticed."

"Well, here's what I saw. He's moving all four limbs well. No broken bones or anything, no cuts except for the one on the head where we fixed him. But there's a lot of bruising that you may not have noticed yet. *Multiple bruises consistent with accidental injury.* That's what I'm writing in the chart. What was that 'yummy yummy' nonsense anyhow?"

"I really couldn't say, doctor."

"Eli needs to learn respect for the police. I'm going to discharge him to your custody."

"I see what you mean."

"Just my job. 'Night, officer."

They took him out. Eli swore and stumbled. Maybe it would happen just down the street, in this precinct anyhow. He might bolt outside the hospital, or there were a lot of quiet corners where he might try to escape, and they would have to take him into custody again, teach some respect. I went into the quiet room. It stank. The scissors were gone, and what can you say about that? So many things happen at once. A doctor could lose track of one small, sharp object, and an agitated patient could easily grab a little pair of scissors.

I went to the bathroom, took the small handful of pills that would reduce my probability of seroconverting if I had actually been exposed to HIV and washed them down with handfuls of water. Soon my shift was over, and I signed over to the next physician.

As I drove away, I saw a speeding police cruiser with sirens on, blazing toward the hospital. There're a lot of cruisers, like crackling fireflies in the night. The police bring in their prisoners when necessary, and the officers come themselves as patients when they're hurt. I didn't look to see the faces of the officers in that car.

AFTERWARDS

—
—
—

DOCTOR SRI WATCHED THE AMBULANCE CREW wheel in the big, motionless man. In resuscitation bay 3, the form wrapped in the blanket was lifted upward by a circle of hands, each grasping the orange cloth. The medics and nurses asked and answered each other at the same time. This heavy form in the bright blanket rose off the ambulance gurney, floated for a moment, and then settled on the hospital stretcher. Around the silent man, a choir of beeping monitors and electronic alarms rang out a desperate melody.

Lines and cables spilled over each other, into him and onto the floor.

"What's the story?" asked Sri.

Zoltan the paramedic said, "Unwitnessed collapse in a hair salon. He was in back. Found in vee-fib. Shocked three times, tubed, epi times three, atropine times two. En route, total six shocks—no response."

"Time down?"

"Call at fourteen-oh-five . . . now twenty-five minutes down."

"All right." Sri placed his stethoscope on the man's chest—no heart sounds. The eyeballs were beginning to dry and stick to the open lids, and the pupils were a fixed size. The hands were a lacy blue web, which spread up the arms to the purple face. Sri felt relaxed, almost placid.

"Twenty-five minutes down?" said Sri. He felt calm because it was too late to make a difference.

"Yeah. Traffic."

"Fine. Bolus Amio three hundred. Pads, and get ready to shock." Hands reached for drug boxes, for the paddles. The monitor's frantic line jumped up and down. Bouncing, bouncing, and wild. Ventricular fibrillation, the heart's desperate spasm.

"Amio in," called out a nurse.

Sri held the paddles in front of himself.

"Charging to three-sixty," said Sri. His thumbs flicked the red button on each paddle. The counter climbed: two-fifty, three hundred, three-sixty. "I'm clear." He placed the paddles on the chest. "You're clear." He looked up and down the stretcher to see that everyone had stepped back. "Everyone's clear." Sri leaned down hard over the paddles. His thumbs found the big orange buttons. With a quiet beep of the defibrillator, the man's body jumped in a moment and softly rustled the sheets in falling back into them. Sri always thought there was a noise in that jumping—like a little bang or a snap. Afterwards, he wondered if he had imagined it, and then he couldn't be sure.

"Continue CPR," said Sri.

Zoltan, whose shoulders were broader than his planted feet, compressed the chest. With his hands overlapped and a closed-mouth smile, he pumped the chest casually, flexed at the elbows. Most people lock their elbows and lunge from the waist to achieve enough force. Zoltan pumped with a delicate stroking motion that pushed the silent man audibly down, down into the stretcher.

"Good output," said Sri. His gloved hand felt for a pulse on the groin of this human shape in the nest of sheets and wires. The blood not clotted yet, but not warm either. At the requisite intervals, Sri ordered injections, shocked the human form, and re-examined. On the monitor, the dancing line became a lazy wave. Sri wrote in the chart.

It was fourteen-fifty when Sri said, "Hold compression." The line was flat across the monitor. "Is the family here yet?"

"No one."

"Well, I think we're done. I'm calling it. Thank you everyone."

Four patients later, Nurse Lillian came to Dr. Sri.

"Mr. Wilhelm's family is in the family room," she said.

"Who?"

"The vee-fib. His family."

They began to walk down the hall. Lillian handed Sri the chart.

"Wife and son," said Lillian. Her voice was light and firm, a tone that might signal the arrival of guests who were expected but not especially welcome.

Is he really dead yet? Sri wondered. Mr. Wilhelm himself was gone, but the Mr. Wilhelm who existed with his family was alive until Sri told them of the death. *This hallway to the family room always feels long,* thought Sri. Sri knew he was wondering idly, because either this death had happened or was soon about to be finished. It didn't matter if it was a secret reality in this hallway. The door appeared. *What if I don't go through this door?* thought Sri. He would not turn away. He had been in the family room many times.

Sri opened the door that had no window in it. He and Lillian entered the room.

"Hi, I'm Dr. Sri. This is Nurse Lillian."

Glancing at the chart, Sri saw that he had not yet written that the patient was deceased. *What if, just now,* he thought, *I forgot that Mr. Wilhelm died?* Sri shook hands with Mrs. Wilhelm and then her son, Tomas. "Pleased to meet you," said Sri. Seeing them, now it seemed unfair that he knew and they did not. He wanted to rush the words. "I'm sorry it's under these circumstances." But first the key phrases. What did he usually say in this time when everything but the facts would be lost? *Each time it feels like I'm rehearsing.* "Your husband arrived here about an hour ago." *I should just say it, to make it real and end it. They already know. A wife knows—some believe that at the moment of death she feels it already.* "He collapsed in a hair salon. The paramedics came immediately, and did everything they could." *I used the past tense. It gives it away. What would I say if the man were alive? I would start by saying he was alive.* Beginning to tell it, Sri felt calm. "They transported him here. We began to resuscitate him immediately. His heart had stopped beating. We did everything we could." That last phrase felt like soap opera, but these words always came out of Sri's mouth. *To talk like this creates a delay, but there's a story to tell. Tell them the story. The story needs to come before the ending so that it makes sense looking back.* "We couldn't restart his heart." So he had maybe tricked himself by revealing the death without saying the actual words. *I still have to say it.* "I'm sorry, but Mr. Wilhelm passed away peacefully about half an hour ago. He was in no pain or discomfort." *That last part, I always feel I might be lying.*

There.

The wife's face held a shattered expectation. Tomas Wilhelm was Dr. Sri's age, with quiet eyes that had the calmness of grey water. The young Wilhelm gazed beyond the space of the small room. This room. Sri had seen its pictures so many times but he could never think of what they showed. Forgotten landscapes, maybe, hung over the soft, easy-to-clean vinyl furniture.

"Heart attack," said Sri. "Most likely."

"He didn't take care of himself," said Tomas, squinting.

"I see."

"He smoked, never exercised, he was a diabetic—didn't care about his sugar."

Sri always felt relief to learn that a deceased person's end was predicted by his life. It made it a happens-to-someone-else event, a bound-to-happen circumstance. There was less to explain, or understand.

"Well, I'm sure there's a lot to remember," said Sri. Relieved at having told his part of the story, he tried to look at his watch without appearing to do so.

"He was in a hair salon?" asked Mrs. Wilhelm.

"Yes, a hair salon," said Sri. "He fell in the back room. They called the ambulance. The paramedics gave him—"

"A hair salon? You mean his barber," said Mrs. Wilhelm.

"I suppose his barber."

"Why was he in the back of his barber's shop?" asked Tomas.

"Well, I don't know," said Sri. *Details. Everyone wants the details. Emphasize the promptness of treatment.* "The ambulance crew shocked him immediately, and——"

"Immediately? The ambulance people were there?" asked Tomas.

"After they arrived."

"I don't think his barber has a back room," said Mrs. Wilhelm. She turned to Tomas, "Did he ever call it a hair salon?"

"It must be the back part of the shop." *How would I know?* Sri looked openly at his watch.

"The haircut place. We'll get the address for you later," said Lillian. "The ambulance people write down something that describes the place. For instance, if they bring someone from a coffee shop they might write *café*. Hair salon, barber. Back room, back of the store."

Sri decided to try his medical speech again. "I can assure you that he received all the treatments that had a chance of saving him."

"What about his car? Where is it parked?" asked Tomas.

"They won't tow it if he's died," said Mrs. Wilhelm. "Will they?"

"Well, you know the parking police," said Sri, and then wondered if he should have said something different. It was true that they ticketed and towed you even after death.

Sri stood, his hand at the doorknob. "Please don't hesitate to ask any further questions—about the medical

issues." Relatives asked things he had no idea about—
whether the car would be towed, or which hairdresser
had given the last trim. Why did they care, now that
these things were in the past? As soon as Sri felt the distance of closing the door behind him, he felt badly for
thinking that. After all, the trivia was their property to
care about, to console themselves with.

The nurse wrote down the address of the hair salon to
help Mrs. Wilhelm and Tomas find the car. Tomas
crumpled it into his pocket; 487 Fenning Avenue. As
they drove from the hospital, neither Mrs. Wilhelm nor
Tomas commented that this was not the address of the
usual barber. It was early evening, and the winter sky
had been dark since late in the afternoon. The gusts of
falling snow were lit by streetlight. The snow com-
forted Tomas, filling the harsh air with softness. The
early black evening made it feel like it was time to be
at home, to sleep and be ignorant. Perhaps to watch television, and to allow the seduction of flickering cone-
light from thirty-nine cable stations.

"I'll take you home, Mother?"

"I don't want to be alone."

"We'll call Aunt Sophie and she'll come over. And
Nana needs to know."

"How will you get his car?"

"I'll find it."

"You can't drive two cars."

"True."

Four-eighty-seven Fenning. Tomas pulled over, found a map and looked it up. It was a street in the area that real estate agents called the Upper Beaches, an attempt to convince house buyers that it was a part of the neighbourhood near the water. No one ever referred to the Lower Beaches but simply the Beaches, unless it was the Upper Beaches. When they found Fenning, it was an awkward street containing both houses and small, brick industrial buildings. An auto body shop, a reupholsterer, a hair salon. Tomas wished that he had insisted on taking his mother home, that he had come here by taxi or by streetcar. He could have walked to find the car, and he felt like walking, like having the repetitive motion of walking quickly in the snow, of seeing his tracks behind himself. He slowed down the car. The window of the hair salon at 487 Fenning was still bright through the slats of venetian blinds. The car was not on the street, though there seemed to be plenty of parking.

"Let's drive up and down," said Tomas.

"Pull over."

"The car's not here."

"I need to get out."

Slowly, thinking of not stopping, Tomas eased the car alongside the curb. His mother stepped out of the car, and pulled her green coat closed in front. She slammed the door quickly, and Tomas sat in the car with the engine running. The radio was off. Tomas watched his mother walk toward the hair salon, and thought about following her. He wondered how much gas was in his father's car, a hatchback. His father often let the gas run low, then filled it up a quarter-tank at a time and said that he was going to wait and see if gas was cheaper tomorrow. His mother had not asked him to come with her, and Tomas saw her go into the hair salon, the blinds on the glass door shivering behind her. There won't be gas in the car, decided Tomas. And his father wouldn't have fixed the muffler yet. This would be left to him. He was angry at his father for leaving these messes, and for dying on a street in the Upper Beaches not known to them. Tomas watched the snow. He let it accumulate, and then flicked the wiper switch on for a moment to clear the windshield. He admired the patterns of the flakes on the glass. At first the snowflakes melted upon contact with the windshield, and then when they stuck they clumped so it was difficult to see the hexagonal patterns of the crystals. *Maybe I should go inside?* he thought. He looked toward the hair salon and saw a man emerge. Tomas turned on the windshield wiper, swept the glass canvas clean, and watched again. He turned off the car and put on his gloves. He had always doubted the uniqueness of each snowflake.

Five minutes, and he thought that two flakes were close, but had to admit there was a minor difference.

Ten minutes, and he flicked the windshield wiper to clear the glass in front of him. It remained grey and misty even with the snow wiped off, because the car was cold and the windows were fogged.

Cold air gusted into the car when the passenger door opened and his mother got in, holding his father's old crushed fedora.

"He forgot his hat," said Mrs. Wilhelm.

Tomas turned the key and the engine started, coughed. He put the car in gear and pulled into the quiet street.

"Do they know where his car is?"

"I didn't ask."

"This is his new hairstylist? Was, I mean," said Tomas.

"There were men waiting to have their hair cut," said his mother blankly. "Your father's hat was there. A girl came out. I think she saw him earlier. I took the hat."

The car slid softly around the white corner of the street. Tomas liked this kind of driving, in the winter snow when all movements were approximate.

"So there *is* a back room in this barber," said Tomas. As if this explained things.

"There is a back room. For ten years your father hasn't touched me. Said it was his diabetes, that he couldn't do it."

They drove around the block. Then in a wider circle around the next streets. To the east, the streets contained residential houses with miniature bright windows. To the west, it was more small brick factories. Some had been converted to lofts, their faux-industrial stainless steel appliances glinting in bare kitchen windows. Tomas drove in larger circles, slowly down the hushed white streets. Four blocks out, Tomas wondered if he had missed a street, or if the car had already been towed. On the fifth block to the east, there was the hatchback. It had been parked before the snow had begun; the smooth inch of white on it like a shroud. There was a ticket. Twenty dollars. ONE HOUR EXCEPT BY PERMIT, read the sign. Tomas swept off the car and wondered what suit to wear to the funeral. He wondered what the car was worth, whether he could sell it without a muffler, and wished it had been towed. In this car, you had to hold the starter key for about five seconds before the engine coughed and then roared. His mother drove the sedan. Tomas followed. She pulled over, and Tomas put on his emergency flashers. He was about to step out of the hatchback, but then he saw his mother come out of the sedan. She walked briskly to a mailbox, stuffed the fedora into its slot. She got back in the car and drove away too quickly. Tomas drove behind her, saw the rear end of the sedan fishtail briefly as she went around a corner without braking, but it was only a moment before the car straightened out and she continued to drive.

Cynthia heard a woman's voice in the front of the salon. She told the man she was with that she needed to go out front. To hear women in the salon made her nervous. Women didn't generally come here, and when they did they were out of place, their motives less clear than the men's. The women were sometimes Jehovah's

Witnesses who would exhort Cynthia to repent, or they would be teenage girls—strung out and looking for work. Cynthia was suspicious of anyone wanting to work here.

A few months ago, there had been a female bylaw inspector and a police officer. The bylaw inspector began, unannounced, to check the rooms to see if they conformed to the municipal code for massage rooms. The inspector quickly and quietly opened her door. Cynthia did not hear her approach because of the penis in her mouth, which, along with the moaning she used to speed things up, had the effect of compromising her hearing. The police arrested her and John, although she later learned that his name was Philip. The officer testified in court that, no, he didn't have a search warrant, that he had simply been accompanying the female bylaw inspector for her safety when he had, quite coincidentally, witnessed the offence in question. The bylaw inspector seemed to enjoy her testimony, describing what she had seen with a triumphant disgust. Cynthia herself answered the questions simply, plainly, as the legal aid lawyer had instructed her. What she wanted was to address the court and say what was clear to her: *Sure I was blowing him. That's what he wanted, to get off, just like you're getting off on me now.* Cynthia told herself that she was immune to sentiment for the penises that presented themselves, like tubular pimples that needed to be burst. In any case, the penises were a clear arrangement: cash in advance. Her money box, a disguised cosmetics case, was next to the lube. The prosecution lawyer made her angry, the way he enjoyed administering humiliation without paying for it. After that, Cynthia raised her price for oral, and become more nervous about women's voices in the shop.

Massage itself, meaning with the hands only for therapeutic purposes, was licensed. Clean towels were required, for instance. Inspectors could always drop in.

When she heard a woman in the front, Cynthia put a towel over the man, who lay naked on his back with his erectness close to bursting. She went outside and found a woman, snow damp on her pea-green coat shoulders, holding a fedora.

"This is my husband's hat," she said, and looked at Cynthia as if it were stolen goods in a pawn shop.

"Take it then," said Cynthia. "Go ahead."

"Did you see my husband?" asked the woman. "Did any of you see my husband?" she asked the three men who sat with their backs to the venetian-blinded windows. One of them smiled and shrugged, while the other two looked deep into the spines of their magazines.

"Lots of people come here," said Cynthia. "For haircuts. Take the hat if it's your husband's."

"Where do you cut hair?"

"Here," said Cynthia.

"Here? Where?"

"Right here. This is a hair salon."

"Well, where's the hair?"

"Excuse me?"

"The hair. There's no hair on the floor. Where are the little cans of mousse, and gel, and spray?" There was one lonely barber's chair in the corner of this front room, its vinyl dull with lack of use. There was a hair-washing sink, over which sat a mirrored shelf that Cynthia suddenly felt was conspicuously empty. The woman's green coat was wet with the melted snow, and she pointed at one of the seated men. "In fact, this guy doesn't even have hair!"

"We cut hair. In the back," said Cynthia. She felt unprepared, not having a shaver or any scissors. *Where's Lorraine*, thought Cynthia, *she's the manager. Back there somewhere, making cat noises.*

"Take me in back," said the woman. "My husband came for a haircut today."

"Do you want a haircut?"

"No," said the woman.

"Well, in that case, you can't go back there. The back is only for haircuts," said Cynthia in what she hoped was a decisive voice.

"Then I want a haircut."

"You just said you didn't."

"Well, I guess I don't," said the woman, who suddenly looked lost.

"Then why do you want to go in back?"

"My husband's dead," said the woman. "I want to see where he died."

One of the men put down his magazine, stood, and opened the door just enough to let in a thin knife of snow as he hurried out. The smiling one picked up the magazine.

Lorraine should explain this. That's why she gets an extra cut for being manager.

There had been that big man, this afternoon. The big man who wouldn't wake up after Cynthia finished with him. She had tried to shake him, then after a moment she'd slapped him hard across the face, swore at him, and called for Lorraine. He didn't move. Cynthia called 911, and Lorraine cleaned up the semen, then used the same hand towel to rub Cynthia's fingerprints off his body and face. Cynthia wanted to leave the salon, but Lorraine insisted that she help get the man dressed. "I'm the manager," she said. They each pulled at one side to get the pants on, struggled to get the cuffs over the bend of his ankles before the ambulance arrived, tucked the limp penis between his legs and zipped up the fly. They gave their names to the ambulance crew, which were not their real names in any case, but were the ones they used in the salon.

"I just finished his haircut," Cynthia told the big paramedic, who thumped on the man's chest as they wheeled in the collapsible gurney. The blue-coated paramedic seemed to notice Cynthia's nipples through the T-shirt she had quickly pulled on, which made the whole interaction seem more normal to her.

Maybe he's not dead, she thought. *It looks like he fainted. Sure, he doesn't get enough, and it was too much for him.* The paramedics talked on their radio, and shocked the man on the massage table. He didn't wake, and they used what looked like a silver crowbar to put a plastic breathing tube down his throat. Cynthia wondered with some satisfaction if he felt it, if he could feel what it was like to have a long tube stuck in your throat and about to burst. Feeling guilty at this thought, Cynthia told herself again that he must have fainted.

"He probably passed out," Cynthia said after they had wheeled him out and the sirens had faded down the road.

"He'll be back next week," Lorraine said. The big man was a regular. The name he gave was Ed.

So, he won't be back. Where is Lorraine?

The woman in the green coat said to Cynthia, "You don't cut hair, do you?"

"It was my manager who took care of your husband."

"How exactly do you take care of people?" asked the woman, and then she grabbed the magazine from the bald, seated man. "How will this little girl take care of you?"

The man's face flushed red, and colour swept over the top of his head. He said nothing.

"Do you want the money back?" asked Cynthia, with a desire to retreat as much as possible from the events of the afternoon. She should have left after the ambulance had gone.

"What?" said the woman.

"Do you want a refund? We don't usually issue refunds, but I can ask my manager if—"

"You think I want the money back?"

"I was just wondering, because obviously you're upset—"

The woman looked at her. *I'm not stupid like you think I am*, thought Cynthia with anger, *I just know what things are worth. I don't want the money, because it's not worth it to me anymore.*

"Give me the money back, then."

"Then you'll leave?"

"How much is it?" asked the woman.

Cynthia turned and went back into her room, closed the door behind her. The man lay quietly like a child who had been told to put his head on the table, and he was deflated under the towel. He looked scared, perhaps wondering what the fuss was about—and whether he was about to be arrested.

"I'll be with you in a minute, John," she said. She was annoyed that she would have to redo the pimple work. Through the thin wall, Lorraine made repetitive squealing sounds in the next room, which one would think were sexual except that Cynthia heard them all day long. They became like TV commercials in the background.

"What's going on?" said the deflated man. "Hurry up."

"You think you can handle me, sexy guy?" said Cynthia automatically, without looking at him.

The cash box had a combination, and Cynthia was careful to keep her back to the man. *I'm not giving*

Lorraine the manager's cut tonight, she thought. When she turned to go outside, with a hundred dollars in her hand, Cynthia saw that the woman had entered the room. She held the fedora in front of her, looked at Cynthia, looked at the man on the massage table.

"Is this two for one?" he asked, nervous.

The woman took the money from Cynthia. "Exactly where you're lying," she said to the deflated man, "my husband died this afternoon. Enjoy your haircut."

The man sat up.

"So," said the woman in green to Cynthia, "did he, you know, before he died, did he get what he was after?"

Cynthia saw that the woman had summoned a great deal of courage to ask this with bravado, and she felt badly for them both.

"I don't know what you mean. You've got the money." She tipped her head to the door and stared straight at the woman, who did not budge.

"Come on, woman to woman, did he do it before he died?" In this instant, neither of the women realized that they each felt an almost identical mixture of hate and pity for the other. The woman in the green coat said, "Don't play dumb. Did he come? Shoot off? Orgasm?"

"I don't think so," said Cynthia, quietly. "No, definitely not. No."

"But he paid."

"It's cash in advance."

"Right, cash up front." The woman stuffed the money into the fedora, turned, and was gone.

"Give me my money too," said the man to Cynthia. "This is bullshit."

Lorraine grunted and swore in the next room, and Cynthia wanted to turn down the volume, or change the channel. She shut the cash box securely, took off her T-shirt, stood up straight and said to the man, "I'll get you off, or you can get yourself out."

He rested on an elbow for a moment, and then lay back on the table. Cynthia felt lighter, and better for having given back that money. That transaction was cancelled, and she turned to this man's pimple.

Two weeks later, the ambulances were lined up outside the hospital entrance, and their stretchers filled the hallway. Nowhere to put them. Some of the paramedics had folding lawn chairs and novels, which they always kept in the ambulances for these situations. They sat next to their orange-wrapped patients and thumbed through the paperbacks. Some played cards, and intermittently they asked the nurse in charge whether any beds were going to free up soon.

One of the paramedics, Zoltan, saw a doctor that he recognized. One who was quiet, and therefore the right person to approach.

"Dr. Sri?"

"Yes."

"I have a question. Let's go over here," said Zoltan, and motioned the physician away from the other paramedics. "I'm having a problem."

"What kind of problem?"

"Personal," said Zoltan, lowering his voice.

"Personal. Like intimate, sexual," said Dr. Sri immediately in an unchanged tone of voice, and it surprised Zoltan that the doctor was so unsurprised at the meaning of *personal.*

"Like that."

Zoltan explained that he had never had this problem before, a performance problem, but that it wasn't exactly a performance problem either.

"Here's how it started," said Zoltan. He had picked up a patient from one of those places, those brothels. They call it a hair salon. He couldn't remember which hospital he had brought the patient to.

"Maybe here? Did I bring this patient to you, Dr. Sri? No, of course you wouldn't remember, there are so many patients. The guy died. He died after, or during, well, the act. We wrote on the call record that it was a hair salon. That's what the sign said. Better for the family to call it a hair salon, so we wrote it that way—as a little courtesy."

Ever since then, when he and his wife would begin to make love, said Zoltan, he would have a vision. A flashback, seeing this dead guy with his pants half on and all these women with their tits half out of their shirts. Then he would breathe fast, get chest pains, then tingling in his hands, and feel like fainting. They hadn't made love properly since that time.

"You've discussed the issue with your wife?"

"No, I haven't told my wife why. I'm not bringing this shit home. I see everything. You know—drownings, things chopped off, blown up. Never bothers me. But I keep thinking of this dead guy, and I can't get it up."

"Sometimes, a little thing is like a trigger," said Dr. Sri. "One little thing happening sets the mind in a particular course."

"What can I do?"

"You need to make love once, without thinking of this. You need to get past it."

"Are there any pills to help me?"

"Maybe with the sexual part. No medication erases memory. Why don't you go away for the weekend. Somewhere calm, where you will think differently. Don't let this pattern settle in, or it will become more of a problem. Think of a beautiful place, and go there with your wife. Have a good meal, a bottle of wine, and just let things happen naturally."

AN INSISTENT TIDE

———
———
———

JANICE LAY IN THE PILLOWED SAND, AND THE water drifted and frothed as high as her calves. The tide was coming in, and she had been lying there for a number of hours. *Is that so? Or did I just arrive?* she thought, unsure now of this point. She knew, however, that the level of the water was rising. Sometimes she heard its hush, its whisper of motion without feeling the cool wash at her heel. It was clear, however, that over ten sighs of the water, over a hundred repetitive flexures of the ocean, the curled breakers were coming closer.

They opened their mouths to her legs, and pursed their whistling lips as they fell and rushed forward, blowing the stream of rising tide up to her thighs now.

I am so still, thought Janice. *Why have I never in my life felt so still before?* There was a wonderful relief of not moving her limbs, of allowing her arms to lie like wet rope over her globe-like abdomen. The water pooled and became a warm slurry of salt and sand in the hollows that held her thighs. She counted the waves. One, a stroke that seemed to touch only the leg hairs. Two, a tingling pain on her skin—as if the drying salt would pull and crack open her pores. Three, *what is this beach?* Four, a rush of briny sea with its sharp sting on her red thighs and then this wave receded. Five, *where is Oliver?* Six, now a panic as if she had split in two, and one half had forgotten the other. Seven, *have I peed myself?*

Warmth spread across Janice's lap, and she felt something shift inside her belly, like a weight about to drop. Above her, in the sky, she saw a bird swirling. Higher, it rose on thermal currents she could not see, but whose rising spirit was evident in the creature's arc upward. *Do birds ever get to heaven?* she wondered. Now a pain, a wrenching fist squeezed her belly. She thought of sitting, of stretching, of turning on her side because this might shift some of the weight of her swollen uterus. She could not sit, could not turn, and was unable to move except to follow the bird with her eyes. It had notched wingtips. *I'm scared he will fall*, she thought. *He? Maybe it's a she bird.*

Beep Beep.

Is the bird making that noise?

Beep Beep.

Why am I paralyzed?

Beep Beep.

Janice grabbed the telephone. "Hello!" she shouted. She sat up, and was shocked by her own ability to move.

"Jan, what's the matter?"

"Oliver," she said. The slats of early afternoon light stabbed through the bedroom shutters. "I was dreaming. Are you at Pearson?"

"Still in New York."

"You said you'd take the morning flight."

"Didn't you see the news? Hurricane warning. Nothing's moving on the east coast. They say we'll be out tomorrow, or maybe the day after. It has to blow over."

"One-day trip. You promised."

"It's the forces of nature, Jan." Now she heard his muffled voice aiming away from his cellphone: "Pull up here. Yellow awning on the right."

She ached to remember the dream that had preceded the telephone. That wonderful coastline. What had been frightening about it? It was then that Janice realized that her underpants, and the hem of the nightgown bunched around her hips, were wet. And warm, with a seaweed smell. Amniotic fluid was soaking into the mattress.

"Oliver?"

"I'm going to wait it out at the hotel. They'll call when they have a plane for me. You want me to get anything? That lox you like?"

"Oliver."

"Listen, cab's pulling up, let me pay him."

She heard a scratch as he put the phone in his jacket pocket, the flap of fabric as he rifled for his wallet. Janice heard the cab door slam. A fumbling noise as he put the phone to his ear.

"My water just broke," said Janice.

"Say again. The water's broken? There's a plumber, the guy we used last time. Sam, or Joe. No, Stan. Number's in my desk." She could hear the honking of a Manhattan morning behind his voice.

"Oliver. *My* water's broken. I'm in labour."

"Why do you say that?" he said. She heard an engine hum and then fade away.

"Because that's what's happening."

"Do you know for sure? You've never had a baby." His voice sounded less and less real—more like a clock radio as he talked. She heard him cup the phone in his hand and tell someone that no, he didn't have any change.

"You better come home," she said. "Right away."

"Go to the hospital and find out if it's labour. I'll call the airport."

Janice put the phone down, and heard Oliver talking in the background. He said her name several times. She put her hands on her belly, experimentally. She had become accustomed to its growth, its weight which for the past nine months had sunk into the centre of her pelvis, streaking her abdomen with stretch marks of glistening purple skin.

What now?

A contraction swelled up—this strong grip from within her uterus. Janice realized that she would not be able to alter the ensuing events. She knew from the prenatal classes that now there would be thinning of her cervix, it would dilate into an absurdly large opening, the muscles of her uterus would begin to squeeze in their own rhythm, accelerating like a heart coming to life, and her baby would emerge. It was a relief to realize that this would now happen despite herself.

"You're two centimetres," said Dr. Ming that afternoon. She removed her right hand from within Janice's vagina, where she had been spreading her fingers to see how wide Janice's cervix was open. She plucked the cuff edge of the glove and pulled it inside out over her fingers in a quick motion that sounded like a rubber band snapping. There was fine white dust in the creases of her fingers.

Janice was on her back, her feet together and knees apart. *If I were not a pregnant woman, I would look like Buddha,* she thought.

"How long, then?" asked Janice.

"That depends."

"Of course," said Janice, *but what does it depend on?* She felt that she should know, and tried to remember her readings, which she had undertaken like exam preparation. Janice had read a prenatal book, *What to Expect When You're Expecting*, a book with line drawings of happy couples called *Birthing for Beginners*, and two-thirds of *Boen's Comprehensive Board Review— Summary of Obstetrics*. She had stopped midway through *Boen's*. It had bored her with its anagrams of treatment protocols and dosage calculations, while shocking her with curt descriptions of obstetric disaster. The term *fetal demise* was used without embellishment. All of this gave Janice a feeling of emptiness, as if she had seen a naked corpse and not known the person's name. Now she wondered if the last third of that book explained what the length of her labour now depended upon.

She hadn't brought the books. That was supposed to be Oliver's job, to pack the red duffle bag before driving her to the hospital: books, Walkman, diapers. He had a long list of essential items. As it was, the only thing Janice brought was her pillow. When she had told the cabbie that she wanted the maternity wing, he drove with a grimness of purpose, but seemed suddenly congratulatory once they arrived at the hospital and Janice still held the pillow over her pregnant belly. *He couldn't refuse to take me,* she thought.

Dr. Ming squirted a spiral of jelly, which had a tinge of blue like ice, on Janice's stretch marks. She pointed the dop-tone wand at the ripe pregnancy and began to search. The fat end of the wand slid through the jelly over Janice's skin. The amplifier, to which the wand was connected by a slinky wire, crackled and then hissed. It was like a shortwave set seeking out a long-range transmission at dusk. Dr. Ming twisted the wand around in a circle as static popped and hushed. Then a beat—a single drum tap. Dr. Ming honed in with the wand to find several more beats. White noise. The speaker made a sucking sound as she lifted the wand, squirted more cold jelly on that spot, and then returned the wand there.

Thump thump. Static. Dr. Ming adjusted. *Thump thump thump,* a clear impulse forward. Humanity's first drum.

For months now, Janice had heard the sound of her baby's heart during checkups at Dr. Ming's office. Each time it felt like a growing voice, a surging message in the fetal staccato of cardiac rhythm. *Thump thump thump thump.* Dr. Ming turned off the machine. The heart rate counter on the dop-tone shined out: 142. Janice remembered from *Boen* that it should be 120 to 160, and was satisfied at being almost exactly average.

"Looks good," said Dr. Ming. "Where's Oliver?"

"On his way. I called him—thought I'd come first," she said, forcing a casual disregard for her husband's absence.

Having found the fetal heart, Dr. Ming buckled an elastic monitor belt over Janice's tight skin.

Oliver's cellphone had a local Toronto number that Janice dialed early that afternoon from the Labour and

Delivery Lounge. His phone rang wherever he was in North America, and gave the illusion that he was nearby.

"How long?" asked Oliver.

"Dr. Ming said that it could be any minute," said Janice.

"Jeez," he said. "I knew that already."

"And you went to New York."

"But is it 'any minute' meaning a few minutes, or 'any minute' meaning like sometime today."

"It's something like that. Oliver, I'm having a contraction." Janice grunted, and gave a low moan which rose and then tapered. She heard Oliver fiddling with something. "It's like a clamp."

"I'm driving, Jan. I got a rental car."

"That'll take hours, forever."

"Nothing's flying, and it's pelting rain."

"How far are you?" At that moment, Janice heard a prolonged honk, the single raised finger of urban traffic.

"Relax, buddy," said Oliver, his voice faint because the phone was not at his mouth. She heard him pick up the phone, and then his voice spoke clearly, "Jan? I'm still in the Lincoln Tunnel."

"Are you kidding?"

"It's bumper to bumper. I'm coming, though."

Again a low grunting cry. Then Janice said, "I have to go."

"Wait!" said Oliver. "Did you bring the champagne?"

"You're in charge of the birth bag."

"I'll be there soon, Jan. Take it slow, okay?"

After hanging up, Janice felt a contraction grip her—a firm hand squeezing. It started like a gentle pressure—a flat palm—but grew and strengthened into a clenched hard fist.

Two hours later Dr. Ming said, "Three centimetres." She withdrew her hand, snapped off the glove, smiled, and left the room.

The pain came hard every four minutes. *Three centimetres. It stretches to ten before my baby comes out,* thought Janice. She called Oliver and got his voice mail.

"So slow," said Janice to Ronai, her nurse.

"Sometimes fast, sometimes slow," said Ronai, who had sad, round eyes. "Do you want laughing gas? Like at the dentist. It doesn't knock you out, but it makes you dreamy."

Ronai gave Janice a mask, which she had to hold up to her own face.

"It won't knock you out, but if you need to rest it will help you relax. If you fall asleep, the mask will drop from your hand."

Two birds wheeled in the sky above the beach, where Janice lay naked and warm. Wet sand was gritty in her elbows and behind her knees. She was now able to extend her arms in front of her, bend her legs at the knees, and raise her head to consider the rising water and the swirling shards of seaweed. Her body was heavy in the sand. The surf pooled around Janice's neck, and as the sea washed out with each wave, it dug a deeper pit around her body. Multicoloured fish had become trapped in this pit, and swam around Janice's ankles and buttocks, nipping furiously at her thighs. The birds suddenly tumbled, having lost their warm upward draft. Or maybe one tumbled, and the other dove after it. Quickly, their wings regained a hold on the air, but now instead of gliding they flapped powerfully upward. *Strange birds—they have faces,* thought Janice. One she did not recognize although it felt like she should, and the other looked very much like . . . Dr. Ming? A large fuchsia fish opened its jaws and attached itself to Janice's belly. She did not try to remove it. *I know that it must bite me,* she thought. *The Dr. Ming bird is watching that fish, and doesn't like it.*

The fuchsia fish gripped her and the beach seemed to funnel into its body. *Where is it going?* Janice opened her eyes on the labour room. Outside, the sky was dark. Evening, so soon. Ronai had turned off the laughing gas and the mask lay beside Janice. Dr. Ming was running the tracings through her hands. They were spooled out of the fetal heart monitor in a crumpled heap. She folded them back and forth on the perforations and spun the paper through her fingers. Janice saw that Dr. Ming was attentive, was interested in this spool of paper.

"What do you see?"

"I need to examine you again. I need to attach a scalp clip to the baby's head, for more direct monitoring."

Next to the bed was a console that had a thin tail of wires in a straw-like tube.

Dr. Ming pulled on a glove. Janice spread her legs and felt Dr. Ming reach up into her muscular centre. She spread her fingers, adjusted the angle of her wrist, and suddenly became still within Janice.

"What's the matter?" asked Janice.

"Don't move," said Dr. Ming.

"What do you feel?"

"The umbilical cord."

"That's wonderful," said Janice, satisfied at this reality that was going to emerge from her. She had noticed a chapter on umbilical cords in the last third of *Boen*. She hadn't read it.

"Actually, it's unusual," said Dr. Ming. She spoke quietly to Ronai, "Put ten litres of oxygen on Janice. Call anaesthesia, stat call, cord prolapse, get the section room ready." Dr. Ming adjusted herself, crossing her left leg over her right as Ronai snugged the straps of a clear plastic mask over Janice's nose and mouth. Dr. Ming looked very comfortable, as if she intended to maintain that pose for the evening. Ronai rushed out. "Janice, we need to change plans," said Dr. Ming. She still had her hand inside Janice, and pressed her fingers hard and upward. They began to feel uncomfortable. "And you need to lie on your left side."

Janice eased herself over, and thought, *This is what beached whales must feel like.* "Are you finished examining me now?"

"Well, yes," said Dr. Ming, "but I can't take my hand out. I feel the cord outside the cervix." Dr. Ming looked at her with a tight smile, a pause, and then a delayed wrinkling of her brow that gave the impression that she wanted to make the situation clear but, like a teacher, would prefer her student to figure it out on her own. She drew her breath in quickly, like a grip of apprehension. "It shouldn't come out before the head. I'm pushing up on the head right now, to try to keep it from coming any further."

Janice imagined her cervix, this narrow opening that needed to be stretched almost to snapping by the head of her baby, which should squeeze through it like a seed spit through teeth. She imagined the cord: its thick, pulsing blood flowing from her to the warm life inside her. It lay floppy in her vagina.

"The head will crush the cord," said Dr. Ming.

"And my baby will suffocate," said Janice.

Dr. Ming nodded, and the corners of her mouth creased with the satisfaction of having laid out certain facts and seeing her patient come to the correct conclusion.

"I have to keep my hand here. If the cord comes any further or the head pushes any more, it will be worse. I'm still going to attach the monitor." Dr. Ming snaked the plastic sheath with the wires along her worried fingers, twisted the device into place, and pulled off the tube.

"Why don't you push the cord back in?" asked Janice.

"Can't. It would tangle. Same problem. Stay calm, still beating 120," said Dr. Ming, looking at the fetal monitor. Janice was unsure whether the doctor was talking to her or herself. "We need to take you for a Caesarean section."

There was a tinny overhead page: "Anaesthesia— stat to Labour and Delivery."

So it was decided. A sudden change of direction. Janice had imagined the increasing pains, the spreading ripples of her own uterus's strength, the impossible stretching open of her body and the emergence of a son or daughter. She knew that things might go wrong, that in some women things did not go forward, that complications arose. She knew that things could come to a point where the danger to the baby outweighed the rhythmic forces of a childbirth's natural progress, and it became necessary to perform a Caesarean section. But she had expected that this point would be reached with a struggle of screaming and pushing and blood leaking out. It should be an epic of successive brinks and hazards. She was surprised that it was just like this. A decision.

"You're sure about the cord," said Janice.

"The cord is pulsing on my finger, and I'm pushing up against the head . . . it's coming down."

Brrr. Brrr.

The telephone next to the bed.

Brrr. Brrr.

It was an old style of telephone, with a heavy C-shaped handset. Janice picked it up and held the handset in one palm and the phone in the other.

"Janice."

"Hi, Oliver." Janice spoke through her oxygen mask.

"I can't believe it. I got a flat. I'm waiting for triple A. I tried to change it, but you know I'm not good with these things. I cut my finger. How is it going?"

"Dr. Ming is just giving me an update."

"Did you bring the camcorder to the hospital?"

"You know what? I forgot."

"Jan, I bought fresh tapes for this."

"I'm sorry, Oliver. I just forgot." A contraction began to well up inside her, and Janice felt Dr. Ming's hand firm, insistent, pressing up against the baby's head.

"Should I stop at home and get it? I'm a couple hours from the border. Or just come to the hospital?"

"If you really want the video . . ."

"Okay, honey. Oops. There's the triple A truck. I'll be there soon. By the way, I got the deal in New York wrapped up. Love you."

Janice hung up the phone and placed it squarely, symmetrically, on the side table. The scalp monitor flashed a new number every two seconds.

126

130

123

"Can you turn up the volume?" said Janice. "I'd like to hear the beats."

"Sure," said Dr. Ming, leaning her torso and left arm toward the box on its rolling stand, while careful to not move her right hand from where it was the placeholder for Janice's umbilical cord. "I can't reach."

"I'm having a contraction," said Janice. She felt it tighten and grow in strength as if these muscles expanded their sinews each time they were exercised. It was like strong hands circling her pelvis, and the end was like a slow exhalation.

She saw that Dr. Ming watched the monitor.

80

85

83

90

"Too slow?" asked Janice.

"Well, it's not just the number," said Dr. Ming. The twist of her eyebrows made Janice suspect that a simple answer was being obscured. "It's the pattern, the timing." Janice looked over Dr. Ming's shoulder, out the door into the empty hallway. There was a second overhead page for anaesthesia.

"It's not good if I have contractions now, is it?" said Janice.

"The nurses are setting up for the section. The anaesthetist is coming."

"And the head is pressing on the cord."

"Yes."

She could not will her womb to stop, now that it had begun its crescendo dance of muscle movements. It was awakening into its final purpose. The birth of a baby, the death of pregnancy. Months ago, Janice had been amazed that it grew, that it claimed a mass which had never before been occupied in her body. Now, the fleshy cradle had become aware of the being formed within it and was trying to thrust it into the world. It was faithful to its program of bearing down, of pushing the head through thinning muscles of the pelvis. *Is my uterus so stupid?* she thought. But it wasn't its fault. It didn't know that the head was crushing the thread of oxygen that allowed the fetal heart to beat, staunching the trickle of blood that fed this new brain just as it began to wonder if it existed.

"Dr. Ming," said Ronai, running into the room in her clogs, "section room's ready."

Then there were more nurses. They took the intravenous bags off poles, attached them to the hospital bed, unhooked certain wires, attached other ones, everyone telling Janice not to move. They put a hairnet on her and repeatedly told her that everything would be fine, like an urgent mantra. One nurse turned up the volume of the scalp monitor.

"Get up on the bed," said Ronai to Dr. Ming. "We'll push it down the hall."

Dr. Ming was crouched, now leaning on her elbow with her fingers still pushed up inside Janice. Ronai put a sheet over them. With Dr. Ming crouched between Janice's legs like a monstrous emerging newborn covered by a hospital sheet, the nurses released the brakes on the bed and with a hollow clang set off down the hallway. Past the pastel-painted nursing station. Past the other rooms, where women laboured and in one room a man yelled "Push! Push!" as a woman gave a long wailing grunt. Past a room where Janice heard the coughing cry of a baby, to the C-section room. Hands on each side of her pushed buttons, raised the bed so that it was level with the operating table, unplugged wires, plugged in wires, ripped down empty intravenous bags, hung fresh bulging ones, and repeated to Janice the dual mantras: "Don't move" and "It'll be fine." In a series of manoeuvres during which all around her seemed to stretch themselves into contortionists, while urging her to be as still as possible, Janice was lifted onto the surgical table and Dr. Ming's hands were replaced by those of Ronai, who slid her fingers in alongside Dr. Ming, allowing the doctor to free herself.

They began to wheel the bed away. "Can I have my pillow?" said Janice to a nurse who was masked but did not wear a surgical gown.

"I'll have to put our pillowcase on it."

It smelled like hot sand.

"Where is anaesthesia?" said Dr. Ming.

"Paged three times now," said a nurse who was gowned and masked in green.

"Page them again," said Dr. Ming.

"I'm feeling a contraction," said Janice. She looked at the monitor. They all looked.

"Three minutes apart," said Dr. Ming.

60

65

60

80

"Have them page any anaesthetist in the hospital," said Dr. Ming. "I'm going to scrub. Call pediatrics."

It took a long minute for the numbers to rise again, for them to reach 100. Then it hovered at 82, then up again to 95.

From where she lay on the operating room table, Janice could see the clock. A minute. Ninety seconds. *The contractions are closer together. My womb is doing exactly what it is supposed to do, pushing the head down.*

Two minutes.

Dr. Ming backed into the room, opening the door with her shoulder. The back of one hand was clasped in the palm of the other, held in front of her as if about to catch her own heart leaping from the centre of her green V-neck surgical scrubs. Her arms were white-clean and dripping to the elbows.

Two minutes thirty seconds.

"Another contraction," said Janice.

"The head's coming down," said Ronai. She sat at the side of the operating table on a black-covered stool, pushing up against the head that surged slowly forward.

Janice no longer found it strange to have a hand pressed up inside her like a finger in a dam. In the birth videos, she had seen that sometimes labouring mothers would touch the head as it came out, to feel that there was a living globe there to push against. A hand connected the pushing. Now, feeling Ronai's fingers inside her made her want desperately to relax. It was a reminder, a scolding that the squeezing of her body had become dangerous.

67

75

80

69

A nurse opened a crack in the door. "Got a phone call."

"Anaesthesia?" said Dr. Ming.

"Husband. Wants to know if Janice needs her foot massager."

"Tell him to drive safely," said Janice.

The monitor was one in which the pitch of the beeping changed with the rate. As it fell slower, it beeped in a sad, low note.

Dr. Ming stepped into a gown offered by a nurse who stood, in sterile gloves, by the operating table next to an open tray of steel blades, clamps, handles, scissors, and spreaders. Janice saw Dr. Ming plunge her arms into the fabric, saw that she kept her hands hidden in the cuffs. Then, the nurse offered a paper-wrapped cord from the gown, which Dr. Ming accepted. The nurse held another cord in place as Dr. Ming spun fully around in front of her. This dance unfurled the gown and wrapped Dr. Ming in a membrane that made her shine green like the tiled walls.

Another contraction.

The nurse tied the two bands at Dr. Ming's waist, then held out gloves. She spread their opening wide so that Dr. Ming inserted her right hand into one, and it became a live thing of latex. Dr. Ming made a fist and released it, to fully animate the pearly synthetic skin. Then the left hand.

66

66

70

75

This contraction was longer, and urgent. Janice realized that her uterus asked no questions, did not wonder whether the baby was doing well, whether the umbilical cord was safely tucked away.

80

85

80

Dr. Ming painted Janice's belly with a red-ochre liquid. It was cold, and ran down to her thighs. Neither of them spoke. Quickly, Dr. Ming taped drapes over Janice's skin, leaving only a rectangle of tight stretch marks tinged the colour of sunburn.

"Chart the time," said Dr. Ming to the nurse who was not gowned. "Chart the time, that we are at twenty-two fifty-five fully ready to perform an emergency Caesarean section but have had no response from the anaesthetist on call."

The monitor beeped a slow, low note.

Why are all these people here? thought Janice. *I'm cold. I'm dissolving into this table. There's the contraction.*

Maybe if I focus hard enough, I can hold it off. I read about Tibetan monks who can make their hearts stop, and then start again.

It's stronger, squeezing at me. It has its own force, but stop! Stop! Why don't they turn down that monitor—that noise is like mourning.

60

50

NO VALUE

NO VALUE

50

60

My womb is choking my baby. Dr. Ming, why is she standing there?

"You don't need the anaesthetist," said Janice.

She looks at me like I'm crazy, but like I've saved her.

"Do you?" she continued. "To cut me open?"

I'll pretend I'm not here. I'll just pretend that it's over already. That I only exist in the future.

"Get any of them," said Dr. Ming. "Someone run and find an anaesthetist."

"Just give me the laughing gas. There's no time, is there?" said Janice.

"You need more than that. There's no time for a spinal, we need them to knock you out."

"The actual operation—you can do it even if I'm awake, right?"

Why do I feel calm, having said that? It's me asking, that's why. No—not asking, I've made my offer.

No one moved.

"They call it a Caesarean section," said Dr. Ming, "because it comes from the time of the Caesars in Rome. They used to tie the woman down."

So simple, that this doctor will cut me open and pull out my baby, who will cry. Then she will stitch me up again like a universe that has exploded from a dense star and then billions of years later condenses into a black hole.

"Get the nitrous," said Dr. Ming. Her eyes did not meet Janice's. "And six of morphine. Give me a fifty-mil syringe of lidocaine." She looked at Janice and said, "Breathe the gas deeply. I'll freeze the skin. We can't stop once we start."

Who is that nodding? It's me.

Dr. Ming ran the long heavy needle under the skin at the incision line, made it swell with lidocaine like a sausage.

The laughing gas, which smells like clouds. A rush of warmth with the morphine injection. It's like a blanket through the intravenous. That jab in my skin—freezing. Why do they call it freezing when it burns, when it's hot like a brand on my stomach? Dr. Ming is picking up a knife. They call them scalpels, to make it official. I'm glad it's her. Why? Because she felt the cord—she knows it's there. She's cutting, I can see her stroking the blade into me.

—

It's true, the skin is frozen.

Oh.

It doesn't freeze deep, does it?

She's cutting muscle, the blade deep inside me now.

My mouth dry, throat too tight to yell.

Breathe the gas.

Where is the clock?

How long? I can't see the time.

The ring of operating lights is like suns, and moons, and stars, blinding me.

Dr. Ming operated quickly, methodically, as if she were alone in the room. A nurse assisted, pulled on spreaders, pushed on the belly as they slipped instruments through the layers of a woman. Dr. Ming directed the operation in short, tight phrases, and silence roared through the operating room. Her movements were fluid, and violent in the speed of cutting the uterus itself.

I need to let go, I may be close to evaporating, vanishing.

What is that noise?

Ripped open.

Myself screaming.

That's what it is—to hear my voice truly for the first time.

But, strangely, as if it's someone else.

The room black and swirling, where are the lights?

—

The strange beach.

The waves are going to crash over me, drown me. Why can't I move?

Foamed tops of breakers swirled high in front of Janice. The water rushed around her head, which lay heavy and aching on the wet beach. The sea pushed forward—hissing along the beach—and as the water fell back in a desperate clamber into the ocean, it dug a trench in the shape of her body around her, into the sand. Deeper, her shoulder blades seemed to settle like broken wings in the warm slurry. Her buttocks were heavy. Water ran around their edges to hollow out bowls for her flesh. She felt as if her balance had shifted, as if there were gravity lower within her that had been removed, lightened, now replaced by a searing torn-open pain. She tried to feel her belly, but found that she could not move her arms. Now the water fell over her, lifted her into a wave free and churning, and threw her tumbling into its froth of bubbles.

Janice saw hands flutter and whirl in the hard sun of operating lamps that shone on her belly. The soft, flat white of the gloves was streaked with red, and the fingers themselves beat like wings. One of the hands held a metal claw that descended into her belly with a needle, stung it, and then flew upward to pull the thread tight. The other hand flew around this thread to tie it, the fingers grasping and tying the thread like the movement of a bird's nest-building.

"I'm closing you," said Dr. Ming.

Janice heard a sputtering, protesting cry. She turned, and glimpsed the exultant blood-smeared child between the green-mantled shoulders of those around the baby-warmer. As Dr. Ming began the last layer of closure, Janice no longer felt pain, because this outermost skin was frozen.

NIGHT FLIGHT

—
—
—

December 9, 17:45 EST—Toronto

My phone rings at home, waking me from sleep. It's dispatch in Calgary.

"Dr. Fitzgerald speaking." I clear my throat.

"Dr. F? Be at the hangar at six-thirty. I'm faxing you the flight plan."

As we talk, it spools out of my fax machine: 19:00—depart Toronto, 22:45—Tampa for fuel, 1:50—St. Therese, Guatemala. Local ambulance to the hospital, rapid assessment, grab the patient and go. 3:20—takeoff from St. Therese. Tampa fuel stop, then the hop to Toronto.

"What's the rush? Ninety minutes ground time?"

"The St. Therese airport closes at 3:30 EST, 2:30 local."

"Can't fly tomorrow, huh? I just got in from Thailand a few hours ago." I had a little nip this morning to settle my nerves, then slept through the day. Now I am jittery and dazed, both from sleep disruption and from needing an eye-opener.

"Flight's booked, Dr. F."

I have given up trying to understand the scheduling of flights. Sometimes we need to fly sooner than a competitor, sometimes it is a rush to get the plane back for another job, sometimes it is an insurance company's whim. I rummage for fresh underwear and socks and pull on my uniform, which is stale and crumpled over the chair where I left it this morning. In the blue flight suit is my passport, stethoscope, PDA, wallet, sunglasses, and my folded wad of emergency U.S. dollars, which I keep cellophane-wrapped in the inside zippered pocket. With a small funnel, I fill my hip flask with vodka. I pocket a fresh package of strong mint chewing gum. I close the vodka bottle.

I reopen the bottle, take a sip before putting it away, feel a bit better already. Just another little sip. Better not overdo it before driving, even if the flight doctor uniform carries some pull with the highway cops.

———

19:10 EST

I'm in the four-foot-wide back seat of the Lear 35. Our planes are kept in a side hangar attached to Pearson International, three highway exits west of the passenger terminals.

"We're supposed to be wheels-up at nineteen hundred," says Niki, fidgeting. We often fly together, and I like Niki because she watches the details. "Already ten minutes behind schedule, Dr. Fitz," she says. She's in the forward seat, next to the stretcher. Behind me, the cargo bay is tight with flight and medical bags. The plane jitters and bounces out of the hangar, ungainly as it turns onto the taxiway. I slip out the flask and take a real slug. It's a good warmth, and I'll be dry by the time we get to Guatemala. The other thing I like is that Niki's not one to say anything.

In front, the pilots activate switches and speak into their headset microphones. Their hands slip back and forth across the glowing instrument panels. The jets' vibration soothes and surrounds the plane, and frozen rain shatters the black of night. A storm's coming— this sleet that blows in from Lake Ontario. I stuff a pillow under the small of my back, a smooth miniature airplane pillow. I belt myself in snugly, the secure feeling of pulling the strap tight. I close my eyes as the plane comes to life at the end of the runway. I'm tired. I slept four hours after getting back from Chiang Mai this morning. Open my eyes again. Another little sip, I deserve it.

Marcus, the pilot, used to fly CF-18s but his wife got sick of living in Goose Bay. The co-pilot, Rafael, speaks Spanish, which is good for a Guatemala run. We taxi to our runway. The pilots have their posture of relaxed focus before takeoff.

Acceleration and disequilibrium come instantly in a drugged moment. The jets roar in thrust down the tarmac, jolt through tens of seconds, the nose lifts, back wheels drag for a moment, and then with a sudden calm we ascend the sky. I am sleepy. The earth shrinks and drops—a camera panning out. I used to watch the cities as we took off, tried to spot their monuments, trace their watercourses. Then I discovered this moment, the powerful sedative effect of hurtling down the runway followed by the sudden forceful calm of pushing up into sky. Takeoff has become one of my sleep drugs, especially in the Lear, where the back seat is a few feet from the fuel tornado urging us forward. I breathe slowly, fade away, and am out before we reach cruising altitude.

21:55 EST

A loss of altitude wakes me. How does my body know? We drop through cloud cover over Tampa. The land mass sparkles with electric light, and the water around coastal Florida is a dark, geographical shadow.

Night over Tampa, coming in for fuel. I like to be awake for landings. I don't expect disaster, but statistically it's upon landing that we're most likely to spin into a ball of flame. I would like to experience that rare moment, to have the privilege of my last thought. A routine of acknowledging these small probabilities reassures me. Marcus is flying. He's slick—was trained to land on aircraft carriers—but I like to be awake.

"Dispatch says the patient had a stroke," says Niki over the deep exhaling vibration of the wings. The flaps point down, poised to lose speed and altitude.

"Info is from the wife?" I ask.

"Here's what we have," she says, and hands me the run sheet.

A handwritten note, rendered into brown pixels by a fax machine, reads:

Dear Sir/Madam,

Here is a summary of recent events concerning my husband, Franklin, which I hope is helpful. December 3: dizzy, bad headache, then got better. December 4: the hotel doctor came, and Franklin was feeling fine. December 5: so dizzy he couldn't walk, had a worse headache, doctor came, sent him to hospital. Diagnosed with stroke. Then got worse and very confused. December 7: he went to sleep, they said a coma, and a breathing tube was put in. Now they say he's stable but they can't help him.

I look forward to seeing you. Many thanks in advance for your help,

Mrs. Amiel

"This is all we have," I say.

"And you've heard about the airport?" says Niki.

"Closes at 2:30 local. They won't wait for us, huh?"

"Adamant. They close, and we've got to be in the air or we're stuck."

I read the fax again.

"Bet it's a bleed," I say.

"Can't tell from that," says Niki, putting up a palm in protest. "Don't be a jinx."

I actually prefer flight evacuation's lack of information. It means that there are fewer options, and it's all about a simple goal: to collect the patient in Location A and deliver him, alive and hopefully not worse, to Location B. We don't claim to fix anyone, or to know more than we can. Not like at the hospital, where everyone must pretend to know more than everyone else, and no one can mind their own business.

"Doesn't matter, we're going to get him," I say. We descend until we're alongside an elevated Florida overpass. The night is an orange haze of city glow. For a moment, the plane skims through the air at the same height as a transport truck on the freeway, and then we drop to the ground.

Out of the plane. First, to the washroom to pee. We clear American customs as the fuel truck rolls up, warning light flashing. The airport caterer arrives on an electric golf cart with our dinner. Dispatch has ordered us the trays of big, hand-filling sandwiches, and pickles, and coleslaw, and white chocolates in the shape of fighter planes all nestled in a bed of tough, bright green lettuce. Can't eat the stuff—it's like paper, simply live packaging to keep the sandwiches fresh. Our flight number is on the cellophane wrappers, and no one is hungry so we put the trays on the floor in the back.

I'm tempted by the flask. Sip just a little. Better watch it, we'll be there soon. The moment of takeoff puts me to sleep. It's something about being pushed back into the seat by the strong hand of exaggerated gravity.

1:55 EST

Descent into St. Therese, a mountain town. It's a steep landing, and Rafael says to hold on, he's flying by instrument. We bank, circle around to get the right approach, the yellow airstrip lights twinkling in the distance like stars turned upside down.

As we descend, I see a cloud of red light to the right of the plane. It is smoke in luminescent red globes, hot and bright from below. Like the earth cracking, opening, and venting anger.

"Fire," I say to Niki.

"Seventy minutes on the ground," she says, looking out the window. "It won't get to the strip."

Neither of us knows a thing about judging distances from the air, about the influence of wind upon flame, or about forest fires in Guatemala. The glowing red clouds roll like fog over the ground. Our plane drops into a cleft in the earth, and the clouds disappear behind the opaque shoulder of a mountain ridge that blocks the burning forest light as we fall toward the airstrip.

"We're down to seventy?" I ask.

Now the landing lights rush beneath us. There is the roar of slowing, the jolt of wheels on asphalt, and the scale of objects becomes human as if we just woke from a dream. At the end of the taxiway is a brilliant bank of floodlights. We swing around sharply toward it. The ambulance is parked just off from the hangar.

Niki says to Rafael, "Find out about the fire, but not until Dr. Fitzgerald and I are on our way to the hospital."

"We will assess the situation," says Rafael. "We will discuss it if it seems right."

Marcus winks and says, "We're not going to get stuck here, so hurry back, boys and girls."

"Radio if we need to get back fast," I say.

Niki rotates the handle to release the doors, whose halves swing up and down like a jaw. A man in uniform stands next to a man in a cream-coloured shirt that is loose at the waist. The ambulance backs up toward the plane, beeping and flashing.

The man in the ironed cream shirt says, "Dr. Fitzgerald? I am Garcia." Dispatch had given us his name. He is our facilitator. The air is damp with a fine, clear smell of wet leaves. Also, I think, a hint of burned cake. Birds wheel and dive over the plane. Excited, they circle and snap. "You must go quickly. The airport will close soon, and they will turn off the lights," says Garcia, pointing to the orange globes along the airstrip.

"Are they always like this?" I ask as I haul out the heavy drug bag. He looks at me, and I realize the pointlessness of my question. I decide to gesture to the birds, "The birds, are they always like this?"

Garcia repeats my question in Spanish. He and the man in the uniform laugh.

"Amigo," says the man in uniform, "they are bats."

Garcia says, "The insects love airplanes. They swarm around when the jets land and the bats go crazy."

The uniformed man takes our passports. He slips them into his shirt pocket, smiles, and flicks his wrist to wave us on. Instinctively, I fondle my emergency wad of American cash—my security blanket. From where we are on the ground, surrounded by the shadows of mountains, there is no fire. We load our stretcher into the ambulance, then the drug bag, portable monitor, hospital bag, airway bag, vent bag, field radio, Garcia, Niki, and myself. Garcia pulls shut the back door. We jolt as it clatters away, and no one has said a word about the flames.

2:05 EST—St. Therese Hospital

Garcia takes us through the front doors into the dark lobby, where a sleepy security guard looks up from his wooden chair. He swings a flashlight at us, nods, and turns it off. The lobby is high-ceilinged, with curving stairs at one end leading up to a second-floor mezzanine. All of this I glimpse in a single arc of the guard's flashlight.

Our stretcher loaded high with gear bags, we follow Garcia through the front building into the courtyard. Between the buildings are walkways roofed with corrugated tin on vine-covered stilts. Between these paths are swaths of grass, the tips going to seed and waving in the courtyard breeze. We ride up the clanking elevator and trundle down a dim hallway.

Outside the intensive care unit, a woman with peeling shoulders sits cross-legged on the floor. Her two greasy braids of sand-coloured hair hang heavily over a blue flower-print dress. Next to her is a knapsack. It is as if she has been kidnapped from suburbia, and in her captivity she listens to a portable tape player.

"Mrs. Amiel?" I say.

She looks up. "Are you here for Franklin?" she asks. She speaks loudly above the headset.

"We don't have much time. The airport will close," I say.

Mrs. Amiel nods as if this is perfectly natural, that the airport would be on the verge of closing just as we arrive to transport her comatose husband. Niki introduces herself and Garcia. Mrs. Amiel takes off her headset and smiles. She says, "Spanish tapes. I'm trying to learn. There's no hospital tape, though. It's all about ordering beer, and how to describe the colours of dogs."

"We're going to speak to the local doctor and move your husband onto our stretcher," says Niki.

"Everything is in Spanish," she says. "They are kind,

but everything is in Spanish." Her smile is hard and dead, speaking the voice that she is trying to keep sharp.

"Garcia will help us," I say.

Mr. Amiel glows under the lamp at the head of his bed. Another three beds like his are in this room, each a shrine to care surrounded by pumps, poles, tired nurses, and the sleep-deprived Dr. Manolas. Mr. Amiel's blood pressure is 65/45, which is a good pressure for a newborn baby. Temperature is 41.8. Hot. I rub his sternum with my knuckles, and he arches his back very slightly. I squeeze his big toenail between my thumb and my pen, and there is the slightest withdrawal of the right leg. The toenail begins to bruise. Garcia translates for Dr. Manolas, the intensivist: Mr. Amiel had a bradycardic near-arrest the day before and was given atropine. Blood pressure is in his boots, even with the dopamine drip. With the back of my hand, I feel Mr. Amiel's hot, dry skin. His tongue protrudes slightly from his mouth to the side of the taped-in breathing tube. One pupil is bigger than the other, and neither of them wink at my bright flashlight. Probably he's already coning: the brain swells and squeezes itself to death in the back of the skull. The smell of skin as it melts into a hospital bed is a rank scent of jungle decay, slightly sweet. Niki checks the lines and the vent settings.

Garcia translates: Mr. Amiel came into hospital still talking, but too dizzy to walk. He was vomiting from the dizziness and unable to drink. Initially, the CT scan of his head was normal. His nausea was treated and he was given fluids. Over several days he became more sleepy, then confused. Three days ago he became comatose, and was diagnosed clinically as having a hemorrhagic stroke.

"And the subsequent scans?" I ask.

"Unavailable," says Garcia after asking Dr. Manolas. "The scanner has stopped working."

"And the fever—it has been investigated? Urine? Blood cultures?"

Garcia speaks to Dr. Manolas. After talking back and forth, he says, "They say the fever is due to increased pressure in the brain. They placed a device—a Thompson bolt—in his head, but they have removed it because they cannot send it with him." So that's why the head is bandaged.

Dr. Manolas shows me a careful record of Mr. Amiel's intracranial pressure. Big spikes, like cliffs. Too high, too fast.

Through Garcia, I ask Dr. Manolas about details, bits of information framing therapeutic pitfalls that he and I both understand. He is intelligent, well-read, and knows that the treatment has not been as modern as his reading. I make my professional sympathies evident and say that I am impressed with the clarity of the flow sheets in the chart. I ask if there has been consideration of neurosurgery. It took a day to get a neurosurgeon three hundred kilometres away to discuss the case on the phone, says Dr. Manolas, and by that point Mr.

Amiel had already blown a pupil. Also, it is hard to appeal to a neurosurgeon without a recent CT, he says. We do not say it directly, but we talk around the regret of a lost opportunity: the narrow time frame in which an expanding death in the form of a bloody intracranial expansion can perhaps be drained, can sometimes be sucked out like an evil spirit to leave the scintillating brain intact. I say that this is an unfortunate case, and that obviously Dr. Manolas has done everything in his power. He speaks in Spanish, looks at Mr. Amiel and then at me. Garcia says, "Dr. Manolas's heart is broken to see that a man is lost far from home."

In the hallway, where the only light leaks from patients' rooms, I ask Mrs. Amiel whether she understands the situation. "He is physically delicate," I say. I try to continue, to explain specifics. I want to clear my conscience by mentioning the proximity of death.

She interrupts me, saying, "Yes, I know. I completely understand the situation. I understand." She nods quickly. "The insurance company didn't want to fly him. Said there was no point."

"But finally they agreed," says Niki.

"We're still negotiating," says Mrs. Amiel. She must be a kind woman, because *negotiation* is a kind term. "In the meantime, I borrowed the money against our house. I'm glad we own a house."

I know what she's paid, and her ardent triumph at having covered this bill shows that she can't afford it. Used to own a house, I think.

"I'm sure that's what he would want," says Niki.

"It'll be touch and go," I say. I was about to tell her that he may die at any moment, and that even if his physiology stabilizes, he's beyond the point where she'll have her husband back. I can't say that now, because the money issue embarrasses me.

As we bump into the elevator, the gauze pad falls off his right eye. The eyelid falls open in a slit, and the eye stares suddenly at me, showing its sleeping world of white conjunctiva and black pupil. I slide the eyelid shut and retape it. Niki and I watch the lines and monitors as we trundle out of the elevator, down the walkway, toward the courtyard. Dr. Manolas pulls the foot of the stretcher. We've got to get in the air, I think. They haven't radioed. I suppose that everything is fine, but we can't be caught on the ground. There's a fire on the other side of that ridge, I tell myself abstractly, as if it will disappear as soon as we take flight.

2:55 EST

The courtyard has a pungent grass-dew scent. The dark hospital windows around us are empty eye sockets that cannot watch, cannot see the way we now walk lopsided, the straps of the heavy bags pulling at our shoulders. Our patient is belted into the stretcher. Niki walks alongside him and every few seconds she squeezes the firm rubber bag that pumps air into Mr. Amiel's lungs. It is the kind of bag that reinflates on its own, that pops back into its original shape.

As we lift the stretcher into the ambulance, I catch the distant burnt cake smell. Dr. Manolas helps to pull the stretcher up, and a sudden guilt comes over me. Fire burns what it touches. I say to Garcia, "Tell Dr. Manolas that we saw a fire from the plane. He should know, so he can see what needs to be done. There are many patients here."

Garcia seems confused, but speaks to Dr. Manolas in Spanish. Then Garcia says to me, "Dr. Manolas hopes to see you again one day, and would like to visit your country. He asks for your email, and prays that God will keep you safe." Niki is in the ambulance, and I heave the end of the stretcher to push it toward her. Garcia says, "You should give this doctor something, as a courtesy. It will be good for you, if you come back here some day." In the dark, broad leaves slap each other in a random, syncopated rhythm. Niki gestures to the Guatemalan ambulance driver about the way she wants monitors placed, lines hung. I zip open the wallet of company money, pull out fifty dollars and give it to Dr. Manolas. Garcia climbs into the front seat. He talks into the radio, and Niki yells at me to get in. "We must go," says Garcia, "there is little time."

I give Dr. Manolas my card with email address, which follows the money and slips like water into a pocket.

"There is fire close by," I say in English, and make gestures that are meant to represent flame. Doesn't he understand me, if he reads English medical journals?

"Dr. F," calls Niki, "airborne in twenty."

Dr. Manolas laughs and holds out his hand. He must be happy with the money and my email address. Our palms slap together, we shake, and all around us the leaves that I cannot see make a sound similar to our hands meeting. I smell a sugary smoke. Does no one else notice?

"Get in!" says Niki.

Dr. Manolas didn't seem to understand my flame gestures, so I make sounds like burning. Maybe it's better to go. What can he do, even knowing that there's a fire? At that moment, I decide that I have said all I need to say. I jump in, and the door closes with a cheap tin clang. Only once the ambulance rushes down the driveway and lurches up the road do I feel like I have abandoned a friend.

Mrs. Amiel is in the ambulance's fold-down seat. Our equipment bags are piled high beside the stretcher. As we swing around a corner, the heavy red oxygen case falls on Mr. Amiel's legs, and he does not flinch. I pull it off quickly. Mrs. Amiel does not react in any way— her face is as wooden as her husband's legs.

As we drive, she recites her calculations to me. She has weighed the sums and circumstances with forced rationality. In the rhythmic way she tells it, I can see that she has done the arithmetic many times. She says, "I thought to myself, I can fly him out now, and maybe at home he'll have a shot at getting better. Or I can wait here. He's not getting better here, and if he dies I'll have to fly the body home anyways. Insurance doesn't pay for bodies." The insurance company refused to fly him out while he was still talking, because they said he was getting the same care he would get in Canada. He didn't need another CT scan, they told her. Once he was living on machines, they said that they wouldn't fly him out because he was brain dead, and there's no benefit in medevacing a brain-dead man. "They say I could pull the plug and he would never know. The last thing Franklin told me was that he wanted to go home, and I promised him I'd try, so I can't turn off the machines. How long could I stay here, then? No further ahead, sitting here? No way, so I called my bank."

The ambulance dives slightly as it charges into a puddle, and water sprays the windows.

"You were here for a vacation?" says Niki.

"On the motorbike. Two-month trip—the idea was to ride to Argentina. We've been on vacation for two weeks, well, just one I guess. Second week in hospital. He thought we should do it before we had kids. Today I sold the bike for almost nothing."

All around is black, shifting shadow. The ambulance lilts drunkenly in the turns, and I keep my hand on the red oxygen case.

"So, Niki," I say. "Looks like a bleed."

She nods.

There has been no CT scan proving this, but every disease has its rhythm, its dancing sequence of steps and turns that acts as a coded storyteller. The pressure in the head tells it, the pupil of one eye wide, the worsening day upon day, the mention of an episode in which the heart slowed—bradycardia—and almost stopped.

3:15 EST

The last stretch of uphill switchback road. The ambulance tires spin the gravel on the shoulder. As we approach the airport, the gates of the chain-link fence roll to either side. The plane is precisely where we left it, but facing down the runway, and the pilots stand chatting with the driver of the fuel truck. Seeing us, the driver climbs into the tanker. Its upright exhaust pipe shakes as it starts, and he swings it neatly away toward the hangar. Marcus looks our way and taps his watch. We back up to the airplane.

"Are you almost ready?" says Garcia, as we delicately unlock the stretcher bearing Mr. Franklin Amiel and his assortment of lines, tubes, and wires from the ambulance to move him across the few feet to the plane. Some of the airport workers stand around us, in their jackets, holding briefcases. "I don't think they will really close, but are you almost ready?" he says.

"Ten minutes," I say.

Garcia slaps shoulders and jokes with the airport staff. They laugh politely, but in their tiredness they do not appear anxious to make allowances for one plane which has appeared in the night to fly away with one foreigner. Garcia takes our passports from the man with the military cap. Niki and I pause, check the passports in the rear lights of the ambulance, and button them in our pockets. I am now afraid to mention the fire. The night is a cool black, and we seem to be at a moment of delicate balance, a moment when we need to walk the suspended narrow bridge of time and step onto the stable earth on the other side of the chasm with our patient airborne. Around us is darkness, and the shuffle of bats' wings above the plane. I strain at the slight suggestion of smoke.

It's not simple to move a critically ill man. It might seem that it would be like moving a parcel, or shouldering a big, warm duffle bag. But it's not, because the tubes and lines splay from every orifice, drape the sides of the stretcher, threaten constantly to be kinked and cut off or tugged out of position. The functions of moving air, of regulating fluid, of voiding urine, which a healthy man keeps secret and neat within closed skin and barely refers to while going through life occupied with desire and philosophy, become visible external concerns. How much urine output? What are the lungs' tidal volumes? Niki has her hand on the endotracheal tube as we slide him forward. I watch it also, for this is the crucial tube that breathes. We move Mr. Amiel slowly, pull the front of the stretcher out, allow its folding legs to reach down and touch the ground. Slowly, forward, now the rear legs of the stretcher fold down. Rolling, easy, and now in the corner of my eye there is a line too straight, plastic pulled tight.

"Stop! Stop!" I yell.

One straight strand of plastic is caught on the hinge of the ambulance door, pulled tight, and then it falls slack and it's already too late. Just like that. The central line is pulled out. Its flexible blue plastic tip lies naked on the ground. A dribble of saline fluid wets the tarmac.

"We've still got a peripheral line. Let's fly," I say.

"We need a second line," says Niki.

"The time," I say. But she's right. It's too risky to fly with just one peripheral line. We've got to put in another, but I'm afraid of the delay because we don't know anything about Guatemalan airport workers, or about fires. Certainly, we can't tell them now about the flames. As soon as we're in the air, we'll radio about the fire. I tell Garcia that we need a few minutes, and he speaks like a jovial salesman to the airport workers. Their expressions do not change, but they also do not move. Niki flicks Mr. Amiel's puffy wrist and swollen arm, looking for a vein.

After four IV stabs into the putty-like flesh of the right arm, it is by some kind of divination that Niki establishes a second intravenous line. I see the air traffic controller's silhouette in the tower and am relieved. Now that we are ten minutes past their closing time, I feel confident that they will stay until we have taken off. Also, I have not yet paid the airport fees. Carefully, as if shifting a bomb, we move forward again into the jet. Done.

The air is fresh and full. It is the breath of jungle, of fetid water, and of breathing leaves. We secure the monitors and pumps to the wall of the plane. I am happy that our patient is on board, that the airport is still open beyond its closing time, and for the live wet soil exhaling into the night. Above the plane, bats wheel and strike. Their soft wings make blowing sounds as they sting and grab at insects. If a bat or bird is sucked into a jet engine, it destroys the turbine and cripples the plane, but somehow this rarely happens. The Lear 35, bright in the centre of the taxiway lights, is an apparition in the night. Someone imagined it into existence on the tarmac. Other planes are parked alongside, surrendered to the sleepy shadows. A strand of burnt sugar smell. I grip the tension of near-gratification, of being about to reach success, and remind myself that once we are in the air we will radio them about the fire. It will be as if we just spotted it on takeoff.

Garcia gives me an invoice on semi-transparent paper—the airport, the ambulance, himself: six hundred and ninety American dollars. I give him eight hundred, and tell him to thank the airport staff. I shout, "*Gracias*," and wave to them. This is my only word in eight languages. I pull the doors of the plane closed, and activate the seals that whirr like a spinning drill. Mrs. Amiel is in the back seat, and she has dropped her smile. Perhaps now that she is in the plane with her husband, now that she has paid the ticket and the voyage is under way, she is freed from her hard-smiling imperative of forward motion. The progress will no longer hinge upon the force of her will. It will be up to jet engines in the night, and she can release this bird of horror, open her hands and allow it to fly up like a dark ghost.

Niki and I buckle into the narrow single seats beside the stretcher. The jets whine. I'm sitting behind Niki, who is closer to the cockpit. I lean forward and say, "Niki, it is a bleed."

"You said that already."

"Did you see his pressure spikes?" I say and tap my head. "He's tight as a drum."

She leans toward the cockpit to speak to the pilots, so that they can hear through their headsets. I wonder if Mrs. Amiel can hear from the back.

"Can you climb slowly?" asks Niki.

"Mountains all around us," says Rafael.

"Can you pressurize the cabin to sea level?" she says. "It would be better."

"We've got to get altitude fast," says Marcus, flipping switches as the jets rise in pitch.

Niki turns, looks at me.

I shrug.

There are mountains.

She faces forward, and there's not much more to say.

Maybe we will be lucky. Relative to the cabin pressure dropping, the pressure in Mr. Amiel's head will rise. We fly with bleeds, and usually we are lucky. The roar begins with a jet kick, the nose of the plane heaves, the wings make an urgent commitment to the air, and now we're up, flung into the dark. Ten seconds, fifteen.

Niki and I watch the cardiac monitor: a PVC, then normal sinus.

I'm tipped backwards in my seat, and as I turn to the window the runway lights flicker off. We're alone in the night.

We watch: normal sinus. Good.

My ears fill. I swallow, make myself yawn, ears pop open and now the airplane screams—full throttle taking us higher.

On the monitor: several PVCs, a run of bigeminy.

"Can you level off?" I call out to the cockpit.

"We're not clear yet," shouts Marcus.

Out the window, I glimpse the red bursting cloud on the ground, spreading heat beneath us, its flames licking leaves, fanning the guilt of my silence.

The monitor: a slow, wide rhythm like the teeth of a saw.

My hand on his wrist: no pulse.

The monitor: still that wide, slow rhythm like television static.

My hand shoved into his groin: pulseless.

The monitor: a jitter of movement, no more.

"Start compressing," I say to Niki.

The Lear is still nose up, and everything is tilted back. I release my belt and reach uphill for the cardiac arrest drug box. Niki is out of her seat, standing with her feet wide, her torso curled in the short cockpit to pound Mr. Amiel's chest.

"So there you go," she says to me as if it's my fault.

We know the story, this twist. Just as Dr. Manolas and I talked around the loss of therapeutic opportunity, Niki and I know this plot without saying it. The bridge of air rescue can lead to this cliff. My ears are tight again. I swallow, they clear. The swelling in the narrow back compartment of Mr. Amiel's head grows as the cabin pressure drops. It squeezes the brain stem, which protests that this will be the last abuse, that its last remaining functioning cells will join their dead companions, and now in their swollen growth they tell the heart to stop. The heart says, Fine! Leave me be, for I too will die now.

I climb downhill to the back of the plane. The compartment of the Lear is twelve feet long, and I tell Mrs. Amiel that her husband, six feet away, is having a cardiac arrest. Prospects are poor. Does she want us to proceed?

"Go ahead, try for a while," she says. "I understand the situation. Really, I completely understand the situation. I did my crying before you arrived."

I say that we will try for twenty or thirty minutes, and return to Mr. Amiel and Niki. CPR. Three epi. Two atropine, Mannitol, D50, bicarb. We take turns compressing, and it aches the upper back to compress in the Lear. We are acting. I am glad for the second IV, because the first one blows after two minutes, and it would be a sorry act if we were injecting drugs into a single blown IV. After twenty minutes I wonder if it looks obvious that we are simply playing our roles. He has no pulse, no rhythm, but we administer the drugs anyway because I said we would try for twenty or thirty minutes. Mrs. Amiel is six feet away, and she has done everything she promised her dying husband.

At twenty minutes I look back at her, and she waves her hands in front of herself like an umpire calling "Safe!"

"No more," she says.

"There's no chance remaining," I say. Sweat runs under my flight suit.

"Stop," she says.

I go to the front of the plane and say, "Okay, let's call it."

Niki stops compressing, and removing this action reveals that Mr. Amiel has been completely inert all this time. The monitor shows a straight, true line.

"We levelled off ten minutes ago," says Marcus. "Didn't tell you. We didn't want to interrupt you."

"Thank you," I say. "Thank you, everyone."

We pull the sheet over his torso, package him neatly, and I move to pull it over his face.

Niki stops me. "Ask her if she wants the face covered. Some people don't."

I go to the back. "I'm sorry for your loss," I say. "Would you like to spend a quiet moment with him?"

"I said my goodbyes already. Days ago," says Mrs. Amiel. Her face is collapsed, but also more relaxed, as if relieved that the anticipated grieving is upon her.

"Do you prefer we cover the face, or not?" I ask.

"It's up to you," she says. "Do what's best."

We have been flying for just over thirty minutes. The Lear does .77 Mach, but the pilots have kept as low as they can, which means flying slower. How far are we from St. Therese? I have no concept of the distance now that we are in our throbbing, hurtling bird of night. We are over the Caribbean. At this moment I remember those burning clouds, that smell like sweet coal embers lighting the jungle floor. I clamber to the cockpit.

"Can you still radio St. Therese?" I ask.

"They're down for the night," says Marcus.

"We have to tell them about the forest fire," I say.

"What forest fire?" says Rafael.

"Don't you remember? We saw it from the air. I didn't want to say anything on the ground." I imagine the flames undulating, spreading, coursing down the hills to the homes of the airport staff with their shares of the American-denomination tip. I feel sick with the sudden panic of guilt, for hurtling past this information in order to get this one patient, and myself, onto this plane. Could Rafael have forgotten? I think of Dr. Manolas and his courtyard hospital, his Thompson bolt and my business card in his pocket. What will they do if the flames come to them? They have no Lear jet. I say to Rafael, "Over that ridge, we saw the fire."

"Oh yes," he says without looking back at me. "We asked them while you were at the hospital. They're burning the sugar cane for harvest."

The smouldering clouds, the sweet hint of an odour drifting into the hospital courtyard. Rafael had almost forgotten this agricultural observation, this detail, until I had asked.

"That fire, it's deliberate?" I say.

"They burn the leaves to process the cane," says Marcus. "A controlled burn. Think of that, when you put sugar in your coffee."

"Controlled burn. Remarkable," I say.

I pull the sheet over Mr. Amiel's face, so now it's just the three of us in the cabin. I sit down, my seat near Mr. Amiel's feet. The sky is a deep blank hole, and within it I see our wingtip lights blinking. I have a restful awareness that Mr. Amiel is officially dead, that we have completed our obligation to the living.

After some time, it strikes me that we are in an airplane. It is night. We have gained altitude and are cruising fast. A bouquet of lights appears in the window—must be Havana. I'm thirsty. This thirst is like the day after a long-distance argument on the telephone with an old friend, when you realize that he is still on the other side of the telephone line, and that what you were fighting about was what you always disagreed about but were never able to say, and you wish that he lived around the corner so you could go out together for a drink. It is that thirst. We are on an airplane with a wife, with a deceased husband, and if we vanished in the sky, then at least for a little while no one would notice.

We haven't touched the catering trays from Tampa. I go to the back of the plane where the trays sit next

to Mrs. Amiel. "There's lots of food. Are you hungry?"
I ask.

"No appetite for days."

"Maybe you should eat. Some crackers?" I say. I
might be a doctor or a flight attendant.

"I can't," she says. Her blue eyes have flecks of
brown in the iris.

Whether to look away now, or in a moment from
now? There is this balance of professing humanity
without invading privacy. Should I keep eye contact for
another few seconds, or turn away? I nod slightly. I turn
away, crouched in the short cabin. I take a food tray. It
has one violet and white orchid under the cellophane,
nestled into the jungle of olives and vegetable sticks.
They breed these flowers to be tough and unwilting.

"Dr. Fitzgerald," she says.

"Yes," I say, turn.

"What do you think of . . . I guess I mean, of how
everything happened."

"Mrs. Amiel, I'm very sorry. This is a terrible thing."
I kneel in front of her in the back of the plane. The
only options are to crouch half-bent or to kneel. "This
kind of stroke could have happened anywhere. Just as
easily in Toronto."

"And if it had happened in Toronto?" she says. "I guess
I'm wondering if things would have gone differently."

"That hospital in St. Therese may be less fancy
than one at home, but I looked at the records and discussed the case in detail with Dr. Manolas," I say. I

look at the brown flecks in Mrs. Amiel's eyes. Without a moment's hesitation and with the greatest tenderness I have within me, I lie. I say, "I think that your husband got the crucial treatments he could have received at home. Sure, they didn't have all of the tests and scans, but he got all the main things that could have given him a chance."

Lies are about belief, about a reality suspended because we want to believe the lie. Both the teller and the recipient must trust each other for everything to hang together. I sense this trust between us and say, "You did everything you could do. So did we. Your husband could have died just as easily in Toronto. I am truly sorry for your loss."

7:30 EST—Tampa

This new rising sun is a second afternoon, since we didn't sleep last night. Rays of light shatter over the elevated expressway, which curls around the airport. Cars flash past the sun like an inverted strobe light—a strobe shadow. We've been on the ground for an hour, and lenses of clean, clear dew appear on the metal skin of the plane.

It's illegal to transport a dead body without the proper documentation.

Permits are needed.

We needed to make a fuel stop in Florida. Niki wanted to connect the ventilator when we got there and just ignore the fact that Mr. Amiel had died. Fuel up, keep on going, and arrive in Canada. She explained this to Mrs. Amiel, who nodded, wordless. Dispatch in Calgary wouldn't go for it. Once they knew that the patient had died, I guess there's no way they could allow it. In accordance with FAA regulations, we have declared that the patient is dead.

The morning stretches into flat, hot light. The Aviation Authority men meet us in a pickup truck. The constable from the sheriff's office arrives wearing tan polyester pants with a holster slung against his hip. The coroner's workers pull up in their van. The FBI agent looks like an out-of-work corporate lawyer. Jiggling belly, crisp tie, and expensive sunglasses. They take statements. They speak to Mrs. Amiel quietly, with sympathy, but there are questions to ask, and yes, there's one more person who wishes to speak to her. Each time I give a statement, I point out how much Mrs. Amiel has been through, and how much it would help her if we could fly home with her deceased husband. There are regulations, they say, that must be followed.

The coroner's workers take the body to the coroner's office, where it will be decided whether to release it or to perform an autopsy.

Some fuel stop.

19:15 EST—Place de Ville suites, Bahamas
Marcus, Rafael, Niki, and I are in a hot tub. The pilots are timed out. No more flying until they rest.

More regulations, and these ones I appreciate. From here, we can see the beach in its round sunset light as we sit in the hot, swirling water.

We said goodbye to Mrs. Amiel in Tampa. Her insurance firm and our flight company haggled back and forth on the phone, and made a deal with her. Something to do with money, such that it was better for her to get a commercial flight home. No point in our medical jet flying her back to Toronto. Dispatch said that we would pick up a passenger in Cuba, and should wait in the Bahamas. The embargo prohibits flying from Florida to Cuba, so we had to go via the Bahamas. After clearing customs in the Bahamas, dispatch told us that the Cuba flight was off, but we should sit tight. They would look for another paying run. I was happy that the pilots were timed out and we could rest. At the hotel, I finished off my flask, and slept through the afternoon under a big, whipping fan with no hesitation, and no dreams. Now, in the bubbling tub, the evening half-light is like a strange illusion. New plan, we've heard. Tomorrow, we fly for Chile.

We drink mojitos in the hot tub. The hotel girl brings a fresh round and says, proudly, that they grow the limes and the mint here, on the grounds.

"And the rum?" asks Marcus.

"That comes from sugar cane," says the girl.

Rafael makes a sound like fire and laughs at me. We read out loud from a pocketbook that Niki always brings. The book has three hundred pages. Each page is numbered with large italicized numerals, and on each page there is a question. As we go around, every person chooses a number and then must answer the corresponding question.

Rafael chooses number 168.

Niki reads, "If you had a choice between being famous and destitute, or rich and anonymous, what would you choose?"

Rafael says, "Wealth. Filthy loads of it."

"And you can't buy the fame," says Marcus. "It's an either-or question."

"That's fine. I would be rich. People hate the famous, and the rich. The best situation is to be rich and unknown. When you need help, not one person will help a famous, destitute man."

"I would choose the fame," says Marcus. "Then you live beyond your death, and the famous always manage to live off others anyhow. Who cares if you leave bad debts? Immortality has no price."

I drain my glass. Mint in my nostrils. The lime and sugar are emeralds melting the ice cubes.

Marcus chooses 207.

Niki reads, "You are offered the chance to live every possible dream in one year. In that year, you will do everything you ever desired, fulfill every fantasy you ever had. You will be completely happy and satisfied. When that year is over, you will die a quick and painless death. Would you take this offer, or would you instead decide to keep on living your life as it is now?"

"This is a trick question," says Marcus. "This is really a question about how happy you are right now."

"But what's your answer?" says Rafael.

"I refuse to answer trick questions," says Marcus.

Niki boos.

"All right. I choose my own life, because I expect to fulfill all my desires in this life and live to be healthy and old. I'd like to stretch it out. Why all in one year?"

It is my turn. I choose page 40.

Niki reads, "Your spouse goes on a business trip far away, and has an affair. The person is someone your spouse will never see again, and this affair will never affect you in any way. Would you want to know about it?"

"Is ignorance bliss?" I say.

"Don't dance around it," says Niki.

"Whether I would want to know depends on a lot of things. Did my spouse seduce the other person, or was she seduced? Maybe it was one of those drunken things that happens. Is my spouse apologetic in telling me, or triumphant? All these things would affect my answer." I am unmarried, so I feel comfortable speculating.

"Drunken things that happen, you say," says Rafael. "Then you allow that these things happen."

"Of course they do. I saw a survey," I say. "Half of men, a third of women."

The bubbles have stopped, and the palm leaves above us make the sound of dry hands rubbing slowly together. Marcus pushes the button on the side of the tub, which makes it erupt again. The forceful thumbs of air press the small of my back—that muscle pain which is about to melt into relaxation.

"How do they get those numbers? Who would tell some pollster about themselves cheating?" asks Niki.

"It's the relief of confession," I say. "Secrets are difficult, heavy. So one day, you're making an omelette, or driving to work. Your phone rings and some anonymous person wants to know if you've had an affair. Of course you tell them. You've been waiting to tell someone for years."

"So what's your answer?" says Niki.

I say, "I don't want to know. How could I ever trust my wife again, if I knew?"

Marcus shakes his glass. Ice. He looks around for the girl who makes the drinks.

"It's about knowing," says Niki. Then she says to me, "But what if you had an affair, or did some horrible thing? Would you tell your wife?"

"Probably. I'd want to come clean. I couldn't carry around that secret."

"That's unfair. You wouldn't want your wife to tell you, but you would tell her."

"That's not the question in the book," I say.

21:55 EST

I am about to fall asleep in the hot tub. Too tired to stand. The pilots have gone already. It's just Niki and me. We're pretty far gone, but we can sleep tomorrow while the pilots fly. It is night, and I love the damp cool fingers of Caribbean evening on my face.

After a long silence, Niki says, "That woman, Amiel, she told me you said her husband got everything that could have saved him. She was glad to know that much."

"I couldn't say anything else."

"That's the right thing to say," says Niki. "Nothing else needed."

"You think?"

"Isn't that what you would want to hear?"

"Absolutely."

I drain my glass, and the sweet mint clears my eyes, my vision. Soon we will have to stand up into the breezy sea air, be chilled for a moment, make our way to our hotel rooms with their hypnotic fans, and rest for tomorrow's flight.

CONTACT TRACING

—
—
—

November 16, 2002 (from the files of the World Health Organization)

First known case of atypical pneumonia occurs in Foshan City, Guangdong Province, China, but is not identified until much later.

February 10, 2003 (from the files of the World Health Organization)

The WHO Beijing office receives an email message describing a "strange contagious disease" that has "already left more that one hundred people dead" in Guangdong Province in the space of one week. The message further describes "a 'panic' attitude, where people are emptying pharmaceutical stocks of any medicine they think may protect them."

Dr. Fitzgerald still had his watch, so on the second day of his admission he timed it. Through the glass, he could see when someone was coming, and it took them a little while to get in to him. Anyone who needed to come into Fitzgerald's respiratory isolation room had to don a second N95 mask over the one that was already pressing a red welt into their face, a clear face shield, a second hairnet, a first pair of gloves, then an isolation gown over the one they were already wearing, then a second pair of gloves, then a second layer of shoe covers. Then they would wave to Fitzgerald to make sure that he was wearing his mask securely before coming in. But this preparation time didn't count. Fitzgerald timed the minutes of human contact starting when the person entered the room, and ending when the person left. Usually, it was one of the nurses. Dr. Zenkie saw him once each day.

They addressed him as Dr. Fitzgerald even though he had become a patient. When he was alone in the room, he didn't want them to call him doctor, because it somehow implied that he should be partly floating above this illness and yet have some control over it. These were the obligations attached to the word, which he had no energy or ability to live up to. Each time he saw a nurse begin her ritual preparations to enter the isolation room, he decided that he would ask her to not call him doctor. However, once she entered and addressed him in this way, he could not ask her to call him anything else. With someone else in the room, he became scared to give up his title, this dark-cloaked word. Suddenly, this label which felt taunting and futile when he was alone became, with someone else present, his best and last and only piece of clothing which, despite its flaws, could hardly be discarded— except for this he was now naked, stuck in this isolation room that was always humming with its dedicated ventilation fans. What would he be if not a doctor? His self before becoming a physician seemed like a half-remembered, dreamed version of himself, a persona that was impossible to resume in his present life. Although he longed to shed the medical shell when he was alone, it was frightening to try to remember how to be anything else in the presence of others.

They took his vitals, and checked his intravenous line. The fever clawed at his skin and he gripped the armrests of the chair to control the shaking while the nurse took his blood pressure. The nurses brought the food as well, so the attendants wouldn't be exposed. Then they left. Seven minutes, was what he timed each day. Seven minutes of human contact in twenty-four hours. Between these minutes, Fitz kept the television on. The same clips played again and again, and encouraged time to evaporate. Each day, the numbers on the television mounted. One hundred and sixty-seven cases worldwide. Eight in Toronto. Thousands quarantined, and now the horrible, fascinating spectacle of new cases blooming, spreading, the numbers bursting bright on maps like dandelions on a mowed lawn after the rain.

March 15, 2003 (from the files of the World Health Organization)

"This syndrome, SARS, is now a worldwide health threat," said Dr. Gro Harlem Brundtland, Director-General of the World Health Organization. "The world needs to work together to find its cause, cure the sick, and stop its spread."

(Initial consultation note of Dr. R. Zenkie, FRCPC, dated March 15, 2003—excerpted from chart with permission of Toronto South General Hospital)

ID: Dr. Fitzgerald, 29 years old
OCC: Flight evacuation physician
CC: Cough, fever
Dear Dr. Chen,
Thank you for this consultation. Dr. Fitzgerald is a previously healthy young man who saw you in the emergency department on March 10 with four days of fever, progressively worsening dry cough, diffuse myalgias, and occasional rigours. I agree with your impression at that time that the chest X-ray appeared typical of an

atypical pneumonia. You prescribed a course of azithromycin and advised Dr. Fitzgerald to rest at home. In the following days, Dr. Fitzgerald became progressively more short of breath and noted his own tachypnea at rest.

It has since become apparent that a patient whom Dr. Fitzgerald transported from Shenzhen, China, to Vancouver, Canada, has died of pneumonia and DIC at the Oceanside Community Hospital and that Dr. Fitzgerald likely contracted his illness, which we suspect to be SARS, from this patient. Dr. Fitzgerald was seen again in the emergency department on March 14 by yourself, and then by myself at your request. Isolation and respiratory precautions were implemented.

Initial physical examination revealed a muscular young man with a good oxygen saturation of 95 percent on 4 litres nasal prongs, however with an O_2Sat of 88 percent on room air. Mild tachypnea, fine inspiratory crackles noted throughout all lung fields, with mild indrawing and accessory muscle use. Chest X-ray reveals diffuse patchy densities and air bronchograms suggestive of widespread consolidation.

We have admitted Dr. Fitzgerald into a negative pressure isolation room. He has developed a coarse tremor. We have continued the azithromycin, have added ceftriaxone, acyclovir, ribavirin, as well as a pulse course of solumedrol. This broad regimen will be continued until there are any developments concerning the appropriate treatment of SARS. Dr. Fitzgerald's clinical condition has *worsened, and today he requires 10 litres of O_2 by face mask in order to maintain an O_2Sat of 91 percent. He is somewhat anxious. Having said that, he is a robust young man who will hopefully improve, although his thoughts have become rather morbid. His coarse and bothersome tremor is not in keeping with the SARS picture that other centres are reporting. There are no focal deficits. Tracing and quarantine of Dr. Fitzgerald's contacts is being undertaken by the Department of Public Health. Several of his contacts have already been hospitalized.*

Thank you for involving me in this timely and interesting case. I will continue to copy you on the chart notes, although you will likely not receive these reports until you have completed your own quarantine period.

Yours truly, Dr. R. Zenkie, FRCPC

Consultant in Infectious Diseases, Toronto South General Hospital

When Fitzgerald was admitted, Chen was quarantined as an unprotected contact. Fitz asked Zenkie about his flight crew. All quarantined, afebrile, except Niki, who had been in the cabin with him and the patient who was now Canada's first SARS fatality. Niki was admitted at Holy Mercy, and requiring an FiO_2 of a hundred percent. It had been a routine patient transfer—Shenzhen to Vancouver. Pneumonia and sepsis. Now the patient was dead, which was also not outside routine, but what was new was that they were sick, they had made others sick, and the whole world was now holding its breath while learning this new word, SARS.

Dr. Zenkie puzzled over Fitzgerald's tremor. This was not part of what most centres were reporting, but of course no one could say what to expect. Fitzgerald knew this shakiness. When he had gotten the fever and cough, he had figured he would blur away the time with some single malt. Probably a viral pneumonia, he and Chen had figured, but best to start the azithro just in case.

For the most part, he had kept the alcohol just below the surface—a quick shot in the back of the plane, one or maybe two with a meal, a glass of comfort before sleeping in the hotel rooms that looked the same all over the world. It was always there, but he told himself that he was disciplined about it. He paced and timed himself to the next one, and figured that as a flight doc he passed the effects off as being dazed from the time change and sleep deprivation. That and breath mints. Niki must know, of course, but Fitzgerald believed that when the tight spot came in a flight, he was up for it and sharp.

Apart from the rationed nips, the binges called him like old friends who were impossible to outgrow, who wanted to visit him on his days off. He would sink down through the first four or five that made him feel right, then swim into the next few rounds where there was a peaceful warm slowness, and then the weight of it would pull him to the bottom of the bottle where it was just one after another, automatic as if the drinking itself would be enough. Enough for what? Enough.

This time, though, the breathing bothered him. When he drank to the point where he usually felt soft and floating, instead the numb edges were fringed with a panic. One night he dreamed that he was in the Lear jet with Ming. She was the patient, but she opened her duffle bag to reveal a newborn child. The baby was blue, floppy, and she threw it at Fitzgerald. It was a girl, mottled and cold, limbs draped down from the naked torso which he cradled. He said, "You're the baby doctor." Ming said, "I just deliver them. The rest is your game." Then she went to the front of the plane to chat with the pilots. Fitzgerald began mouth-to-mouth and chest compressions. On the infant, the mouth-to-mouth was little breaths puffing out a single birthday candle, the CPR was a tap-tap-tapping on the chest, as if using a manual typewriter. Tap tap. Firm. Not too hard or fast—lest the spindly metal arms with the letters on their tips become jammed. The plane dropped—a weightless moment—air pocket? Turbulence? Then a hiss, and the oxygen masks dangled from the ceiling. Fitzgerald tried to hold a mask to his face and deliver rescue breaths to the limp baby. Breathe the mask, puff the baby, but he couldn't keep it up. Too much switching, fumbling, he needed both hands to hold the baby, but one hand to grab the mask and one hand for compression. He was faint, vision clouded. Ming and the pilots chatted casually, their masks strapped to their faces. Fitz would have to stop breathing for the baby, just suck on a mask himself. At this point, when he had decided to abandon the child but had not yet given up the baby to hold his face to the mask, Fitzgerald woke—shaking, gasping. Drank from the bottle next to his bed.

It was perhaps because he was drunk that he waited a couple more days to return to hospital. By March 14, the sparks of plague headlined news broadcasts. Public Health phoned, left messages. Fitzgerald listened to all eleven urgent voice mails that exhorted him to check his temperature, to call Public Health, to report to hospital if he had a fever or any respiratory symptoms. A man in an isolation mask came to the apartment building, and on the short-circuit monitor Fitzgerald watched him stand in the lobby, buzz Fitzgerald's apartment, pull on latex gloves. Fitzgerald didn't answer. He was drowning in lung fluids and tried to flush this away with alcohol, but even when the alcohol began to recede his lungs were still filling from illness, so he returned to the hospital. Chen was on duty, again.

And now the withdrawal. Of course, Fitzgerald had his own diazepam stash at home for the shakes, but he hadn't brought them with him to hospital. It didn't hurt anyone, he told himself, and he only "treated himself to a session" when he had some time off, and then weaned himself to that "cool place" before he was scheduled to fly again. Now he wished he had brought a bottle, never mind diazepam.

—

(Initial consultation note of Dr. R. Zenkie, FRCPC, dated March 18, 2003—excerpted from chart with permission of Toronto South General Hospital)

ID: Dr. Chen, 31 years old

OCC: Emergency physician

CC: Shortness of breath, fever

Dear Dr. Chen,

Thank you for this consultation. As you know, you developed a fever and some mild shortness of breath on March 17, which was the third day of your quarantine after contact with a probable SARS patient, Dr. Fitzgerald. You alerted me and, after we discussed the matter on the phone, you presented to the hospital (travelling appropriately with an N95 mask in a private vehicle) and were admitted directly into a respiratory isolation room. At present, I note that you have only mild shortness of breath not requiring supplementary oxygen. Your X-ray findings demonstrate diffuse infiltrates consistent with an early case of SARS. You are otherwise healthy. Ceftriaxone, azithromycin, acyclovir, ribavirin, and solumedrol have been initiated. Since we agreed that no other physician should be exposed by becoming involved in your care, I will address you in the consultation notes.

Contact tracing is being carried out by the Department of Public Health. Thank you for another interesting consultation, although I regret that you have now come under my care. As per your request I will ensure that your wife,

Dr. Ming, who is currently under quarantine, receives copies of the medical record.

Yours truly, Dr. R. Zenkie, FRCPC

Consultant in Infectious Diseases, Toronto South General Hospital

At quarter to midnight, Dr. Chen was admitted to the respiratory isolation room adjacent to Dr. Fitzgerald's. These rooms were fishbowls, walled with glass and humming with the fans that created a negative pressure environment, sucked the air out to be filtered. Each of the rooms had a television and a phone. From inside the room, the occupant could see nurses and doctors passing in the hallway, appearing and disappearing with the casual nerve of those who had not been imprisoned. There were curtains that could be drawn on the inside, but the cardiac and saturation monitors that trailed wires from Chen and Fitzgerald's bodies were always watching them, a peephole even with the curtains drawn. Fitzgerald wrote the extension number of his phone on a piece of paper and held it up to the glass. Chen called him.

"Sorry," said Fitz. "I gave you this SARS thing."

Chen said, "It's an infection. It's not you."

"Did you give it to anyone?" Fitzgerald knew that Ming and Chen had married a year ago, that they were now Mr. and Mrs. Chen, although she still used Dr. Ming. "You still single, or what?"

"My wife's in quarantine. Afebrile, though. She's

been on call a lot this week so we haven't seen each other much. Maybe for the best . . . considering."

"Right."

"It's late," said Chen. He looked up at the curtains.

"Sure. Hey, what's your phone extension? We can catch up."

Fitzgerald realized that there was a time when he would have simultaneously wanted Ming to have contracted this illness and yet given anything for her to be healthy. Now this was all far away, dull and subject to illumination by the impartial swinging spotlight of infectious illness. He was glad that Chen was here, a familiar face.

The next morning, Fitz turned up his oxygen to fifteen litres per minute. He watched TV. SARS was now in Canada, Germany, Taiwan, China, Thailand, Hong Kong, Vietnam, and Singapore. The numbers seemed to grow by multiplication instead of addition. The cloud of humidified oxygen that blew into his face left him breathless, and through the glass he saw Chen talking on the phone. He talked for a long time. Hung up. Looked like a man who was adapting to being a fish in a tank. Seven minutes, Fitz thought. The windows of this ward looked over the back of the hospital where there was now a tent, and a line of hospital staff waiting to be screened for entry. As if the hospital was worth lining up for. The nurse who brought lunch (forty-five seconds) was one he had not met before,

Dolores. Her eyes were red. She told Fitz that this was no longer a regular ward, that it was the new SARS unit, to which nurses had been assigned by lottery.

Earlier that day, Dolores had sat down in the cafeteria for the second SARS Strategic Meeting among a masked, garish army of yellow and blue isolation gowns. None of the Toronto South General nurses knew that there would be a lottery. The creation of a dedicated SARS unit was explained by the administrator who wore a grey dress and a mask. It would be simple. All of the ward nurses had to be entered in the lottery. If someone didn't want to be in the draw, there was a sheet of paper they could sign, said the administrator. If you signed this paper, you were out of the lottery but you also forfeited recognition of your seniority. Seniority was what nurses built over a career, what entitled them to a better choice of shifts, to the first pick of holidays, to be the last one laid off in a spasm of restructuring, what made a nurse somebody. A masked union rep sat next to the administrator, nothing else for her to say. If you signed the paper, you had to leave the room. You weren't fired, but would possibly be reassigned, depending on what was required after the results of the lottery.

Some who had recently graduated from nursing school got up quickly, signed the paper, and were gone. They didn't have much seniority, and some had small children. One nurse stood and asked if they could exercise their retirement instead of signing the paper. The union rep looked like she was about to answer, but then turned to the administrator instead. The two of them murmured mask to mask. The union rep stood and said, "This situation does not annul any previously determined benefits."

The union rep and the administrator conferred, and produced another sheet of paper for nurses who wanted to exercise their retirement. Another small number stood one by one to sign. They looked at their colleagues, but because of the masks could not tell whether the glances were farewell smiles, gazes of consolation, or eyes met as a warning. Most of the nurses who signed the second sheet of paper had been at the hospital since before many of the younger nurses were born. One had actually delivered one of the junior nurses because the doctor couldn't get there in time.

Dolores kept her seat. Her divorce settlement had only just been completed. There were the three kids, the second mortgage, and the twelve years of seniority which were too many to throw away. In one box were everyone's names. In another box were yellow and red tags. One by one, the union rep drew a name, the administrator drew a tag, stapled the name to the tag. The red tags meant the SARS unit. Dolores's name was drawn, and then out came a red tag.

Afterwards, those with yellow tags tried to suppress the relief and laughter of a near miss, embarrassed at their good fortune while standing amid those who held red tags. Those who had been selected for the SARS unit only met the eyes of others who held the same colour tag. Some cried openly, or left the room to do so. One woman with a yellow tag offered it to her friend who had a red one, and who was just back from her honeymoon, but the trade was refused. Grief and trauma counsellors were available in the next room, said the union rep over the murmur. No one offered Dolores a trade. Management left the room once the lottery was completed.

March 18, 2003 (from the files of the World Health Organization)

Data indicate that the overwhelming majority of cases occur in health care workers, their family members, and others having close face-to-face contact with patients . . .

After lunch, and the noontime vitals and IV replacements (two minutes, fifteen seconds), Fitzgerald called Chen. Through the glass, they could see each other's monitors. Chen had been on the phone all morning with Ming and his family members. Fitzgerald had been flipping between news channels. They compared and discussed their vital signs, which were all abnormal. Chen said, "You remember Sri's funeral?"

"Sure. Everyone was there—even though it was the day before the royal college exams."

"Ming and I were talking about it. One day he felt a little itchy, thought his eyes looked a bit yellow. Did you know he had me order the labs? Dead within a year. It was astounding."

"Pancreatic cancer," said Fitz. "Nasty."

"Did you know that Sri once made eggs Benedict for a patient?"

"Eggs Benedict?"

"You know, poached eggs with that lemony sauce."

"Must have been a good cook."

"We were juniors, and Sri had this patient, Mr. Olaf. Cannonball lesions all over his lungs, brain mets, all his family dead in Sweden. He had written a will on lined paper, that his clothes and books should go to his land-lady. Olaf had no visitors, and I remember Sri saying how sad it was that he was all alone. He was always smiling, though, reading his Swedish Bible, and the chaplain came every day. So one day we're rounding, and Mr. Olaf has this look . . . as if he's figured out some amazing thing. You can tell he's just bursting to tell us what he's thought of, and right in the middle of our rounds he picks up and says, 'Doctors, excuse me, sirs, but may it be possible to kindly arrange for me to partake in some eggs Benedict? Perhaps with bacon?'

"The staff guy was Arnold. He writes an order in the chart: EGGS BENEDICT. Later that day, we're in a fam-ily conference and Sri gets paged. He goes off, comes back, says that the nurses are upset at the order, saying it's an inappropriate order to put in a medical chart, yada yada yada, and who do the doctors think the nurses are, anyhow, personal chefs? Later, Sri calls the kitchen himself and asks them if they make eggs Benedict. He finds a cook who says he can make it, but that he doesn't think he's allowed to deviate from the regular menu. Sri calls again. He finds some other guy who says he'd be happy to make anything, but he doesn't know the Benedict variety of eggs. Meanwhile, the nurse has decided to make it into an *issue*. You know how it is, once an *issue* is created. The nurse asks the dietitian to consult, because of course Olaf has high blood pressure and high cholesterol. The dietitian doesn't know what this is all about, but she writes dietary recommendations in the chart—a low-salt, low-fat diet. Arnold sees this, so he just writes: LOW-SALT, LOW-FAT DIET AS PER DIETITIAN. Next day, Mr. Olaf is eating his low-salt, low-fat porridge and tea with no sugar or milk for breakfast while we're rounding. Doesn't say a word until the end of the rounds, when he shyly says, 'Excuse me, doctors, sirs, I apologize humbly for my lavish request of the eggs Benedict. But would it be possible to restore the regular food?' You should have seen him, poking that hard porridge.

"Arnold writes DAT on the chart. Later, Sri is paged while we're in a seminar. He goes off, comes back, says another nurse is peeved about these contradictory orders. First, eggs Benedict, then low-salt low-fat, then DAT. Sri cancels all the previous orders and writes DAT—DIET AS TOLERATED again. The next morning, I see he's got some little containers with him. I ask him what they are, and he says it's his lunch. But later, when we're rounding, there's Mr. Olaf with a great big spread of eggs Benedict and bacon and home fries, digging in like he's found a preview of heaven. All the time while we're rounding, he's smiling and nodding at Sri, grinning like a madman."

"Sri was a good guy," said Fitzgerald. "I barely recognized him at the viewing—that open casket thing they do."

"Lost a lot of weight. I hadn't seen him since he got sick. So fast, eight months. At least a few times I saw Sri with his little stack of containers, then Olaf died a week later. One day, I think he had waffles."

Fitzgerald said, "Isn't it amazing how weight loss changes the face? Especially when the body is supine. Changes the way everything sits."

"Gravity shapes everything," said Chen. "First, I couldn't believe that he was gone. Then, I couldn't believe that I couldn't believe it. After all, how many dead people have we seen? How many have we watched die?"

Fitz coughed, and it took him like a shaking fist, forced him to put down the phone until he was able to stop and wipe the perspiration from his face. He picked it up again and said, "You want to order something?"

"What, fancy eggs?"

"I'd like a seared tuna steak with wasabi mashed potatoes and vintage port."

"Pan-fried crabs," said Chen, "with lots of scallions and garlic."

"Scallops. Big, fat Nova Scotia scallops browned in butter with asparagus, wild rice, and a bottle of Gewurztraminer."

March 19, 2003 (from the files of the World Health Organization)

Brother-in-law of Guangdong doctor dies in a Hong Kong hospital.

Both of them watched TV all day. Switched between the stations. Mostly stayed on the news, the SARS clips over and over again: mask shortages, enforced quarantines, panic spreading like flight trajectories between cities. Later that night, after dinner, Fitz called Chen. Through the glass, Chen saw Fitzgerald hold the phone, a spasm of coughing, his hands shaking like the tailpipe on a cold car. Chen said, "This shakiness business of yours. I know you have a few from time to time."

"What?"

"Booze. Are you withdrawing?"

"I guess."

"Get some diazepam."

"No way. Zenkie's writing it up. 'Tremor: A Novel Aspect of the SARS Syndrome.' You want to take away his paper?"

"What if you seize?"

"Fuck it. I'd rather be famous. The Zenkie-Fitzgerald Tremor—an atypical manifestation of SARS. I'm going to be a co-author."

"You better tell Zenkie, and get some diazepam."

"Right, I'll tell him and in forty seconds the whole hospital will know."

Chen was about to say that it didn't matter, because after the night when Fitz had arrived for a shift with the sweet smell on his breath, his speech slurred, and was asked to leave and stop seeing patients, it didn't make a difference whether people knew he was withdrawing. But Chen didn't say it, because maybe Fitz didn't know how much people had talked in that indelible way. Fitz had resigned from the hospital the next day, signed on with the flight company. Chen said, "Instead, you'll seize and die."

"Who said death was so bad?"

"Did someone say that?"

Fitz had a coughing fit, and then, "When did we forget what it meant to die?"

"Probably at night."

"Yeah, it would have been late."

"One night . . . I was very tired," said Chen. "There was this hysterical family. You know the kind—they stare at you when you sit down to write a chart, they grab you to tell you that they read something on the Internet. Their mother was going to die. It had taken me a long time to convince them that there was no other way. Every half-hour I would get paged, and the nurse would say, 'They want to speak to you again.' Don't you hate that? When it's not even a particular problem, but they just want to speak to you? Finally I told them that Mom wasn't going to die tonight, that they should save their strength for the next day."

"And as soon as they left, she died."

"Of course."

"Always the way."

"It was three o'clock. I had been running back and forth from emerg and it had finally quietened down. I told the nurse that she didn't need to check on the woman until the morning. We both knew."

"You didn't call the family."

"I just couldn't. I was exhausted. I called when I woke up, and filled out the death certificate as if she had just passed away. By the time they got to the hospital and started their wailing and carrying on, I was out the door."

"That's not so bad. They needed the sleep. Imagine if they came in at three o'clock? The whole floor would be awake, and then you'd be fucked."

"Later, I felt like maybe I should have called. But I just felt that way kind of theoretically. I didn't really care."

"You took care of the patient, right?" said Fitz. "The rest is your own business. What's your temp today?"

"Thirty-nine." Neither of them wanted to take too much antipyretic. Both of their livers were already reeling from the cocktail of drugs.

"I'm forty," said Fitz. Even through the glass, Chen could see the sweat-glaze on Fitz's skin, and a slight collapse of facial features. "One morning, I was post-call. I went to that park in Kensington, you know the corner stand where they make fresh chocolate croissants and serve latte out the window? Yeah. Those mornings when the weather is so fresh, and you're kind of stoned but awake, on those days sometimes I wouldn't sleep, I would take the ferry to Centre Island. Wander around. Watch the moms and kids on the toy train."

Fitzgerald didn't mention the rum he put in his post-call latte. Not a lot, just enough to soothe. He said, "That was my plan. I had my nice big latte, my warm croissant, and the sun was just up. This woman is walking across the park. She goes up to this picnic table where this guy looks like he's asleep, slumped over. I don't know why she does this, but she tries to wake him up. He doesn't wake up. She shakes him. He's just lying there, and I'm drinking my latte thinking either he's dead, or he's a heroin addict. I decide that he's probably not dead because he's too floppy, unless he just died, so he's probably a junkie. People gather around while this woman slaps the guy and shouts at him. I laugh because she tries to move him and obviously she's never moved anyone before—his head just flops back and goes *bonk* when she drags him onto the ground. On the dirt, mind you, it's nice and soft. I zip up my jacket, because otherwise you can see my scrub top. This woman freaks out. She starts to scream, 'Call 911, call 911,' and all these people look at her like maybe this is performance art? Finally, someone takes out a cellphone and calls.

"I imagined what would happen if I went over there. He would be fine, just a junkie on junk, but I'd be standing there all doctor-like and therefore unable to escape. Or, maybe he would be dead. Then I'd start CPR, although if he was dead all that time it wouldn't matter, but if I was playing Mr. Doctor then I'd have to do something to make it look good, I'd have to do mouth-to-mouth and he would vomit in my mouth, and then whether he was okay or dead, by the time the ambulance guys came, either some homeless guy would have stolen my croissant and latte or it would be cold."

"But then . . ." prompted Chen, and he saw from Fitzgerald's slump that the funny ending and heroic anecdote that these types of stories usually concluded with would not come.

Fitzgerald said, "So the woman starts CPR. She hasn't even checked for a pulse, and in fact I think I can see him breathing, so she would totally fail an ACLS course. Anyhow, she's doing it like squirrel CPR. *Boop boop boop* on his chest. Must have seen it on TV. She's got the two-hand thing going, elbows locked, but she's barely touching the guy. I figured that if he was actually alive, her CPR wasn't going to hurt him much, and if he was dead, none of this would matter. Then the ambulance came. I had to watch, because I was convinced that he was breathing, just to see whether I was right. Sure, they tubed him. I heard him sucking on the tube, and they weren't pumping him. See? I knew he had vital signs."

"Sometimes you can tell from a distance," said Chen.

"Sure," said Fitzgerald. A coughing fit. He wondered if he would have told the story if the ambulance crew had started CPR, if in fact the guy had died. No. He knew that he would have just kept it to himself. As it was, Chen was the first person he had told.

"Did you go to Centre Island?"

"Yeah, but that whole incident soured my day."

"It's cute out on the Island, isn't it? All the rides, and the kids in the swan boats, driving those little cars."

"I like it out there," said Fitzgerald. Fitzgerald thought of a ferry trip to the Island with Ming before she met Chen, and was surprised that he could remember this without bitterness, without needing to know whether Chen knew that Ming and Fitzgerald had once spent a sunny afternoon on Centre Island. He felt good, that it was mostly a pleasant memory of a woman whom he now hardly knew, and of himself as a person remembered. A slight pang, of course, but after an unusual length of sobriety he was able to see that this was mostly a pang for his present aloneness, and that there was no truth to representing it otherwise. "Listen, if I go down the drain, and I think I will, I don't want to be tubed or resuscitated or anything. It's not worth it."

(Portion of progress note of Dr. R. Zenkie, FRCPC, dated March 20, 2003—excerpted from chart with permission of Toronto South General Hospital)

. . . and as his clinical situation continues to worsen, Dr. Fitzgerald has indicated his wish to not be resuscitated should he deteriorate to the point that he requires

intubation. He has told me that should this occur, he would not want to expose other staff to the SARS infection by performing such a high-risk procedure, since he judges that in this instance his chances of survival would be slim. I am inclined to wonder whether Dr. Fitzgerald may be suffering from an acute situational depression, and therefore may not be competent to make this decision. At this point, I am refraining from writing a DNR order, because of my doubts about the state of Dr. Fitzgerald's mental health.

Yours truly, Dr. R. Zenkie, FRCPC

Consultant in Infectious Diseases, Toronto South General Hospital

(NB: Also on March 20, Dr. Zenkie ordered diazepam 10 mg by mouth every one hour as needed by Dr. Fitzgerald to treat persistent tremor. No other explanation of this order is noted in the chart.)

Dolores explained to the daycare director that she, herself, had no fever, no respiratory symptoms, that she was screened daily at the hospital and checked her own temperature at home at least twice. Certainly, her children were perfectly healthy. She had had no unprotected contact, she said, and could not be considered to be a suspect or probable case. The daycare director said that it wasn't that she had any problem with the situation. No, it was just that the parents of the other children felt . . . uncomfortable. Dolores asked why those parents didn't just keep their kids at home, then. Well, that would be unfair to them, said the daycare woman, and it wasn't that she was forbidding Dolores's kids from coming, it was just that maybe they should . . . think about things a bit. Already, Dolores's children had told her that the other kids wouldn't play with them, had been told not to by their parents.

Dolores found a babysitter who could provide both daycare for the little ones and after-school care for Dolores's older daughter. Dolores told her that she worked in the sanitation industry, and explained to the kids that they shouldn't tell anyone that Mommy was a nurse. Why not? her daughter asked. Because people are silly, Dolores said. For how long do we keep it secret? her son asked. Dolores said that she wasn't sure how long it would be. It might be a while.

On March 21, Chen saw that Fitzgerald sucked on his oxygen with all the heaving muscles in his chest, that he ate ice from a cup next to him. Chen called Fitzgerald and asked how he was doing. Great, replied Fitzgerald.

"Hey, you remember that guy, that old German internist, the one who did his residency in India? He would talk that crazy German-accented Hindi to all the Indian patients. They loved him. What was his name, Glug-something? Gland?"

"Gerstein."

"Were you there when he convinced that woman she needed a spinal tap?"

"Remind me."

"The one-in-a-hundred thing . . ."

"Oh, of course," said Fitzgerald. Both he and Chen began to laugh. Dr. Gerstein had been their attending when they were consulted about a patient with a headache. Her story raised suspicions of a subarachnoid hemorrhage, and the CT scan was negative. Dr. Gerstein explained to the woman, in the German-accented Hindi-influenced English he had learned in Bombay, that even though the CT scan was negative, there was a one percent chance that it could be wrong, and a lumbar puncture was necessary in order to be certain.

"One percent," she said. "I'm scared of needles."

"A subarachnoid could kill you," Dr. Gerstein said.

"But one percent. That's one in a hundred. You would put a needle into my spinal cord for one in a hundred?"

"Actually, into the spinal canal. We would avoid the cord."

"Maybe I'll take my chances," the woman said. "One percent isn't bad."

At that, Dr. Gerstein made for the door, leaving Dr. Chen and Dr. Fitzgerald standing at the woman's bedside. They did not know whether to follow him. They knew that this woman needed the lumbar puncture, and that sometimes Gerstein would abandon difficult tasks, such as convincing a patient of the wisdom of medical guidance, to his house staff. At the door, Gerstein turned, widened his stance. He made his hands into a pistol and raised them, pointed the two-fingered barrel straight at the woman.

He said, "I just picked up one of a hundred Mauser pistols that were sitting here outside the room. One of them is loaded, and I don't know which one. Regardless, the gun is trained on your forehead. I'll leave it up to you. Would you like me to pull the trigger?"

The woman's eyes were fixed on the muzzle of Gerstein's fingertips.

"The safety is off, shall I pull the trigger?"

Chen and Fitzgerald's chests thumped in sudden fear. Gerstein stood absolutely still, stared down his gun barrel until he smiled—not ironically, not exactly kindly, but mostly with sadness at the reality of decision making.

Fifteen minutes later, clear cerebrospinal fluid trickled into the needle embedded between that woman's fourth and fifth lumbar vertebrae.

"Like a gunslinger in a western," said Chen. "High noon at the spinal tap corral." Both he and Fitz were laughing.

Fitz said, "You think we'll die?"

"Maybe." The laughter continued.

"Me, more likely. I'm on a hundred percent." He knew that Chen was only on four litres of oxygen per minute. "It's not so bad," said Fitzgerald. "If we die with only a few hundred others, we'll be SARS martyrs. If thousands get it but they find a cure and our deaths help, then it's worthwhile. If this thing just goes wild and the whole world dies by the millions, then we'll miss the worst of it. See? Can't lose." By the time he had finished saying this, they were both sober.

"When I try to remember, I can't recall when I learned about death," said Chen. "How it's ordinary, but like a sudden hole in the world. I learned it, then I forgot, or maybe I just began to ignore it. Ming and I were talking about kids. Maybe next year."

"I'm a fuckup anyhow. Better for me to croak. You stick around." The mention of Ming made Fitzgerald angry and sick with himself, his drinking, his aloneness. He told himself resolutely that losing her hadn't influenced the shape of his life, but when he drank he did not believe this. When the bottle sank him below the comfort zone, Ming was one of the if-only-it-had-been-another-way things that became vivid. Fitzgerald decided from Chen's comfortable manner with him that Ming had never mentioned Fitzgerald, and only once at a departmental party had they all been in the same room. He and Chen had never been very close, but when you do months of "team medicine" together, you end up acting like buddies out of necessity. Now, being in respiratory isolation together, calling each other on the phone, it was like those times.

"Not what I meant," said Chen.

"That's the way it is. I told Zenkie to write a DO NOT RESUSCITATE on my chart."

"You're being crazy."

"Of course not. It's just common sense. Look, everyone who gets tubed dies. While they're getting tubed, the resuscitation team catches it. Then some of the people who tubed the guy who died get so sick that they need to be tubed. And so on. They should cut us off from everyone, like a leper colony."

"This is early, a new disease. There're intubated people who haven't died yet."

"Come on. You think we ever beat outbreaks? They run their course, they burn themselves out. It's just a question of how many people get burnt up in the process. Spanish flu, forty million dead, more than the First World War."

"Something like that."

(Transcript of Dr. R. Zenkie, FRCPC, dictated March 22, 2003—never transcribed because of deviations from standard dictation format—recovered from electronic transcription system with permission of Toronto South General Hospital)

ID: I am Dr. Ronald Zenkie, infectious disease consultant and avid nature photographer

CC: Fever, shortness of breath, heightened awareness of societal paranoia

(nervous laugh)

To whom it may concern,

(pause for coughing fit)

I am taking the unusual step of dictating my own admission note. Today, I woke with chills and myalgias. My temperature, measured orally, was 39. Over the day, I have become progressively more short of breath, and have developed a cough.

I think I have a cold, just a regular cold, but these days you never know.

(pause for coughing fit)

Erase last sentence, please.

It is probable that I am suffering from a relatively innocent upper respiratory tract infection. However, it must be noted that I may be perceived as being at high risk for contraction of SARS, and thus it is appropriate that I mandate my own admission to the SARS unit in the interests of public safety.

How about that, huh? Down with the ship.

(prolonged bout of laughter and coughing)

Shit.

Erase last sentence and expletive, please.

I have discussed my clinical responsibilities, which will be assumed by Dr. Waterman, who will act as the interim attending staff on the SARS unit.

Yours truly, Dr. R. Zenkie, FRCPC

Consultant in Infectious Diseases, Toronto South General Hospital

(Addendum to SARS Bulletin 14, issued on March 25.)

To All Staff,

We are sad to inform you that after a short illness, Dr. R. Zenkie has succumbed to SARS. Our condolences to his family, and thanks for his twenty-six years of service to the Toronto South General Hospital. Staff members who have been in contact with Dr. R. Zenkie have been contacted personally, but are reminded that they are now on work quarantine. All such staff should leave their homes only to go to work, using a private vehicle such as a personal car or a taxi. Masks must be worn between home and hospital at all times. At home, all such staff are reminded to sleep in separate rooms from their spouses, to sit at a minimum distance of 1 metre (3 feet) from family members during meals, and preferably to eat in a separate room. There should be no physical contact with children or other family members. All staff on work quarantine should shower at work, or shower in a separate area of the home from their family members, because of the possible aerosolization of SARS infectious material within showers. Body temperature should be measured a minimum of twice per day, and any oral temperature greater than 38 must be reported immediately. Dr. Zenkie is survived by his wife, Amita, who is admitted in our SARS unit and asks that donations be made to UNICEF in lieu of flowers or gifts. The memorial service for Dr. Zenkie is indefinitely postponed, and we would remind staff that all gatherings of hospital staff outside of the hospital are forbidden.

Yours truly,

SARS Action Management Team

The morning rush. The line behind the hospital trailed out of the tent and into the parking lot. There was an April drizzle but people did not huddle close to each other's umbrellas. Those with umbrellas stood their ground, and those with bare heads stood at a more than socially polite distance from each other, and gradually became wet. Arriving for the day shift. Dolores eyed the boxes of masks to see whether the blue ones, which were the least constrictive, were available. There were no blue masks. Only the white, itchy ones.

She saw that some people produced blue masks from their pockets and bags. They had hoarded the comfortable masks, she realized. Dolores had not done so, but decided that the next time she saw a box of the blue masks she would slip five or six of them into her purse. If it rained tomorrow, she thought, then she should bring an umbrella. Or maybe not. If she brought one, someone might try to stand too close to her.

Ahead, people filed past the dispensers of antiseptic handwash, squirted the bottles, and rubbed their hands and forearms. They gathered up their daily bundle of isolation gowns and scrubs, stood one by one in front of the masked screeners so that body temperatures could be measured with the ear probe, and to answer the same screening questions asked the day before. Dolores saw that one man had his temperature taken a second time. He shook his head. Then a third. He protested. A fourth. A look of resignation. A screener pushed a second mask at him and led him out the side flap of the tent, to somewhere else. Dolores saw that there were security people at each corner of the tent. They did not move, but they, like Dolores, watched this happen. What was the difference between being led away and being taken away? None, she decided, when a security guard stood at each corner of the tent, when everyone had instructions to follow.

Dolores began to feel warm. The line murmured, looked down, continued to move forward and present their ears for temperature measurement. Yes, she definitely felt warm. It was 7:20, and she should already be getting a signover report from the night shift, but she definitely felt a heat. Then she coughed. A cough. One, and was there another? It did not seem so, but her body temperature was intense, her heart beating. She was not yet inside the tent. She was still in the portion of the line that stood in the drizzle, that was still connected to the outside world of wind and water, a world that did not exist inside the hospital. Suddenly, Dolores wondered who would pick up the kids from the sitter and bring them home if she couldn't? Their father now lived three time zones away, her closest family was two time zones distant. What would happen if she got to the front of the line and had a temperature? They couldn't live with the babysitter. They would end up in a foster home until she got better. 7:23. Or what if she didn't get better?

No one noticed, Dolores thought, as she ducked out of the line, as she made for her car. She did not look back to see whether anyone followed her with their eyes. Now, she had missed report. All the way home she felt hotter and hotter, more and more inflamed. A fit of coughing at a red light, but maybe she had just swallowed wrong? Told herself to drive carefully. She slammed the car door, rushed into the house in her wet shoes, made for the bathroom, and only once the digital thermometer was in her mouth did she think, *But if I have a temperature, then I don't want to be in contact with my kids.*

The metal wand under her tongue, she remembered with a panic the report she had read that speculated that SARS infectious material might remain contagious even for days outside of the body. What was she doing? What was she thinking? She was in the process of contaminating her children's home. Whereas all this time she had been thinking only of the problem of picking up her children from the babysitter and bringing them home, now she wanted more than anything to keep them away from this place—this place that she was now transforming into a cesspool of disease. She felt a tickle, a scratchiness, needed to cough, needed to hold the thermometer under her tongue.

Beeeep.

36.6. Afebrile. No fever.

Dolores sat on the toilet, drank a glass of water. The cough seemed to be gone. She took her temperature again, and wrote it down on a scrap of paper from her purse. And again, shoes still dripping onto the bathroom mat. Wrote down the second temperature. Did it five times, all of the temperatures perfectly normal. The cough was gone. She averaged the five temperatures. The average was 36.5. Normal.

The phone rang. It was the nurse in charge of the SARS unit. Dolores had been seen ducking out of the line.

"No, no," she said, "not a fever. Just dizziness. I get this sometimes, these horrible episodes of dizziness. Usually lasts a few days.

"No, not a fever.

"No, don't send public health, no, it would be a waste.

"Definitely not.

"I checked five times.

"Yes.

"Yes.

"I know exactly what it is, so book me off the schedule for at least three days."

(Transcript of an evening news clip of April 3, 2003—reproduced with permission of CBC Television)

Today, an unusual occurrence at the Toronto South General Hospital SARS Unit: This morning, alarms indicated a breach in the SARS respiratory isolation rooms. What is known as a Code Orange alert was activated, placing the facility in Disaster Response mode. After several minutes, the Code Orange was deactivated. Hospital officials assure us that there was no external breach, and that no unprotected hospital staff were placed at risk. Initially, hospital officials refused to explain the incident, but with speculation heightening throughout the day, a statement has been released. It seems that a SARS patient, Dr. Fitzgerald, became unable to breathe and collapsed within an isolation room. As the SARS medical team donned their protective gear in order to enter the room and administer treatment to Dr. Fitzgerald, the SARS patient in the room adjacent to his, Dr. Chen, broke through the glass partition between their rooms with an intravenous pole, in order to initiate emergency treatment for Dr. Fitzgerald. The Code Orange alarm was activated by this glass being broken but, once again, hospital officials insist that no unprotected staff were exposed. Dr. Fitzgerald is reported to be in critical condition. Dr. Chen is reported to have cut his arm on broken glass, but is otherwise stable. The hospital declined to comment on their assessment of Dr. Chen's actions, which they described as being "outside standard protocol." Dr. Chen was reached briefly by phone, and stated, "In a critical situation, it takes too long to put on the SARS gear, and people die in the delay, but I've already got SARS, so I don't need the protection."

Extreme measures at urgent times.

Meanwhile, on the world front, the number of cases has exceeded two thousand. Chinese authorities have announced three hundred and sixty-one new SARS cases and nine new deaths. In Hong Kong, there is strong evidence that the disease has spread beyond its initial focus within hospitals, with secondary and tertiary cases almost certainly occurring in the community at large.

BEFORE LIGHT

—
—
—

21:00—Eighth-floor apartment balcony, south of Queen and Spadina

The sun has left the city. The day collapses into a violet glow—this new purple sky which is the warm birth of night. I look down into the bright windows of houses, at two shadows of boys under a street light, and over the convulsive writhing of a tree's body in the wind. I resent night, the long awakening darkness that will be flickered by red, yellow, and green at intersections, slashed open by arcing headlights, this void gasping for breath, and punctured by the sudden smash of fist into shouting mouth. I see an ambulance hurtle straight up Spadina Avenue, like a bullet shot into darkness.

21:25—Bedroom of apartment

I'm in bed. I tell myself not to look, not to check the time. Not knowing makes me anxious, so I open my eyes again, glimpse the glowing orange numbers: 21:26. I flip from my right side to my left side. *Breathe slowly,* I think. I've been lying here for seventeen minutes: nine minutes on my left, then eight on my right. I feel sad and cheated. I resent my overnight shift in the emergency department, which starts at 23:30. I can never sleep before this late shift, and I always feel desperately certain that if only I could nap, if only I could drift off for a few minutes, it would be much better. I turn onto my right side. The door's edges are rectangles of light. I swing my anxious legs out of bed. I sit. I stand and open the door. Ming is reading, and the living room lights shine brightly.

"Hi," I say.

"What's wrong?"

"Can't sleep."

"Try to rest. Resting is good."

"I hate my job, Ming. I despise it. I have to get *out* of this. I can't do this forever." I stand in the doorway in my T-shirt and underwear.

Ming doesn't look up. "You hate everything before your night shift. In general, you sort of like your job."

"Right now, I hate it." I am aware of the whiteness of my naked legs.

"Fine. Hate it. Feel better?"

"A little."

She looks up. "You should lie down."

"Can you come and snuggle?"

"Sure."

I turn on the air filter for its white hiss. Ming takes off her pants and we lay down. I tell myself to pretend that we're going to bed for the night, that we will be safe until morning. If I could just believe this. Then, with my wife's warm back pressed against my belly, I would sleep. It is urgent that I sleep. I am panicked that I should sleep. The fact that I have to work through the night makes it absolutely crucial that my consciousness fade, that drool begin to fall from the corner of my mouth onto the pillow, that I dream in that liquid way which permits all possibilities. *Sleep, dream,* I think. But this imperative makes me more and more aware that I am not asleep, which makes me force my breathing to become long and drawn out, and then I feel breathless.

In medical school, they once brought a relaxation specialist to our class. She guided a hundred and seventy-seven students, all sitting in the tall and echo-filled lecture hall, through an exercise. We visualized looseness spreading from our toes, to our ankles, to our knees, to our bellies, as tension flowed out of our skin. Some people put their heads on their desks, pens fell from their hands, and they snored. I couldn't get past my ankles. My toes felt too big to relax. My feet ached. I couldn't make my ankles go limp. I asked myself whether the stronger minds were those who were able to allow the relaxation to take them over, to submit to the slackness of their bodies, or those like myself whose knees and necks continued to fidget and fight. Then I became irritated with myself—*why did it matter who had the stronger mind?*

Ming coughs, and shifts. She is lying still for my benefit, but it's not quite the same because typically she falls asleep first. That's how it works. Usually, I become aware of her breathing passing into the involuntary wind of a sleeping body, and this is a trigger for me. This is the thing that must happen before I can let go, before I begin to forget my waking self. Ming coughs a second time.

She says, "I forgot. I have to make a phone call."

"Can you snuggle a bit longer?"

"It'll be too late to call." She touches my thigh. "Sorry, you want me to come back after I'm done?"

"It's okay," I say. I turn so that our curved backs touch each other, and she climbs over me to get out of bed.

"Relax," she says. "You need it."

22:50—Kitchen

"Have you had enough?" asks Ming.

I have just eaten two big bowls of the leftover stir-fried shrimp on white rice from dinner. I ate them with a gluttonous determination that I feed myself, that I need it, that at least my night should be fuelled.

"I guess," I say. Already, I feel the beginning of nausea. My night shifts are underlined by a persistent, hanging, sick feeling.

The bottom cup of a pot of tea sits before me. The tea bags steeped while I drank three successively stronger cups, each with two heaping spoons of sugar.

23:20—Lakeshore Boulevard

My shift starts in ten minutes. I'm the second car at the light, stopped right before the Gardiner on-ramp. The first car is a gleaming, bright-white F150 crew cab. *Who drives a pickup truck in the city? Small man, big car. Custom chrome bumper. Loser.*

The light's green, buddy. Fuck, get a move on!

The light's green, after all.

Braaaaaaaap.

I thumb the horn long and excessively as I pull out, floor it in second, and blow past the F150. He's talking on the phone, giving me the finger, stomping on the gas now, and trying to cut me off as I duck in front of him in the final metres before the ramp and gun it onto the Gardiner eastbound.

Sucker, I think. I feel justified in driving this way. I sometimes see people driving recklessly and I wonder whether they really have such a worthwhile place to be. What makes them feel so important? Don't they realize how terrible car accidents happen? But right now, just at this moment, I have somewhere important to go. I am a linchpin of the city's emergency safety net. I am a night-shift martyr, and if Mr. F150 doesn't notice the green light, he should be dusted off with a vigorous horning.

Coming off the ramp, I'm in third. I zing the tach past five thousand before shifting up, gunning the engine of my silver Benz. I have a mild sense that I should be embarrassed, that I'm a doctor driving a cliché. The F150 is trying to keep up. *No way, man.* I once thought I would defy stereotype, that I would always ride transit. At some point I realized that Mercedes are such nice cars. *It's about the quality,* I tell myself and anyone who sees the car. *And you would be surprised how little I paid for it. It's an excellent used-car value.* It is a shiny CLK 430. Sporty. I can't deny that. I should be embarrassed, but really I'm not. You see, just below the silver paint is a layer of feigned sheepishness, which masks a sense of justification, because really I feel like this car is my due. *Shouldn't I have a kick-ass car? Don't I deserve it?*

I hit one-thirty in fourth, pass a taxi on the right, shift up, move back into the left lane. Mr. Pickup Truck is trying to follow. His heavy chrome lurches to the side as he changes lanes. *Laughable!* I want the cops to stop us. They will pull us over and I will show them my Dr. Chen badge. We will recognize each other; they bring people in to me all night long. I will shrug and say, You know how it is, officers. Hospital—the emergency department. They need me. The cop will wave me on, saying, Night, doctor, and I will zoom away. They will bust the pickup truck instead. I see the custom bumper flash in my side mirror. I pull ahead and cut him off.

I've never been pulled over before. The pickup truck now darts three lanes to the right, passes a panel van, and surges forward. I tap the accelerator, amazed at how quietly this car does one-sixty. *Do they take you to jail for speeding?* Now, I slow down. I'm suddenly concerned that I may not have the man-to-man, doctor-to-cop macho charisma required to get off a speeding ticket. I slow to just a little over the posted limit, see the F150 approach from behind, pass too close, and sweep in front of me.

Go on, little man. I'm above this sort of thing. He pulls away.

23:35—Toronto South General, emergency loading entrance

Six ambulances, two coppers. The ambulances are angle parked outside, backed into the spaces. The police cars have their noses forward and engines running. It is festive, frenetic, a late-night party. Inside, the fluorescent lights cry out, scream brightly, and the waiting room bubbles with faces. The full daytime lighting gives an out-of-earthly-time feeling, like in a convenience store before dawn. Eyes and hands and shouting at this masquerade ball. Stretchers in the hallway with ambulance crews. Five, I count. Sixth must be in the resuscitation bay.

The charge nurse says, "Twenty-two in the waiting room, six hours behind. Got your runners on, Dr. Chen?"

A man in a purple windbreaker asks, "Are you a doctor? You the doctor?"

"They keep telling me that," I reply.

23:40—Room 8. Mrs. Withrow: eighty-two years old with dizziness

"Hello, Mrs. Withrow, I'm Dr. Chen."

"Thank you so much."

"Pleased to meet you. Don't thank me yet." I pull up a chair. "I understand you've been dizzy." I was taught that sitting creates the perception of time. I cross my legs and maintain good posture.

"Extremely, terribly dizzy."

"How long has that been?"

"Oh, a while."

"A while." I nod. "How long is a while?"

"It's been bad for *quite* a while. Also, my foot is sore."

"Quite a while." I nod again. "All right. Would you say that a while is like a day, or a week, or like a month, or for instance a year? Give me a rough idea."

Mrs. Withrow ponders this, she gazes up, looks at me with confidence and says, "Let's just say a while." She presses her lips with finality. "What is your diagnosis, doctor?"

"Let me ask you this, Mrs. Withrow: When did you start thinking of coming to hospital?"

"I've been thinking about the hospital for a *long* time. But just recently I decided to call an ambulance."

"How long ago is recently?"

"What do you mean by that?"

"Recently," I say. "When you say 'recently,' do you mean just this afternoon, or today, or a few days, or a week?"

"I didn't catch the question, doctor. I'm sorry. My hearing aid's at home. Could you speak up?"

I drop my voice into a theatrical baritone. "Mrs. Withrow. Are you dizzy right now?"

"You don't have to shout. I'm not deaf, just hard of hearing."

I stop. Open my mouth. Close it. "Right now, are you dizzy?"

"Well, no, not at all. I feel better already. Thank you."

"That's wonderful," I say in my deepest, operatic boom. "I'm so pleased to hear that you feel better."

The overhead speakers: "*Doctor to resusc now. Doctor to resusc now.*"

I stand up. "Excuse me."

23:46—Resuscitation bay 1. Mr. Santorini: forty-eight years old with chest pain

He breathes hard, looks scared.

Jill hands me an electrocardiogram. I read the twelve punctuated, jagged lines on the grid paper in the way that my ancient predecessors peered into tea leaves, or gazed at bones thrown in the sand. The electrocardio-gram tells fortunes, is a sudden lightning-strike omen.

I say, "Mr. Santorini, I have some bad news and some good news."

"What's the good news?" he gasps. He is sweating, melting into the stretcher.

"I'll tell you the bad news first."

"Doctor, it's a thing I have: good news first." He wipes the sheet at his forehead.

"The good news is that we have a treatment for your problem."

"What problem?"

"That's the bad news. You're having a heart attack."

"I disagree," he says. "That can't be."

I say to Jill, "Two IVs, he's had aspirin? Great. Nitro point four q five times three, chest X-ray, trop, coags."

"He's got no veins," says Jill.

Mr. Santorini is a big man. Not huge, but big in the pudgy-fleshed way that makes it difficult to get intra-venous lines into veins.

Jill says, "Lenny! Lenny, come here, you try his other arm."

Lenny draws the curtain open. "What?"

Jill says, "He's infarcting. I can't get an IV. Try the other side."

Lenny says, "Oh." Then he disappears.

Mr. Santorini says, "It's not a heart attack. It's some-thing else. I rollerblade like a fiend—you should see me. An hour a day, like a maniac. I'm an exercise *addict*,

I can't be having a heart attack." A bead of sweat is suspended at his chin.

"Exercise is great, Mr. Santorini." I have the clot box out. I draw up sterile water to mix the thrombolytic. "Jackrabbit Johansen, you know him? Legendary skier. Phenomenally fit. Died of a heart attack. Listen, I have to tell you about something. We have what's called thrombolytic, a great treatment for your problem. It's a clot-busting drug. A heart attack occurs when a clot is stuck in your coronary artery, and this medication opens that up, could save your life. There's a little risk with it. Just a very small danger, but we have to inform you of it. A very small, *tiny* number of people who get this drug have a stroke."

"Wait a minute? Stroke? What are you saying? Can you die from stroke?"

"That's possible, but unlikely. Rare rare *rare.*"

"I can't be having a heart attack. You should see me on blades. Flash, they call me. Listen, I need a phone. I need to make a phone call."

"The thing about this treatment is that we have to give it as soon as possible."

Jill yells out, "Lenny! Where is Lenny? These damn agency nurses, why can't this hospital staff the place properly? You know, Dr. Chen, this place is so screwed up."

I stand out of Mr. Santorini's field of vision and hold a finger to my lips at Jill. She giggles. This seems very funny to her.

I say to Mr. Santorini, "We have a motto: time is muscle. Time's ticking, and it's your heart muscle. So you see, I really want to give you this treatment, as long as you accept this incredibly small risk of stroke." I inject water into the vial of powdered thrombolytic.

Jill has got the needle into a vein. I see flashback: blood in the barrel. The metal has bitten the vein and we're on our way. Jill says to me, "All day it's been just myself and this unbelievable agency nurse, this Lenny character. Am I supposed to do everything? It gets to the point that people will die, and there's nothing I can do about it." Mr. Santorini's arm jumps as she begins to feed the cannula and the needle jolts. Jill keeps it in the arm with her thumb, says, "Sir, don't move."

I say, "It's very important we get the IV into you."

"Jeez, that stings."

"We need the IV to give you the heart attack medicine," says Jill, as she connects the tubing to flush the line.

"Are you people listening?" asks Mr. Santorini. "I can't be having a heart attack."

"You got it?" I say to Jill. I swirl the vial of powder and water to dissolve it. The box says to swirl, not shake.

The line doesn't run. She says, "It's blown. This is pathetic. Am I alone?" She says louder, "What does it take to get some help in here?"

I stand again where Mr. Santorini can't see me. I wave my hands, bare my teeth, and mouth *stop it!* at Jill, who laughs.

Lenny appears. He says, "I can't find any IV sets—the cart is empty."

"Good Lord. Get Wanda. Page Wanda."

Lenny says, "Just tell me where. Is there a stock?"

"Lenny, just page Wanda to come do it."

Mr. Santorini suddenly cringes at his chest, puts a fist to it. "Oh, wow. Yesterday I fell. Maybe I pulled a muscle or something. Give me something for the pain and I'll go home."

On the twelve lead monitor, I see his ST segments rising, his heart being starved of oxygen, the muscle becoming liquid and dark like an apple with a soft, rotting core.

"Sir," I say. "Do you pay your taxes?" I fix my gaze on him, to take his attention away from Jill's new jab at his arm.

"Of course. I have a slick accountant, but sure I—"

I come close to his face. I look straight and unblinking into his eyes. "Do you know why you pay your taxes?" The drug in the vial is now dissolved. I draw up the clear liquid, a little more than the exact dose.

"I have to, otherwise—"

"You pay your taxes so that I can be here at midnight after having spent many years in school, and so that I can tell you without a shadow of a doubt that your heart is in the process of infarcting and *we need to use your tax dollars* to do something about it." I say it nicely—like I would sell a used Hyundai if I were a car salesman.

"Oh," he says.

Wanda rushes in. On each side, the nurses tourniquet and flick his arms, probe for veins.

"We have the state of the art, the best, the latest. This is the Cadillac, Mr. Santorini. This is recombinant thrombolytic. It was a breakthrough twenty years ago, it's been refined since then, and it's superb. Minuscule risk of stroke. Hardly ever happens. I want the best for you, because you are an upstanding citizen, a taxpayer, and a rollerblader. You owe it to yourself, and I owe it to you." I flick the bubbles to the top of the syringe, squirt out the tiny pocket of air, and plunge the barrel to the exact dose. "You want to blade again?"

"Whaddya—"

"Yes or no. You want to rollerblade again, Mr. Santorini?"

"Of course I do."

"Then you need this treatment. If you want to blade, you need this drug."

I watch his arms, Jill on one side and Wanda on the other. Almost simultaneously, I see the red burst in each barrel of the IV sets.

"Got it?" I ask. They have. On each side, we have a line. Both run well.

Mr. Santorini suddenly arches his back, holds his chest. "Jeez, it's like a *moose* sitting on my chest. Oh my *God*. Okay, doc, whatever you think."

"Twenty-three fifty-four, pushing the lytic," I say,

plunging the syringe into the happily running tube in the right arm.

1:30—Twelve patients waiting, three hours behind

From midnight to three is running time. Tired and thirsty. The patients pace the waiting room, or shake their stretchers. This part of the night is for fighting. It has escaped the civility of day and evening, but has not yet slipped into the dreaming, drugged morning before light. These hours are the child who kicks and screams himself to sleep. The cop asks the nurse, How much longer? The patient says to the clerk, Where is the doctor? The nurse says to me, Come and see this guy first. He's driving me crazy. The patients develop additional medical problems while they wait. They construct opinions about how they should be treated. Opinions! Later it will be easier, because they will be like sedated animals and they won't care, but now it is all arguing and pushing. I sit when I'm in the patients' rooms, to promote the illusion of time. While I write in the charts, while I jot the orders, I stand because it forces me to keep moving.

2:20—Room 17. Mrs. Amin: thirty-nine years old with hiccups

I cure Mrs. Amin's hiccups by bringing her a large plastic cup of ice water and a thin white straw. I have her plug her ears tightly, pushing both her right and left tragus (that little triangle of springy flesh that arcs backwards over the ear canal).

I cheerlead, "Go, drink, go, go, don't stop!" She follows my instructions and drinks the entire glass of water through the straw without pause, without releasing the pressure over her ears. The hiccups stop. I love it.

"Miraculous," she says, smiling. She does not hiccup.

I love doing this because hiccups are of no significance, because this entertaining clinical intervention works, and I have no idea why it works. There is delicious freedom in doing something I do not understand, which cures a condition of no importance.

After this long, drawn-out clinical encounter (six minutes), Mrs. Amin says, "While I'm here, could you look at this rash?"

"How long have you had it?"

"Four years."

"We focus on emergencies."

"I've been waiting three hours. You can't look at my rash?" Already, she has thrust her arms out, pulled up the sleeves to show me her angry, peeling elbows. It looks like psoriasis.

I say, "Looks like psoriasis."

"I've got three creams, none work."

"Great. See your family doctor."

"I would like to see a dermatologist."

"Wonderful. Your family doctor knows a good one."

"I've been here four hours. You could call a dermatologist."

"We don't have dermatologists."

"Pardon?"

"This hospital has none. Even if we did, they wouldn't come at two-thirty in the morning. Dermatologists like to sleep. That's why I'm here, because I don't like to sleep so I have nothing better to do than look at your rash."

"Excuse me?"

"That's right, I am so *happy* to look at your rash that I can't contain myself. Nothing else to do! I don't need to see the other fifteen patients who are waiting with their heart attacks and broken bones. Thank goodness for your rash, because I would otherwise be bored silly." I am afraid that she will begin to hiccup again, but there is no sign of it.

"Doctor, isn't this an emergency ward?"

I can't think of anything to say except, "Yes."

Mrs. Amin scrunches her eyes at me, says, "Isn't this an *emergency* ward?"

"Your psoriasis is *not* an emergency. It's not related to the hiccups, for which you came here and which I have cured although they were also not an emergency, so consider yourself very fortunate."

Mrs. Amin stares at me.

I say, "I will now leave, shortly after which you must walk away from this hospital. Thank you."

"What's your name, doctor?"

"Dr. Chen."

"Can you spell that?"

"C-H-E-N. Let me write it down for you. I'm going to write my physician registration number, too, and the name of the head of the department, and his phone number. Can I help you in any other way?"

"We'll be in touch."

"I look forward to it. Move along, then."

I feel satisfied, a wormy little righteousness. I hold the curtain, "Go on. Out." She goes. I sit down to write the chart, and I document the encounter completely, such that there can be no question about the appropriateness of my words and actions. I describe our discussion of the hiccups, my differential diagnosis of hiccups, my successful hiccup treatment, and the follow-up plan for further hiccup care. I write that the patient mentioned that she had chronic psoriasis, that I examined the rash, that I informed her of our lack of a dermatology service, and that I encouraged her to follow up through her family doctor who is providing ongoing care. It is the most complete and verbose note I have written all night, and it is almost legible. There are fifteen lines of somewhat readable text to describe the nine minutes between 2:13 and 2:22.

2:45—Three patients waiting, less than twenty minutes behind

4:55—I feel strangely alert lying on this stretcher

At night, the minor area of the department is closed. I am in a darkened room, curtain pulled, socks dry-sticky on my feet. I have inclined the head of the stretcher upward because there are no pillows in the department. My shoes are at the side of the stretcher. On the rolling steel tray, next to suture kits and vomit basins, is my jumble of accessories: pager, mask, Palm Pilot, pen, wallet, energy bar, extra pen, vial of stool test reagent, extra mask. With all of these things removed, I am suddenly weightless.

I am alert, I am aware, I think that the wavy blue curtain resembles water. Hallway light glows through it as if I were in a cave behind a waterfall. I feel so vivid and wired that I don't notice the approach to sleep.

5:25—Suddenly awake

"Dr. Chen."

A face, a curtain pulled aside, I can't see who.

"Unnhh?"

"Dr. Chen!"

"Yeah. I'm awake!" A panic, a heart-pounding proclamation, "I'm awake." *Did I say that twice?* I'm not sure what I said and what I dreamt.

"Brady at thirty. Pressure of fifty on nothing, ETA three minutes."

The voice: I think it's a nurse. *Where're my glasses? Did I fall asleep?* Of course I did—that strange instant sleep I can't remember happening, where one second I had the awareness of waterfalls and curtains, then now this fuzzy face-voice. *Shit, where are my glasses? Brady at thirty. Probably new heart block.* Stumble into shoes. My feet night-swollen, I stuff my wallet, my Palm Pilot into pockets. The nausea. *Where the heck—Oh, screw the glasses. No, I need the glasses, I can't run this thing blind.*

Sick feeling.

I stand at the sink. Heave, dry heave, spit, gargle a little water. Feels a bit better. Stunned, echoing awakeness. Brady. *Jeez, couldn't wait a few hours?* I feel around the tray, then the cart next to it. I pad around until I feel the wire of my glasses. Aha! Once on my face, they make the light glaring, hard. Now that I can see, I realize my headache.

I check my watch. I slept half an hour. Fifteen more minutes would have been great. There's such a difference between half an hour of sleep and forty-five minutes, forty-five minutes and an hour, an hour and two. Two hours is bliss, a revelation of humanity, a soft dawning morning. An hour is enough—enough that the night has been broken and I can stand on it, casually shuffle my feet over its back. Forty-five minutes is like a deep breath, like a good sigh, a fresh drink, but it is just a moment's reprieve and sad in its ending. Half an hour is laying down and being smacked awake, then the sick feeling.

Dry heave. Hands on the sink. The motion of vomiting feels good, as if expelling the nausea although nothing comes out. Spit. Rinse.

Shuffle down the hall, face greasy-cold.

"Dr. Chen!" It is Magdalena, coming down the hall. It was also her before, I realize. Her voice is more urgent, and I seem to hear better now that I have my glasses.

"Oh, yes, I'm awake. I'm fine, I'm awake."

"The brady-hypotensive just pulled up."

"Excellent. That's just great," I say with thick-tongued deliberateness. "Thank you, Magdalena."

Shuffle faster.

5:28—Moonwalking, making war

Stretcher rolls in, trundles across the floor. The medics, the nurses, me: we move, talk, act as a crowd—bouncing off each other. We mill and grab, become a mob. *Beep beep*, always the monitors, *beep beep*. The blanket is a stunning orange. I say, "Move him into the bed." The sagging form of man. I say, "Accucheck, please, bolus a litre." It feels like those films of men on the moon who jump and take a forever leap, who launch a golf ball that disappears against black sky while the narrator says, *All skies would be black without our oxygenated atmosphere. Beep beep beep.* The guy has a shit blood pressure. His skin is the white on blue web-lace lines of death. "Atropine point six going in," I say as I inject. This is also my nightmare of war; the enemy invisible, shots in the dark, everyone rushing, confused, but in one tiny panicked place all is such calm because the end is near or the end is far, but there is no way to know. Somewhere there is a truce. Nurses and medics shout to grab this, hand me that, push it here, get the blue box. I say to the tall medic with the goatee, "Tell me the story again. Once more." He speaks in a loud voice, pedantic, eyes on his notes—a recitation over the ritual. He recounts how they were called, what they found, what they gave him already. I'm pushing drugs again. I say, "Atropine point six. Get me a rhythm strip, Clarice. Clarice! Put that down, it can wait, get me a rhythm strip." I believe there is music on the moon. In the documentaries, there's always music. Bach, or Mozart. Once, I saw Neil Armstrong with a soundtrack of Erik Satie's piano *Gymnopedies*—the astronauts suspended on delicate melody. Like that, floating, I call the orders, touch the patient, feel his belly, put my stethoscope on his side. I shine light in his eyes, they squeeze reflexively: dreamy, unreal. I say, "Atropine point eight." Each small move is accentuated. I say something, call out an order, and someone begins to do it, like my own golf ball hurtling away. But maybe it is not heard, so it is not done. Maybe it is done but by the time it is done, I change the order. The patient has changed already. The soldiers run, stab at shadows, hurl themselves at machine sounds. *Beep beep.* I trace the rhythm strip. Aha, a Mobitz II. "Let's put on the Zohl," I say. Fighting in space, I think they too would use a weapon called a Zohl.

The hydraulic hiss of the ambulance doors. Another crew, another stretcher. I say, "Hi guys, join the party." The charge nurse angry—why didn't you call? The medic defensive—we called, this is the bradycardia. The charge nurse to the first medic crew—what's going on here, did you call? The goateed medic shrugs—sure, we called. Two patients, same story. I say, "Maybe they both called, did we think it was one crew?" The charge nurse waves the second stretcher into the next bay. The battle extends, now a voice overhead asks for more combatants, for float nurses. I give the orders for each bay. I think I am being clear but maybe I am not. I say, "No, not that one, give it to the other guy." I pull back the curtain between the two stretchers, to see them both. I am floating, moonwalking. I am somewhere between the two monitors, *beepbeepbeepbeep*. The rhythms, the drugs, the orders: this is all back there somewhere in my medically sublimated subconscious, like bicycle riding. Floating, everything so slow. Then the second guy in failure, fluid filling the lungs, spilling over. Bad pressure, heart failure. I think, *Bad.* I say, "Dopamine, please." The first guy paced—it's not picking up well. "Put it up to sixty," I say. The second guy in vee-fib. Over him now with the paddles: Shock. "All clear!" Shock. "All clear!" Shock, the body jumps.

Start CPR on the second guy. Gravity is diluted, and it is so slow . . . it all happens drifting sideways. I say, "Push Amio three hundred." It's as if it's compressed into one single moment of rushing, shouting, wrappers on the floor, blood on the arm, foot poking out from under the sheet. I am over him again with the paddles, another zap of electric current. Again. "All clear!" Shock again. No good. "All clear! Shock."

On and on, five minutes, ten minutes. The second guy getting cold.

The second guy dead.

"What's happening, doc?" says Zack.

I say, "He died."

"What do you need?"

"Get me a transvenous pacer." I turn away from the second patient.

The first guy's external pacer is not picking up reliably. I puncture a hole in his groin, thrust the large-bore metal needle home, thread the wires up into the heart. *That's better. He's picking up well now.*

I call cardiology to take him upstairs.

6:10—Sitting behind the desk in the resuscitation room

The five bays fill my field of vision. I have the feeling of morning although there is no natural light here. A sunrise on the dark side.

I pick up the phone and call the desk clerk. "Mo," I don't know her full name, only know her as Mo, "it's Dr. Chen."

"Hi."

"You know that pizza place on Gerrard? They also deliver chicken wings, right?"

"It's six in the morning, doc."

"Maybe shawarma, or something?" I am hungry, craving meat.

"Just Tim's. You want a soup? But they don't deliver."

"Soup. Oh, nah. Forget it."

"Doc, wait a second—"

"Yeah."

"What's the name of the guy in bay four? I gotta do the papers."

"What guy?"

"Bay four."

"It's empty. There's no one there." I'm looking at it. Empty. A cleaner sweeps up a mess.

"But wasn't there—"

I wonder if Mo wants the name of the cleaner. Then I see what she means.

"Oh, you're right, there was someone there."

"What's his name?"

Mo is asking about the man who was there until five minutes ago, until he was wheeled into the pink room to wait for the coroner. I make that leap of understanding.

"Oh, the dead guy?"

"Right. What's his name?"

"Umm . . . I don't know, let me see. I think the papers are here. Didn't the ambulance guys leave the call sheet? Must have. Hmm . . . I was writing in the chart. Now, where the heck. Well, that's a good question, Mo. Maybe if I—"

"Never mind, doc, I'll come look for it."

"Sure. Sorry."

Hang up.

Things like this confuse me. Lost papers, cleaners.

Until 6:55

I rush through the department. I run from room to room, write on charts, wake up patients, send them home—tell them persuasively that all their tests have proven to be normal. In a frenzy of thread and needle drivers, I sew up two men who slashed each other with broken bottles of cheap shiraz. They cry and hug each other. The security guard has confiscated the bottles. I refer patients to specialists. I make phone calls. I wake surgeons and internists. I cast a broken ankle. The debris of night is falling into the hospital. I fix the broken fist of a drunk engineering student who does not know how to punch.

Dr. Pielou, the internist, comes to me with a chart in his hand.

He has just woken up, and he's ready to fight. He says, "Dr. Chen, you are referring Mr. Stanley with cellulitis."

"I am."

"This is *cellulitis*."

"That's what I wrote on the chart: recurrent infections. Both legs."

"Why don't you put the patient on antibiotics and send him home, Dr. Chen?"

"You'll understand when you see the patient."

"No, I won't. I refuse to see him. This is unacceptable. Can't you handle a *cellulitis*?"

"Dr. Pielou. Go see the patient and you will understand why you have to admit him."

Dr. Pielou sits down on a rolling chair, crosses his right leg in a delicate way over the left. There is only one chair. He says, "I would like you to *explain* to me why you are referring this patient with *cellulitis* before I go and see any such patient, Dr. Chen. I don't want my time wasted."

"Within two seconds, when you walk in the room you *will* understand. Stop wasting both of our time."

"This is a poor consult, Dr. Chen." He tut-tuts, and shakes his head, which causes his second chin to wiggle from side to side.

"You want to know why I am referring Mr. Stanley?"

"Yes."

"Shall I tell you?"

"Enlighten me, Dr. Chen."

"The patient is fat, Dr. Pielou."

He uncrosses his legs, pulls his white coat tightly over his belly and says, "Many people have weight issues."

"No, not just fat," I say. "Mr. Stanley is morbidly obese."

"What exactly is your point, Dr. Chen?"

"No. No. Actually, the truth is that this patient makes the notion of morbidly obese seem skinny. I would prefer not to express these thoughts out loud, but since you insist, let me describe the patient to you." I leer over Dr. Pielou, coming very close to the chair and looking down at him as I wave my hands in illustration. I speak too loudly. The nurses stare. I say, "Mr. Stanley's arms hang over the edges of the stretcher. Not the elbows. With the elbows *inside* the stretcher, the flesh of his arms wraps and hangs over the railings of the stretcher.

Have you noticed how most legs are longer than they are wide? This patient is amazing. You will be fascinated, because the width of the legs is similar to the length of each segment. It's incredible. The legs, instead of being tubular, are more like two globular structures, with feet emerging from the ends. Therefore, Mr. Stanley cannot see his legs to determine whether the infection is getting better or worse. He cannot put his legs up, because they will fall on him and knock him unconscious. He cannot walk. He has a specially reinforced, motorized wheelchair. If I give him oral antibiotics, the tablets will become lost in his elephantine digestive tract. If I send him home, he will come back as a huge septic mass of blubber. That is why *you, Dr. Pielou,* must perform the *heroic* task of admitting the patient to hospital and saving him from himself."

I look down at Dr. Pielou, who cranes his neck in order to maintain our fixed, hard eye contact. I tower over him, lean forward and hope that he will tilt backwards so far that the chair will fall over. I am not tall enough to achieve this, so I turn and walk away.

The rolling chair scuttles across the floor as Dr. Pielou loses balance and tumbles to the ground with a soft smacking sound. I turn, and he is pulling himself up. He says, "Dr. Chen, control yourself."

Still walking away, I say, "Thank you for seeing the patient, Dr. Pielou."

7:00—The morning doc comes. I'm happy to see her
"How was it?" she asks.
"The usual."

7:15—Southbound on the Don Valley Parkway

Windows down, sunroof open, the rush of morning air is a tornado in the car. Despite this, I'm sleepy. The music pounds loudly—U2's *Passengers: Original Soundtracks 1.* I need the thumping, driving rhythm to disrupt my sleepiness. I have a cold bottle of water from the hospital fridge. I sip. I make myself sip again, even though I'm not thirsty. The bottle sweats and I roll it on my neck.

The traffic is not stop and go, but all the lanes are full. It is rush hour cruising with sudden spasms of acceleration and deceleration.

My eyes are about to close. A grey Saab cuts me off. *Beeeeeep.* I honk.

I slap myself on the right cheek.

Shout out loud, sing to the music, "Boopity boop!" rocking my head. There're no words in this section, so I'm just shouting, "Boppity bop!"

My eyes pull tight, shut.

On the left cheek, I slap myself hard.

Those muscles above the eye are so weak. The eyelids are determined to snap shut like springs, like traps. Slam on the brakes, thrown forward. *Jeez. Almost, too close.* The line of brake lights is suddenly alive in front of this angry snake halted. I've stopped a foot from the grey Saab.

"Daaa daaa daaa," I shout. Slap myself.

The woman in the Malibu on my right looks at me, both of us sitting here in our cars. *Did she see me slap myself? Oh well, it's no one's business.* I slap myself again. She looks ahead, rolls her window up.

"BAPPITY BOOPITY ARRRRRRRR!" I yell for the stimulant effect.

I've tried to figure out the risks. What's more dangerous? Is it the mornings when the drive is slow, and I have more time to fall asleep? Or, is it the mornings when the drive is fast and I have less time to fall asleep, but the consequences of unconsciousness would be more dire? I can't decide. Driving slowly, I wish for the fear of driving fast while sleepy, because sometimes this fear wakes me up.

I call out letters, spell words like a drill sergeant, like drill bits to bore holes in my sleepiness. "C-A-R-C-R-A-S-H-F-E-N-D-E-R-B-E-N-D-E-R-T-O-W-T-R-U-C-K"

Slap the left cheek.

The curved ramp onto the elevated Gardiner, and then . . .

Just that moment, it comes so quickly, dark rest—sweet.

The whole car shakes, vibrates, I jerk my head up, guide the car off the shoulder, off the rumble strips. I see the woman in the Malibu is behind me now, keeping her distance.

"BOPPITY BOO!" I scream, turn the air conditioning

on high, the music loud. I pinch my thigh hard, rub my forehead with my knuckles. Another slap.

7:35—Parking garage. My spot, my car in one piece
I'll just lie here for a minute. I'll just put the seat down, so the neighbours won't see me.

8:05—Parking garage. My spot, my car in one piece
A cracking sound.
I say, "Unnnnnh."
A faraway voice.
My eyes slit open and I see it is the building caretaker, rapping on the car window. I say, "Morning, Mitchell."
"Morning, sir. I was knocking for a while, getting worried, about to call the ambulance."
Jeez. I better get up. That's the last thing I need. An ambulance.
I get out.
"You all right, sir?" he asks in his thick-tongued speech.
"Just fine."
"Big night on the town, then?" he winks.
"You know it."

8:10—Our bed. Ming is gone. Her ward rounds start early. The sheets are rumpled but not warm
Lying there.
For a moment, I feel so awake. I feel a beautiful alertness, as if the sorrow and calm and joy and exploding

furious vengeance of the world have all settled into me and shown themselves to be the same. Yes, all of an identical essence, different reflections of one basic feeling, one notion, in the way that water is at once an iceberg, the surf, a cloud. Why would I ever sleep?

Gone.

Out.

12:01—Lying in bed. Undecided whether to sleep more

Mostly, I feel that if only I do not speak, if only I refrain from uttering a single phrase, then everything will be all right. If I talk, it may allow things to spill from me. It could set in motion a vertiginous unbalance, a confusion leading to madness, or a hunger that may cause me to eat until I burst and die. If only I do not speak, I will be fine. I may go see a matinee. Movies are mostly mime, and will not lead to a dangerous escape of words.

I listen to the street.

Bells ring. So familiar, at noon.

The church bells are the sky, are the ether of blue and breeze, and they vibrate from a distance so that the notes intermingle and warble with the hiss of air conditioners. All of this sizzles over the popping rumble of streetcars. The light through the blinds falls diagonally in fat stripes on the floor, and is warm on the carpet whose stains are highlighted and made attractive, important.

GLOSSARY OF TERMS

These explanations are provided for the purpose of clarifying the narrative in this work of fiction. While they are believed to be accurate, this is not a medical dictionary. The glossary is not intended to explain medical conditions in any therapeutic way, and does not replace an explanation of any of these terms by a medical professional if they are relevant to your personal health.

8–o tube—refers to the size of an endotracheal tube. This is a typical size for an adult male. See *endotracheal tube.*

Abdomen—the part of the body cavity below the chest.

Accucheck—bedside test to determine a patient's blood sugar level.

ACLS—advanced cardiac life support. These are standardized protocols for treating cardiac arrest and arrhythmia.

Acyclovir—an antiviral medication.

Amiodarone—anti-arrhythmic medication. See *arrhythmia*.

Amnesia—loss of memory resulting from injury, disease, drugs, or psychological disturbance.

Amniotic fluid—fluid contained within the amniotic cavity, the amniotic cavity being the space that contains the embryo and is enclosed by a membrane, the amnion.

Ampoule—sealed glass or plastic capsule containing one dose of a drug as a sterile solution for injection.

Antidote—drug that counteracts the effect of a poison, or the overdose of another drug.

Arrhythmia—deviation from the normal rhythm of the heart.

Arytenoids—two pyramid-shaped cartilages that lie at the back of the larynx next to the upper edges of the cricoid cartilage. See *cricoid cartilage; larynx*.

Atrial electricity—refers to the electrical impulse normally generated in the atria that regulates the normal rhythm of the heart.

Atropine—drug that inhibits the action of certain regulatory nerves and can be therapeutic in some instances of bradycardia.

Bicarb—refers to bicarbonate, a medication used in cardiac resuscitation to treat one of the metabolic disturbances (acidosis) that may accompany a near-death physiological state.

Bigeminy—condition in which alternate ectopic beats of the heart are transmitted. Normally, the heart beats at the rhythm dictated by one centre in the atrium. In bigeminy, the "ectopic" beats are triggered by an abnormal centre of rhythm.

Blown pupil—refers to a non-reactive, enlarged pupil, and is usually an ominous sign of structural disturbances within the skull. Normally, pupils react to light by becoming smaller, but a blown pupil does not. This may be a sign that a patient is "coning." See *coning; pupil.*

Bolus—rapid administration of fluid or medication.

Brady—refers to bradycardia, an abnormally slow rhythm of the heart.

Bronchogram—an X-ray appearance indicating the presence of fluid in the lungs.

Bypass—refers to cardiac bypass, a surgical procedure in which blocked coronary arteries are circumvented, or "bypassed" by the grafting of vessels that provide blood circulation to the heart.

Caesarean section—surgical operation for delivering a baby through the abdominal wall.

Cannula—hollow tube designed for insertion into a body cavity.

Catheter—flexible tube for insertion into a narrow cavity or blood vessel so that fluid may be introduced or removed.

Ceftriaxone—an antibiotic.

Cellulitis—infection of soft tissue.

Central line—intravenous access to the veins of the body that are not normally close to the skin's surface, such as the jugular, subclavian, and femoral veins.

Cerebrospinal fluid—clear watery fluid that surrounds the brain and spinal cord.

Cervix—necklike part of the uterus that projects into the vagina and is capable of wide dilation during childbirth.

Coags—refers to coagulation profile, which is a laboratory measure of the clotting time of blood.

Code blue—refers to cardiac arrest, a situation in which a patient has ceased to breathe and circulate blood spontaneously.

Code orange—refers to a disaster situation.

Collateral circulation—alternative route provided for blood by secondary vessels when a primary vessel becomes blocked.

Compression—within a cardiac arrest, this refers to the act of compressing the chest wall, so as to produce movement of blood through the heart.

Conduction—transmission of electrical impulses.

Coning—refers to the displacement of the brain's structures by an increase in pressure within the skull. This frequently leads to permanent damage of brain tissue, and often to death.

Conjunctiva—mucous membrane that covers the front of the eye and lines the inside of the eyelids.

Contact tracing—the practice of locating individuals who may have come in contact with a patient known or suspected of having an infectious illness.

CPR—refers to cardiac-pulmonary resuscitation, emergency manoeuvres employed to maintain the circulation of oxygen and blood within a body that has ceased to do so itself.

Crackles—sound heard in the lungs through a stethoscope, signifying the presence of fluid in the lungs.

Crash cart—refers to a trolley stocked with the equipment and drugs necessary to initially manage a cardiac arrest. *(Author's note: Typically, one of the wheels is jammed, and the particular sizes of equipment needed are missing.)*

Cricoid cartilage—cartilage, shaped like a signet ring, that forms part of the anterior and lateral and most of the posterior wall of the larynx.

Cricoid pressure—pressure applied to the cricoid cartilage, in order to occlude the esophagus or to reposition the airway for better visualization during airway management. *(Author's note: Although this term is frequently used, it is somewhat of a misnomer in the context of airway repositioning, which, more correctly stated, involves pressure on the thyroid cartilage, found adjacent to the cricoid cartilage.)*

CT—refers to computed tomography, a diagnostic tool that uses an X-ray scanner to record "slices" of the body and then integrates these data to give a cross-sectional image.

Diazepam—tranquilizer with muscle relaxant and anticonvulsant properties.

DIC—disseminated intravascular coagulation, a process in which the body's clotting mechanisms act inappropriately, often resulting in life-threatening failure of multiple vital organs.

Dopamine—drug used to increase the strength of contraction of the heart.

Dop-tone—refers to a portable fetal Doppler monitor, which allows rapid assessment of fetal heart rate.

Endotracheal tube—a semi-rigid tube that is positioned within the trachea to provide oxygen to a patient and prevent stomach contents and other material from entering the lungs.

Epi—refers to epinephrine, a medication that acts as a cardiac stimulant.

Esophagus—structure that moves food from the mouth to the stomach.

ETA—refers to estimated time of arrival.

FAA—refers to Federal Aviation Authority.

False cords—refers to arytenoid cartilage. See *arytenoids*.

FiO$_2$—fraction of inspired oxygen, a measure of the amount of oxygen in the gas a patient is breathing.

Flashback—the appearance of blood in the hub of an intravenous catheter as the catheter is positioned. See *catheter*.

Float nurse—nurse who is not assigned to a specific area, but who is available to help where the workload is highest.

Focal deficits—specific neurological findings that imply an area of discrete dysfunction within the nervous system.

FRCPC—refers to Fellowship of the Royal College of Physicians of Canada.

Heart block—condition in which conduction of electrical impulses generated by the normal pacemaker of the heart (in the atrium) is impaired, so that the rate and action of the heart's pumping is impaired.

Heart failure—condition in which the pumping action of the heart is inadequate, resulting in back pressure of blood and fluid filling the lungs and liver.

Hemorrhage—bleeding.

Hemorrhagic stroke—stroke in which the cause is bleeding into the brain tissue. See *stroke*.

Hepatitis (B, C)—two strains of illness that affect the liver and are transmissible by contact with bodily fluids.

Hilum—a hollow on the surface of an organ, such as the heart, where structures such as blood vessels and nerve fibres enter or leave it.

HIV (1, 2)—refers to two strains of human immunodeficiency virus, an illness transmissible by contact with bodily fluids.

Hypotensive—abnormally low blood pressure.

Internist—medical doctor specialized in internal medicine.

Intracranial pressure—pressure within the skull.

Krebs cycle—cycle of enzyme-mediation reactions that occurs in the cells of all animals. This is a crucial final step in the conversion of food into energy. *(Author's note: Many an hour have been spent by many a student pondering the intricacies of this aggravatingly complex process. Certain chemical reactions in this cycle frequently appear in dreams.)*

Laerdal bag—bag used to push air into the lungs, either via a tightly sealing face mask or an endotracheal tube.

Laryngoscope—instrument for examining the larynx, and for visualizing airway structures in order to place an endotracheal tube within the trachea.

Larynx—organ responsible for producing vocal sounds, which is also the passage conveying air from the pharynx to the lungs. Within it are the vocal cords. See *pharynx*.

Lumbar puncture—procedure in which cerebrospinal fluid is removed from the spinal canal using a hollow needle inserted unto the lower back.

Lumbar vertebrae—five bones of the back.

Lymphoma—a malignant tumour of lymph nodes.

Lytes—refers to electrolytes, the concentration of salts within the blood.

Mac-3—refers to a type and size of laryngoscope. See *laryngoscope*.

MCAT—refers to the Medical College Admissions Test.

Mitochondria—molecular structure found in every living cell that is the site of energy production for the cell.

Mitral regurgitation—failure of the mitral valve to close, allowing blood to flow backwards from the left ventricle to the left atrium. Mild cases have no symptom or consequence, but severe cases can be dangerous. See *mitral valve.*

Mitral valve—valve in the heart between the left atrium and left ventricle that normally allows blood to pass from the atrium to the ventricle but not backwards.

Mobitz II—a disorder of the heart's electrical activity that is potentially dangerous and unstable.

Neuroleptic—class of medications used to treat psychosis. See *psychosis.*

Neuron—cell that transmits electrical impulses to carry information from one part of the body to another.

Neurotoxic—substance that is poisonous or harmful to neurons. See *neuron.*

Nitro—refers to nitroglycerin, a medication that promotes the dilation of blood vessels and may relieve chest pain associated with the heart.

Normal sinus—the normal rhythm of the heart.

Pacemaker—device used to produce and maintain normal heart rate in patients who have a heart block. See *heart block.*

PEA—refers to pulseless electrical activity, a state in which the heart has spontaneous electrical impulses but these impulses do not result in movement of the heart's muscles or circulation of blood.

Pelvis—the lower part of the abdomen. See *abdomen.*

Periodic table—chart that details the earth's primary substances.

Peripheral line—intravenous line that uses veins that are close to the skin.

Pharynx—muscular tube that acts as a passageway for food from the mouth to the esophagus, and as an air passage from the nasal cavity and mouth to the larynx.

Phosphorylation—combination of an organic molecule with a phosphate group.

Poisoning syndrome—constellation of signs and symptoms that appear in a patient as a characteristic manifestation of the patient's exposure to a certain type of poison.

Psychosis—mental disorder in which the patient loses contact with reality.

Pupil—circular opening in the centre of the iris. The iris is the coloured portion of the eye.

Purkinje system—part of the heart's electrical conduction system.

PVC—refers to premature ventricular contraction, meaning an isolated contraction of the ventricle without the normal regulatory impulses of the heart's electrical system. Single PVCs are benign, but multiple PVCs may be a worrisome sign.

Quarantine—period for which a person is kept in isolation to prevent the spread of a contagious disease.

Recombinant thrombolytic—thrombolytic medication that is produced by molecular synthesis instead of by extraction from natural bacterial cultures. See *thrombolytic*.

Renal—meaning to do with the kidneys.

Repolarization—late phase of the sequence of electrical events in the heart.

Rhythm strip—prolonged paper strip showing the heart's rhythm. This is typically thirty seconds to a minute long, permitting a more complete assessment of the rhythm.

Ribavirin—an antiviral medication.

SARS—refers to Severe Acute Respiratory Syndrome.

Scrub—refers to standard surgical clothing. Also known as "greens."

Septic—state in which an infection has led to a patient's widespread, systemic illness.

Solumedrol—steroid medication, used to reduce inflammation and sometimes used in conjunction with other medications in the treatment of severe infections.

Spinal canal—space in which the spinal cord is found.

Spinal cord—portion of the central nervous system enclosed in the vertebral column.

Stethoscope—instrument for listening to sounds within the body.

Stroke—sudden brain dysfunction caused by interruption of blood flow to the brain.

Stylet—wire placed in the lumen of a catheter to give it rigidity while it is passed into a cavity.

Subarachnoid hemorrhage—bleeding into the subarachnoid space surrounding the brain, usually secondary to a cerebral aneurysm that has burst.

Supine—lying on the back with the face upward.

Thorax—the part of the body cavity between the neck and the abdomen. See *abdomen*.

Thrombolytic—medication that breaks up blood clots.

Thyroid cartilage—see *cricoid pressure*.

Thyrotoxicosis—syndrome due to excessive amounts of thyroid hormone.

Torso—external structures of the thorax. See *thorax*.

Tox screen—refers to a toxicology screen, a range of tests that may analyze blood or urine samples to identify the presence of substances within the body. Typically, this is used to identify poisons or substances of abuse.

Toxicology—study of poisonous materials and their effect on living organisms.

Trachea—the air passage between the larynx and the lungs. See *larynx*.

Tragus—projection of cartilage in the pinna of the outer ear that extends back over the opening of the external auditory meatus. *(Author's note: Or as Chen would say, " . . . that little triangle of springy flesh that arcs backwards over the ear canal.")*

Transvenous pacer—pacemaker device that is inserted via a vein, necessitating access via a central line. See *pacemaker*.

Trop—refers to troponin, a protein that is released by cardiac muscle if it is damaged. The measurement of troponin's presence in the blood often serves as a marker for cardiac damage.

TSH—refers to thyroid stimulating hormone, and can be used as a measure of thyroid function.

Vee-fib—refers to ventricular fibrillation, a state in which the heart's muscles move chaotically, and not in a purposeful way. In this state, blood is not delivered to the body. Unless reversed, ventricular fibrillation is followed by death.

Vent—refers to a ventilator, equipment that maintains flow of air into and out of the lungs of a patient who is not able to breathe independently.

Vertiginous—refers to the state of vertigo, in which a person feels that his surroundings are in a state of constant movement.

Vocal cords—two folds of tissue that protrude from the sides of the larynx to form a narrow slit across the air passage. See *larynx.*

VSA—refers to vital signs absent, a state in which normal indications of life, such as breathing, pulse, and blood pressure, cannot be found.

ACKNOWLEDGEMENTS

I thank those who have helped me begin to learn the art of writing, especially Margaret Atwood, Maya Mavjee, Kim Moritsugu, Howard Norman, Jane Urquhart, and Michael Winter. I am especially grateful to Margaret Atwood, whose generosity, wit, and brilliant advice have been inspirational.

Many friends and fellow writers have commented upon these stories, and I am grateful to them. In particular, I thank Richard Munter and Sam Hiyate for their early feedback and support for this book. I have a deep gratitude towards my parents, my wife, and both of our families, who have always encouraged me in both medicine and literature. Thanks to Anne McDermid, my agent, and her excellent staff.

Although this is a work of fiction, it is informed by

what I have learned from becoming and being a doctor. For this reason, I am indebted to all those who have taught me medicine: senior physicians and nurses who have shared their wisdom, my fellow medical students and now colleagues, and the patients whom I have been privileged to care for.

ABOUT THE AUTHOR

Dr. Vincent Lam was born in London, Ontario. His family is from the expatriate Chinese community of Vietnam. He studied medicine in Toronto, and is an emergency physician. Dr. Lam's non-fiction has appeared in *The Globe and Mail* and *The National Post*. His fiction has been published in *Carve*. Dr. Lam's first novel, about a Chinese compulsive gambler and school headmaster in Saigon during the Vietnam War, will be published by Doubleday Canada in 2007. He lives with his wife, Margarita, and his son, Theodore, in Toronto.

A NOTE ABOUT THE TYPE

Bloodletting & Miraculous Cures has been set in
Walbaum. Originally cut by Justus Erich
Walbaum (a former cookie mould apprentice)
in Weimar in 1810, the type was revived by the
Monotype Corporation in 1934. Although the
type may be classified as modern, numerous
slight irregularities in its cut give this face its
humane manner.

BOOK DESIGN BY CS RICHARDSON